MELODY

MELODY

STEEL BROTHERS SAGA
BOOK TWENTY-EIGHT

HELEN HARDT

WATERHOUSE PRESS

*For all musicians, and especially operatic
bass-baritone Eric McConnell*

PROLOGUE

Sixty years ago...

"It's priceless," my mother says. "But I'm giving it to you. I don't have any daughters, and one day you'll find a woman you'll want to marry."

"Not anytime soon, Mum." I shake my head.

Not that it's something a guy talks to his mother about, but I've got a lot of wild oats to sow before I even think of settling down.

"I never liked the color," Mum continues, "but it comes from somewhere in Australia. Your grandmother came from there."

She hands me the burgundy velvet box that houses her treasure. The ring she never wears.

The ring that—if it's indeed priceless—should probably be locked in a safe somewhere.

Which is exactly where it's going now.

I won't be using it for at least ten years.

CHAPTER ONE

B r i a n n a

Every time I see Jesse Pike perform, my heart nearly explodes.

He's on stage now at the Snow Creek Cinema singing with his band, Dragonlock, which now includes my future cousin-in-law Rory as a co-lead singer. The two of them are pure magic together.

But the real magic on the stage is Jesse himself—tall and handsome with long dark hair curtaining his shoulders and those amazing dark eyes. I've been pining for him since I saw him perform with his band when I was a mere fourteen years old. He was twenty-four at the time, and anyone else would have told me it was a simple girlhood crush. Puppy love.

Even then, I knew it wasn't. I've compared every guy I've dated to Jesse Pike, and they've all fallen short.

The song ends, and once the applause dies down, Jesse takes the mic. I gaze at him, stars in my eyes, the perspiration on his forehead making him even more attractive to me. I can almost smell his musk from my front-row seat.

"Thank you all so much," he says in his deep voice. "You all know the band, but I'll introduce them anyway. We've got Jake Michaels on guitar. My cousin Cage Ramsey on keyboard and bass. Dragon Locke, our band's namesake, on drums. And the beautiful Rory Pike, my little sis, on lead vocals. I'm Jesse

Pike, the other lead vocalist."

More thundering applause. The band members are all handsome, and my cousins all have a thing for Dragon. He's hot in that dark way of his, but he doesn't compare to Jesse.

No man does. Not in my eyes.

He doesn't know this yet—and neither do my parents—but I'm going on that international tour with them in January. I've finished my college degree early, though I'll walk at graduation in the spring with the rest of the awesome foursome—my cousins Gina Steel and Angie and Sage Simpson.

Mom and Dad think I'm going to begin working with Dad come the first of the year. Of the four of us—my brothers, Dale and Donny, and my sister, Diana—I'm the only one who shares our father's interest in our orchard of Palisade peaches and apples. I've been following my dad, Talon Steel, around the grounds since I could walk, asking questions, learning about the trees and the fruit, and assuring him I'd never leave his side.

That's still my plan—with a slight detour along the way.

Getting Jesse Pike to fall head over heels in love with me.

The applause dies down again, and Jesse continues, "We've got a major treat for you tonight. As you all know by now, Dragonlock has the honor of going on tour as the opener for the amazing Emerald Phoenix."

Clapping and shouting. I know what's coming. My brother Donny is engaged to Jesse's sister Callie, so they let our family in on the secret. Emerald Phoenix is *here*. Jett Draconis and Zane Michaels and the rest of the band. Rockers galore, all gorgeous, though Jett is happily married to his wife, Heather, who's also here.

And not one of them makes my heart race the way Jesse Pike does.

I never cared that he was a struggling musician. I'm a Steel heiress. I don't have to marry for money. Not that I would, anyway. I've watched both my brothers, my cousin Ava, and my cousin Brock—the biggest womanizer on the planet—fall in love in the last year. They've all found something truly special. Something way more important than money. And two of them, Donny and Brock, are marrying into the Pike family.

I aim to be the third.

"It's our privilege to introduce to you, for a special engagement... Emerald Phoenix!"

Wowza.

If the crowd was excited about Dragonlock, they're about to wet their pants over Emerald Phoenix. They're going batshit crazy with their screams and hoots and stomping.

The members of Dragonlock exit the stage, and Jett Draconis and his band take their places.

"Thank you," Jett says into the mic. "We're thrilled to be here tonight as a favor to Jesse, Rory, and the band. We're excited to have Dragonlock come on tour with us. We know they're going to be a smash. Now... let's rock!"

★ ★ ★

"Your arias were wonderful," Angie says to Rory during the after-party at my parents' sprawling ranch house.

Mom and Dad offered up their house as a favor to the band since it's way bigger than the Pikes'. They have a small ranch adjacent to ours and unfortunately lost most of their vineyards in a brush fire earlier this year. Jesse and Rory are excited about the opportunity the tour gives them to make some money to help. Our family has offered, but the Pikes turned us down.

"Thank you." Rory smiles, fidgeting with the red star sapphire ring on her left hand that once belonged to my aunt Melanie's grandmother. "I'll miss singing opera, but that was my swan song. I'm devoting myself to rock and roll now."

"Good call," I say. "You're fabulous at both, but you and Jesse together… Just *wow*."

Rory squeezes my hand. "Thanks, Bree."

Rory's a classic beauty, and she's always been considered the most beautiful woman in Snow Creek. Jesse looks just like her in male form. He's a freaking god.

I've got to get him to give me a look before we go on tour. Once all the Emerald Phoenix fans in the UK and the rest of Europe lay their eyes on him, he'll have his pick of women.

"I wish I were going with you on the tour," Angie says. "You're going to have a blast."

"I wish you were too," I reply.

I didn't plan to graduate early. I had enough credits, but I figured I'd sail through my last semester with some easy electives and have my last hurrah with sorority and fraternity parties.

Then I found out about the tour, and I chalked it up to fate. Early graduation was a possibility, and it would free me up to go on the tour. Since Callie is engaged to Donny, I talked the two of them into going along for the first couple of weeks, which gave me an excuse to go since my brother will be there.

Yeah, it's farfetched, but it got me there. Then, when Donny and Callie fly home, I'll make some excuse to stay on.

Now… I just have to tell Mom and Dad.

That's what tomorrow's for.

Tonight, I'm partying.

With Jesse Pike, I hope.

CHAPTER TWO

Jesse

Amazing. Most of the women here at Talon and Jade Steel's house for the after-party—even the married ones—are flocking around Jett Draconis and the rest of Emerald Phoenix.

Groupies.

The only groupies Dragonlock has ever had are the awesome foursome, as my little sister Maddie calls them. The four youngest Steel women—Brianna Steel, Gina Steel, and Angie and Sage Simpson. All gorgeous, of course—all the Steels are—but way too young for me.

The awesome foursome isn't giving us a look tonight. They're more interested in Emerald Phoenix—Zane Michaels, Bernie Zopes, and Tony Walker. Everyone knows Jett is happily married. In fact, his wife is here tonight. She's a real sweet thing. Her name's Heather.

Now that two of my sisters are engaged to Steel men, I don't feel quite as out of place at the main Steel house. I've been here many times. I've played at many Steel parties. But tonight, I don't feel like an outsider.

My cousin Cage Ramsey brings me a beer.

"Thanks." I take a long sip, letting it cool my throat. Nothing like an ice-cold brew after I've been singing all night.

"Where's our harem?" Cage asks.

"What do you mean?"

"The awesome foursome. They're usually flocked around us." He narrows his gaze. "You in particular."

I let out a laughing scoff. "More like Dragon. And you and Jake."

Cage chuckles and then glances around. "All of us, then. Where *is* Dragon, by the way?"

"Probably off smoking a joint. You know he always has to have a little weed after a concert since we won't let him get high before."

"Yeah, what is it with him and weed? I never could stand the stuff."

"Don't know, man."

The truth of the matter is, I *do* know. Dragon hasn't had an easy life. He keeps to himself, but one night—one of the only times I've ever gotten high because I actually don't like the stuff—he confided in me. I understand our drummer a lot better now, but I'm sworn to secrecy. And I get why he smokes after a performance. It numbs him a little bit, relaxes him. I've got no problem with it, as long as it doesn't affect his performance, and so far it hasn't.

There are reasons why Dragon shouldn't smoke or drink, but so far he's kept clean from the harder stuff.

"Ah ... there they all are." Cage gestures to the pool house in the giant Steel backyard.

The members of Emerald Phoenix stand there, flanked by pretty much every woman here, including the awesome foursome.

"Guess I can't blame them," I say. "Emerald Phoenix is an amazing band."

"Except one of them seems to be missing ... " Cage looks

around. "Brianna. Where's Brianna?"

I shrug. "How the hell should I know?"

"Those four are usually inseparable."

Brianna Steel is the most beautiful of the awesome foursome. She looks the most like her father, Talon Steel. Of course, her older brothers, Dale and Donny, are adopted, so they couldn't look anything like him. But Diana favors their mother, Jade. Brianna, though... She's taller than her older sister, taller than her mother. Nearly as tall as her father when she wears those sexy cowboy boots of hers. The original Steel Brothers are all ranchers, cowboys. Most of their kids, though? They chose different paths. All except for Dale and Brock Steel... and Brianna.

Brianna Steel is temptation on a stick. I've known her a long time because Donny and I went to high school together. We've had this idiotic rivalry since then because he was chosen most valuable player for the football team our senior year. It should've gone to me. Well... that's not exactly true. We were both equally valuable players. He got it because of his name. It's no secret. We all knew it.

I wasn't happy when he started dating my sister Callie, but she made us shake hands and make up. So we put up with each other now.

Begrudgingly.

Silly, I suppose. It's been fifteen years.

But yeah. When Donny and I were eighteen, his little sister Brianna was eight.

That's how I remember her. A really pretty kid with a spray of freckles across her nose, long dark hair in pigtails, and jeans and cowboy boots, a cowboy hat on her head. Always a cowgirl, that one. She used to follow her daddy around like a puppy. Whenever I saw her at that age, she was either with Talon or on a horse.

She still has that light spray of freckles across her nose. But now that cute little kid—after two years of braces and a lot of filling out—is a damned beautiful woman.

She's got legs that go on for fucking ever, and a luscious rack she inherited from her mother, who's the daughter of Brooke Bailey, a supermodel who was famous back in the day.

Brianna Steel could sure be a supermodel. She's got the height, the perfect facial features, the silky-smooth hair.

Like I said, temptation on a stick.

Until I remember my rivalry with Donny—and his eight-year-old sister with her hair in pigtails in the stands cheering our team on.

Good thing I'll be leaving after the holidays, off to the UK and then the rest of Europe. I haven't been in a relationship for a while, and I'm not the casual sex type, but... with a smorgasbord of European lovelies at my fingertips ...

Yeah, I'm rethinking that.

Cage and I plan to fuck our way through Europe.

I'm looking forward to it.

CHAPTER THREE

Brianna

Jesse's talking to Cage. The rest of the awesome foursome plus Jesse's youngest sister, Maddie Pike, are fawning all over the members of Emerald Phoenix.

It is kind of a cool thing, having a famous rock band at my house. Even my mom is getting a little twitterpated.

Aunt Melanie and Aunt Ruby are sitting on the deck with my brand-new aunt, Lauren Wingdam, who has gorgeous blue eyes and medium-brown hair that she wears stylishly short.

It's a long story.

Apparently my uncle Ryan has a different mother than my father, Uncle Joe, and Aunt Marjorie. We had a big family meeting two weeks ago about it.

It took a while to digest everything. I haven't spent much time with Lauren yet, and since Jesse isn't giving me any attention at all, I walk toward my three aunts.

"Hi, Aunt Ruby, Aunt Mel."

"Brianna." Aunt Melanie smiles. "Come sit down with us for a moment."

I take a seat next to my new aunt. "Hi, Lauren. Did you enjoy the concert?"

Lauren fans herself with her hand. "I did. I've always been a rock and roll enthusiast. I'm sure Jack loved it as well."

Jack Murphy, with reddish-brown hair and his mother's blue eyes, is my newly discovered cousin, Lauren's son. He's around here somewhere.

"This must be a lot for you to take in," I say. "I suppose you never imagined having this many relatives foisted on you at once."

Aunt Lauren nods with a smile. "It's been something, all right. But honestly, I'm thrilled that you've all been so accepting of me."

"I knew they would be," Aunt Ruby says. "We've known about Ryan's true parentage for the last twenty-five years."

"Not all of us," I can't resist saying.

Just one of the many things my parents, aunts, and uncles chose to keep from my generation. They thought they could protect us, or some such nonsense.

"I know," Aunt Melanie says, again with a smile. "If it's any consolation, Bree, Aunt Ruby and I wanted to tell all of you a long time ago. We got outvoted."

I hold back a frown. "Yeah, I heard all about it. Donny and Dale leveled with me. I kind of understand. And I kind of don't."

"You're a smart girl," Aunt Ruby says. Then she turns to Lauren. "I just wish we'd known about you. You're a full-blooded Steel."

"I'm still not used to thinking of myself that way," Lauren says.

"You'll get used to it soon enough," I say with an eye roll. "Lots of parties here at the main house. We Steels throw a party every time someone passes gas."

Aunt Ruby erupts in laughter, though Aunt Melanie narrows her eyes at me. Then she laughs as well.

"I suppose, Lauren," Aunt Melanie says, "you may as well find out what kind of people we are. We don't mince words."

Lauren returns the laughter. "My kind of people, then." She turns to me. "I understand congratulations are in order. You've graduated college."

I give her a smile. I like Aunt Lauren. "Yeah. A semester early."

"So what do you plan to do now?"

I shift my gaze between Aunt Ruby and Aunt Mel. I haven't told my parents my plan to go on tour with the band. I probably shouldn't tell my aunts yet.

"Well . . . My plan was always to stay here on the ranch. I've been working with my father since I could walk. Dale, Brock, and I are the only three of all the Steel kids who have taken an interest in running the ranch. Unless you count my cousins Bradley and Henry. They run our nonprofit foundation, which is related to the ranch but doesn't require getting your hands dirty. And Dave, who works on the financial end with Uncle Bryce."

Aunt Lauren raises her eyebrows. "Really?"

"Donny's an attorney, Diana's an architect, Gina's an artist, Ava runs a bakery in town, and Angie and Sage . . . I don't think they know what they want to do yet."

"So you, Brock, and Dale all work on the ranch, then?"

"Yes, ma'am."

"I'm sure your father's excited to have you come work with him full-time," Aunt Ruby says.

Guilt takes a swing at me. I still have to talk to Mom and Dad about my plans to go to Europe with the band. I've sworn Donny to secrecy, but he insisted I tell them soon, which I'm choosing to interpret as the day before I leave.

HELEN HARDT

"We haven't really talked about it yet." I rise. "It was nice talking to you. I hope you feel welcome here, Lauren. Or should I call you Aunt Lauren?"

"Lauren is fine." She smiles. "But I could get used to Aunt Lauren if you want to call me that."

"Well, that's what you are. I'll see you later, Aunt Ruby, Aunt Mel, *Aunt* Lauren." I smile as I spy Jesse standing under one of the gazebos with a bottle of beer. I walk toward him . . . but my brother waylays me.

"Hey, sis," Donny says.

"Hey. Where's Callie?"

"She and Rory are talking to Jett Draconis's wife, Heather."

"Oh."

"And I need to talk to you."

"What about?" I ask, mustering as much innocence as I can.

"When are you going to tell Mom and Dad?"

"Maybe on the way to the airport?" I give him a sweet smile.

"No way, sis." He gives me that big-brother look. "You promised to tell them soon. And by soon, I mean tomorrow."

"What?" I grin. "You mean you're not going to make me tell them tonight?"

"Not in the middle of the party with the whole town here. But tomorrow. Capisce?"

I poke him in his chest. "What are you? Some kind of blond mobster?"

Donny chuckles. "You're funny, sis." Then his demeanor snaps back to big brother in a flash. "You've got to tell them. Dad especially. He's all excited about you starting work in January."

I sigh. "I'll tell them. What if they pull some kind of weird parental shit on me? Forbidding me to go or something?"

"You're over eighteen, Brianna. Mom and Dad can't *forbid* you to do anything."

"True. They can't cut me off either. I gained control of my trust fund when I turned twenty-one."

True words. But as the youngest of all the Steels, I've always been the baby, and they've treated me as such.

"They wouldn't do that anyway," Donny says. "But you *do* owe them the courtesy of letting them know that you're going to be gone for several months after the first of the year."

I twist my lips. "I know ... I just hate disappointing Dad."

"You don't have to disappoint him. You don't have to go on the tour."

"Are you kidding me? I've never been to Europe, Don. Neither have you."

Despite our fortune, we Steels aren't world travelers. We're homebodies. Brock and Rory went to England a couple of weeks ago to visit Ennis Ainsley, who was the first winemaker here when my grandfather opened the winery. That was the first time Brock had been overseas. Ranching is a full-time job, and though we've got lots of dedicated employees who can keep things running without us, my father, aunts, and uncles like to have their hands in things.

"You want me to be here when you tell them?" Donny asks.

"No ... " I bite my lower lip. "Well, yeah, I would, but I've got to do this myself."

"Good. I agree with you."

"Do you think they'll be *really* upset?"

"I don't know, Bree. With all the shit that's gone down

with our family lately, they probably don't want you leaving the country."

"*You're* leaving the country."

"Yeah, but I'm ten years older than you are, and I'm going because Callie's going to support Rory. Plus, we're only going to be gone for the first couple of weeks. You want to go the whole time, like some kind of Deadhead."

"A Deadhead? Like I'm following the band around?"

"Yeah." Donny furrows his brow. "Isn't that *exactly* what you're doing?"

I have no answer for my brother.

I have no answer because he's right.

"Why do you want to do this anyway, Brianna? Ever since you put on your first pair of cowboy boots, all you wanted to do was work on the ranch. Now you've got a degree in agriculture. Lots of new knowledge, and the best teacher in the world in Dad. I don't get it."

Donny is painfully oblivious. He's going to hate me going after Jesse Pike.

Too bad, how sad, though.

Jesse's been my one and only since I was fourteen years old.

No one knows this, not even the awesome foursome, but...

I've been saving myself for him.

My virginity—a gift I can only give once.

And I'm going to give it to Jesse Pike.

I look toward the gazebo where I saw him a moment ago.

He's gone.

CHAPTER FOUR

Jesse

I finish my beer, toss the bottle in a nearby recycling bin, and decide to enjoy the night. It's clear, as the majority of nights in Colorado are. Here in the country, the stars are brilliant and plentiful.

I walk away from the yard, up one of the many winding paths, and I find Dragon sitting against a tall tree, his coal-black hair bound behind him in a band. The sweet yet pungent scent of marijuana still hangs in the air.

"Hey, Dragon. You doing okay?" I rub my arms against the chill. It is December, after all, and without the outdoor heaters, it's pretty brisk.

He glances up at me, his hazel eyes a bit bloodshot. "I'm good."

"You want to come join the party?"

"Not particularly."

I sit down next to him. He offers me a smoke.

I shake my head.

"One day you're going to take me up on it."

"Doubtful. I stopped smoking five years ago."

"And you really don't miss it?"

"Not really. You ask me every time, and my answer's the same, bud. I'm not into weed."

Dragon leans back against the tree trunk, twists his back as if he's scratching an itch. "I just need to take a load off after the performance, you know?"

"We get it. Nobody's giving you any shit about it. Long as you don't come to practice or a performance high."

"I haven't yet, have I?"

"Nope."

I'd be able to tell, too. I know Dragon better than anybody does. When he's high, a little bit of his classic darkness fades.

Plus he's the best drummer in the business. The band needs him.

"What are you doing over here anyway?" he asks. "Don't your groupies miss you?"

I let out a soft scoff. "What groupies? I'm kibble when Emerald Phoenix is around."

Dragon lets out a low chuckle. "Then I guess I'm kibble too."

In truth, Dragon gets a lot of attention. More than I do, usually. Something about his dark demeanor seems to attract women like flies to honey.

But I get enough attention. I certainly don't envy Dragon. I know his backstory, and it's far from pretty.

"I'm a little afraid," Dragon continues.

"Afraid of what?"

"This whole thing, Jess. I love playing. Love being in the band. Love all you guys. You're like my brothers, man. The brothers I never had." His bloodshot eyes widen. "What if we take off? What if we become famous?"

"That doesn't sound like a bad thing to me, Drag."

"No. I mean, I could use the cash for sure."

"You and me both."

"What I mean is that when you're famous, people want to know about you." He pauses and lights up a joint, takes a long drag. "They look into your stories. Into your life. I don't need that shit hauled out."

"It won't be."

"Can you guarantee me that?"

I pat his shoulder. "There aren't any guarantees in life, bro. I can't guarantee that I won't be hit by a truck tomorrow."

Dragon flinches. "Jesus, Jess. Way to go dark on me. Isn't that my job?"

I chuckle. "Listen, Dragon. Everything's going to be fine. Seriously, what are the chances we'll *ever* be as big as Emerald Phoenix? Kind of a million to one, whether we open for them or not. What this *is* going to do for us is get our name out there. We'll be more than just some bar band who goes on tiny little tours. We might actually get some downloads of our songs. Make some decent money. Go on a few regional tours even. We're not going to be Emerald Phoenix, Dragon."

The truth of my words hits me like a brick.

We will *never* be Emerald Phoenix. Opening for a big name is never any guarantee, and while it will lead to some publicity, most opening acts never make it big.

Then there are the one-hit wonders. A band has a big hit, and then you never hear from them again. That could be us as well.

Whatever happens, I won't let Dragon get lugged through the mud. I'll always have his back, just like he's had mine.

The two of us have been through some shit together. Shit the rest of the band doesn't even know about. Shit my sisters and my parents don't know about.

And they never will.

I tilt my head back. The stars are easy to see through the bare branches of the cottonwood tree we're sitting under.

"You ever wonder if fame is worth it?" Dragon asks.

"Honestly, bro? I'm not sure I was ever looking for fame. I was looking to make a living doing what I love. I watched Rory give up on her dream of being an opera singer. She became a teacher. A good one. But I never wanted to give up. Eking out an existence as a rock band made me happy, even if it didn't make me rich."

"Rory's with us now," Dragon says.

"Yeah, she is." I look back into Dragon's eyes that look more green than brown in the light of the moon. "She completes the band, Dragon. The only thing we need now, if anything, is a bass player so Cage doesn't have to pull double duty. But even without a bassist, we rock, man."

"Yeah, we do. It's just . . . " He takes another toke.

I shake my head. "Dragon, you've got a major fear of success."

He lets the smoke out of his lungs and scowls. "What the hell does that mean?"

"It's kind of like a fear of failure. Except it's not."

He wrinkles his forehead. "Exactly how high am I? You're not making a lick of sense."

"Fear of failure keeps you from trying. Fear of success is worse. Once things start to happen for you, you rebel against them. We can't do that, Dragon. We've got to see this thing through."

Dragon is silent for a moment as he watches the ashes burn on his joint. "Maybe I *am* afraid of success. You and I both know why."

I'm not the hugging type, but I pat Dragon's arm. "It's

going to be okay. You've got to remember that rock bands are an entity. Fans don't think of us as individuals. They think of us as a unit."

"That won't stop the tabloids from doing their research."

"Then we'll just have to erase everything about your past. You've already done that for the most part."

"As much as I could."

"Listen. Two of my sisters are engaged to Steels. They have access to all the Steel resources. I'll see that you're covered. Okay?"

Dragon shakes his head, chuckling. "Listen to you. I never thought I'd see the day where you might ask a Steel for a favor."

"Not for myself. But for a good friend? You bet I would."

Dragon brings the joint to his lips. "Brothers to the end. Sure you don't want a toke?"

"I'm sure." I take the joint from him and put it out with my boot. "And you don't need any more."

"When you're right, you're right. I guess it's time to get back to the party." He rises and rubs his hands together. "Besides, it's fucking cold out here."

I stand as well. "Dude, that's the smartest thing you've said all night."

CHAPTER FIVE

Brianna

Once the Emerald Phoenix band members take their leave, Angie and Sage find me near the gazebo Jesse vacated.

"Where's Gina?" I ask.

"She went home," Angie says. "She's still… You know, digesting everything about her dad. About her newfound grandmother."

I nod. "Yeah, I get it. It's rough for all of us, but probably especially for Ava and Gina, knowing that they're not descended from Daphne Steel."

Sage smiles. "She'll be all right. She loves the holidays, and then we'll be back at school for the last semester, partying and having fun."

"Yeah, I know she'll be all right. I just still…" I push my hair behind my ear. "I can't imagine some of this. How our parents kept all of this from us for all these years."

"That's what bugs Gina the most, I think." Angie takes a drink of wine from the stemmed glass she's holding. "She's pretty mad at Uncle Ryan and Aunt Ruby."

"What about Ava?" I ask.

"Ava knew about it before Gina. Plus, she's engaged to Brendan Murphy. That's the thing about Ava. She doesn't let Steel drama get her down."

"Sometimes I wonder if she wishes she weren't a Steel," Sage says.

"I don't think so," I say. "She's just a . . . different kind of Steel. Frankly, I admire her. I mean, I don't want to give up my trust fund. Do either of you?"

"God no." Sage giggles.

"Maybe I could," Angie says. "If it were for a good reason. Like if I could help people, you know?"

"Good for you, Angie." I give her a smile. "What would you want to do?"

"I don't know. Help battered women maybe. Or better yet, help mentally ill people. People who suffer from the same issues as our grandmother."

I nod. "Yeah, I could see that. So does that mean you've decided what to do after you graduate?"

"Well . . ." A smile breaks across Angie's pretty face. "Yeah. I've only told Aunt Melanie about this, and I've sworn her to secrecy. But I've been applying to medical schools. I'm going to take a gap year first, but then I'd like to study medicine and become a psychiatrist like Aunt Mel."

"So that's where your desire to help the mentally ill came from." I give her a hug. "Good for you, Ang. You'll be a great doctor."

"Yeah," Sage says. "And since when do you *not* tell me these kinds of things? We're twins."

"Fraternal twins, not identical."

"So what? We grew in Mom's uterus together. We don't have secrets, Ang."

"Right. We don't. Not anymore." Angie meets her twin's gaze. "Don't tell anyone. Not even Mom and Dad. Only Aunt Melanie."

"I think it's great," I say to Angie. "What about you, Sage? What are you going to do after college?"

"I am *done* with school, that's for sure. My degree is in business, so I'm thinking I'll probably work for Dad on the business end of the ranch. Show Dave I'm as smart as he is."

Uncle Bryce, Sage's father, is a financial wizard and our chief operating officer. "That sounds ... not even *remotely* fun," I say, laughing.

"Growing apples and peaches doesn't sound like a lot of fun to me either."

"Are you kidding me?" I look out into our vast backyard, imagining the green orchards from blossom to fruition. "I get to be outdoors. Plus I get to help run the business. The best of both worlds."

Angie and Sage don't know I'm leaving yet. I can't tell anyone until I tell my parents. Only Donny and Callie know, and if I start telling the awesome foursome, it won't remain a secret for long.

"Have you seen Jesse?" I ask.

Sage looks around the yard. "Nope. Dragon seems to be missing, too. Cage and Jake are by the pool house. They're holding court over some townies."

"And you two aren't there?"

Sage's eyes light up. "We're headed that way. Come with us."

"Yeah, okay."

Wherever Jake and Cage are, Jesse and Dragon will eventually be. We walk toward the pool house, passing a table where my mom and dad are sitting with Uncle Bryce and Aunt Marj.

"There you girls are." Dad motions us over.

"Great party, Aunt Jade." Angie smiles.

Mom nods. "Thank you, Angie. Glad you're having a good time."

"It's hard not to have a good time with all the handsome rockers around here," Sage says.

Uncle Bryce looks at her sternly. "You stay away from those rockers, young lady." Then he smiles.

Aunt Marjorie laughs. "Give it up, Bryce. Our babies are grown up."

I don't say anything, but Uncle Bryce doesn't have much to worry about with regard to Angie and Sage. Neither of them is interested in settling down anytime soon, especially Angie, if she's going to give medical school a whirl. Juggling that time commitment plus a relationship won't lead to anything good.

But that's still a secret for now.

Honestly? The one they should all be worrying about is me.

Because as soon as Jesse Pike gives me a look, it's over. If he asked me to marry him tonight, my answer would be a resounding yes.

Too bad he's never looked my way.

That's not exactly true. He always helps me with my pool form when we're playing at Murphy's bar. Sometimes without me even asking him to.

Every time he puts his hand over mine to correct the way I hold the pool cue . . . my flesh burns.

I've never thought of myself as a groupie, but damned if I'm not following him to Europe on a tour.

"Do you girls want to join us?" Mom asks.

I'm busy scanning the area for Jesse.

"We're going to go talk to Cage and Jake, I think," Sage says, smiling.

Angie nods, and the two of them walk off.

"What about you, Bree?" Dad asks. "Sit down with your old folks for a while?"

"Okay." I move toward an empty chair, but then—

Dragon and Jesse appear, walking toward Cage and Jake. My skin reacts with an arousing chill.

"You know, maybe I'll join the girls. After all, I won't see much of them once they go back to school."

"They don't go back to school for three weeks," Mom says.

She raises a good point. "True, but there's something I need to talk to Sage about. I'll be back in a flash."

Perhaps I *will* be back in a flash. If Jesse Pike doesn't give me the time of day.

Of course, that's never stopped me from hanging around him before.

I hope he doesn't look at me as if I'm an annoying little sister. I'm the same age as his youngest sister, Madeline Pike. We call her Maddie, and she's the honorary fifth member of our awesome foursome. In fact, it was Maddie who coined the group's name.

I think sometimes she feels left out, but we try to include her as much as we can. The problem is that the four of us are family, so we're naturally close.

But Gina's not here tonight, and Maddie is. She joins Angie and Sage. Maddie's a beauty in her own right, nearly as gorgeous as her sister Rory. Brown hair, brown eyes, killer body.

Luckily, she's Jesse's sister, so she's not competition.

Angie and Sage aren't really interested in Jesse, not seriously anyway. They're my only other competition tonight.

Some townies are still here, making googly eyes at the

band members, but I'm not worried—

Until one of them grabs Jesse's arm.

I arrive just in time to hear her say, "You and your sister have the voices of angels. My God, where did all that talent come from?"

I recognize her. She's a waitress at Lorenzo's. Her name is Sadie, and she's beautiful. She's a little older than I am, too, which doesn't bode well for me.

"Our father," Jesse says in his deep drawl. "He's a musician, and he taught Rory and me from a young age."

"What's his name?" Sadie strokes Jesse's arm lightly.

A fire of jealousy ignites in my gut. Yeah, not liking this.

But Jesse doesn't seem to react to Sadie's touch. "His name is Frank Pike. He was here earlier. But he's not a pro. You wouldn't have heard of him."

"If your talent came from him, why isn't he a pro?"

I head closer, ease into the conversation. "I know why. Rory told me. His music is his hobby. He was afraid he wouldn't enjoy it as much if he tried to do it for work."

Jesse turns and looks at me. "Where'd you come from, Bree?"

"My mom and dad always said I came from heaven." I give him a wide smile.

His lips quirk upward. "I might beg to differ."

"Hi, Brianna," Sadie says. "Do you remember me?"

"Of course I do, Sadie. We met at Murphy's. You work over at Lorenzo's with your roommate, Nora."

"Yeah, that's her." Sadie gestures. "The blonde talking to Cage."

I glance over. Sure enough, there she is. She's not even trying to hide what she wants. She's all over him, sliding her hands up and down his arm.

"Seems Cage may be getting lucky tonight," I say.

"Oh, don't be silly." Sadie smiles adoringly at Jesse, still holding on to his arm. "Nora is just a touchy-feely kind of person."

"Of course," I say.

But that's a bunch of crap, and we both know it.

And if Sadie doesn't get her hand off Jesse . . .

I remember Nora being all over Donny *and* Henry at a previous Steel party. She likes blond men. Cage fits her type.

Sadie continues her love affair with Jesse's forearm, gazing into his eyes. "I love the covers you and Rory did. But the best were your original songs. Do you write them?"

Jesse looks down at Sadie's grasp on his arm. "I write some. Cage and Jake write some."

"What about Dragon?"

"He's not much of a writer." Jesse glances around. "Where the hell did he go anyway? He was just here."

"I don't know," Sadie says.

I dart my gaze around the yard. Then I see him. Dragon Locke is over by the pool house talking to my older sister, Diana.

Lordy. That's like looking at night and day even here in the dim light of the stars.

Dark Dragon and professional architect Dee.

"There he is. He's with my sister."

Jesse quirks his lip. "Diana? Now that's something I didn't see coming."

"I don't think anything's coming," I say. "Diana's a friendly sort. She talks to anyone."

"I know that," Jesse says. "But she is so *not* Dragon's type."

"You can say that again. He's not her type either. But they're probably just having a conversation, Jesse."

"Yeah, maybe." He shakes his head.

"What do you mean by that?"

Jesse frowns slightly. "What I mean is, Dragon's not a big talker. You all probably know that."

"True," I say.

"He does seem to keep to himself." Sadie looks to Dragon for a moment, her fingers still clenched around Jesse's arm. "But tell me more about you. How you got started with this band and all."

CHAPTER SIX

Jesse

Sadie's a pretty girl. I don't know how old she is, but I know she's older than Brianna Steel, who's a beautiful girl.

People like to say my sister Rory is the most beautiful woman in Snow Creek.

She is gorgeous, of course, but since I'm her brother, I don't see her that way.

If I had to choose the most beautiful woman in Snow Creek, she would be the young woman standing beside me now.

Brianna Steel.

She's tall, built, with long sable hair and mesmerizing dark eyes. Perfect proportions, perfect classically beautiful features.

And way too young for me.

I'm not looking for anyone, anyway.

One-nighters aren't my style—even though I plan to screw my way across Europe. But that's different. I'll be leaving after each gig. A hookup with someone here at the party? No thanks. I live here. I know these people.

Take Sadie, for instance. I'm pretty sure she'd be happy with one night of loving and then leaving.

But Brianna? She's way too good for that kind of thing.

Besides, it's too weird, with my rivalry with her brother and all.

It's bad enough that *he's* hooked up with Callie.

"If you ladies will excuse me," I say, finally wrestling my arm out of Sadie's grip.

Sadie isn't deterred and grabs my arm again. "Oh, don't go. You haven't answered my question yet."

"What question?" Right, she asked me about the band. "You mean about how the band got started?"

"Yes. I'd love to know the whole story."

Guess I have to deal with her vise grip on my forearm a bit longer. "I've always been interested in rock and roll. I got to go to college for free on a football scholarship. But I wasn't good enough for the pros—"

Sadie gasps. "Wait a minute. You played football?"

"Yeah. I was quarterback."

"You're kidding me."

"I don't kid."

Brianna laughs at that one, though I'm not sure why.

"Something funny, Bree?"

Brianna shakes her head, still chuckling. "No. Go ahead."

"Yeah, I played in high school. I was all-state, and just a hair short of making all-American. Got a scholarship to the University of Wyoming and went there, played football, but majored in music."

"How fascinating."

Fascinating? There's not really anything fascinating about my life. Or is there? I'm about to go on tour with a famous rock band. Maybe that *is* fascinating.

"So then what did you do?" Sadie asks, her eyes wide.

"Once I got out of college, I thought about going to grad

school and getting a master's degree in music. By then my sister Rory was starting college, and she wanted a classical career in opera. But I've always been a rocker at heart, and I didn't think a master's was worth the time and money. I got my undergrad for free while I played football, but I was going to have to pay for a graduate degree. So I said no, returned to Snow Creek, partnered up with my cousin Cage, and we recruited Jake and Dragon."

"When did Rory join the band?"

"Only recently. She tried for an opera career, but New York didn't know what was good for them, so she ended up back here and taught music. She would sing with us every now and then, but she never joined the band officially until recently."

"The two of you together are like a dream," Sadie says.

"I agree." Brianna steps between Sadie and me, forcing my arm out of Sadie's grasp. "Seriously, you two are. I've always loved your voice, Jesse, and though I'm not a huge opera fan, I've always loved Rory's too. When she sings with the band, lets her inner rocker out? She's amazing."

"I have to agree," I say. "It was actually Rory's idea for us to share lead vocals, and for me to leave the guitar to Jake. That's what drew Emerald Phoenix to us at a recent engagement we had. First half of the night, I played guitar, and we rocked so hard. Then Rory wanted to switch things up. So I said what the fuck? We tried it, and it was amazing. Jett said that was what convinced him that we should be his opening band."

"Wow." Sadie's eyes are dark-blue circles. "What an amazing story. How did Jett Draconis happen to be at your performance?"

"His agent told him about us. She had seen the previous performance. She wasn't signing any new acts at that time, but the opener for the Emerald Phoenix tour had dropped out, so they needed a quick replacement. Selena, the agent, sent Jett and Zane to see us. I guess the rest is history."

Sadie smiles. "So you've been discovered."

"Seems," I say. "Of course, none of us are counting our chickens before they're hatched."

Sadie bursts into giggles. "You guys and your ranching clichés."

I want to roll my eyes, but I resist. That's hardly a ranching cliché. It's as old as the hills.

"Did you ever think of giving up?" Sadie asks.

"Are you kidding me? Only about a thousand times. There were years where we eked out a living. Then there were years when we didn't make a penny. All of us have day jobs, of course. I work on my family's ranch. So does Cage. Jake drives for Uber when he has to, and Dragon . . . "

Dragon works at a dispensary and sometimes takes his pay in weed, but he may not want me to say that.

"And Dragon?" Sadie prompts.

"Odd jobs."

Brianna lifts her eyebrows at me. She knows where Dragon works. There's a dispensary in the next town over, Barrel Oaks. Snow Creek doesn't have one, and they won't as long as Donny Steel is the city attorney. He's sworn to keep the town clean. Most of us in town don't care one way or the other. Those who want weed go to Barrel Oaks and get it. I'm not sure Donny cares either, but his mother, the former city attorney, does. Different generation, and all.

In truth, Dragon shouldn't be smoking weed or drinking. He had a problem with narcotics earlier in his life, but somehow, he's managed to stay away from the hard stuff even though he still uses alcohol and marijuana. Unusual for an addict, but I don't give him any guff about it because he stays sober for rehearsal and performances. He's a genius on percussion.

Besides, he needs an escape. He's had a damned rough life.

He almost took my sister Rory to bed a month or so ago. Luckily, Brock phoned her, and she called it off. Dragon spilled his guts to me about it a week after.

I almost popped him one that night.

I also made him promise never to go near any of my sisters again.

He made the promise.

And I believe him.

I trust Dragon, and he trusts me. Hell, I'm the only one who knows his story, but I swear to God, if he ever goes near one of my sisters again, I won't stop myself from beating him senseless.

Sadie opens her mouth to say something when her friend Nora grabs her arm. "We're heading into town to Murphy's. You all want to come?"

"Sure," Sadie says. "Come on, Jesse."

Hitting the bar is the last thing I want to do. I'm exhausted. Cage, of course, is hoping to get laid, so he'll go. Normally I love an evening at Murphy's playing pool, but tonight I'm just not up for it.

"You all go without me," I say. "I think I'll be getting home."

"Oh, please?" Sadie begs.

"Next time." I smile.

I can tell by the look in her eyes that Sadie wants to stay here, but she already told Nora she'd go. So she heads out with

Cage and some townies.

Jake is nowhere to be found. He must've left already, or he's going with them. Dragon is still by the pool house with Diana.

Really strange.

So I'm left standing here next to Brianna Steel.

"Nice to see you, Bree."

"Yeah, you too." She smiles.

She truly is beautiful.

Beautiful . . . and Maddie's age.

"Shit," I say.

"Yeah?"

"Where's Maddie? Did she go off with them?"

"I don't know." Brianna looks toward the deck. "Donny and Callie are still here. Maybe they know where she is."

"Good enough. Let's go."

CHAPTER SEVEN

Brianna

"Hey, guys," I say when we reach the deck where Donny and Callie are sitting where my aunts were earlier. "Have you seen Maddie?"

"She went on home," Callie says. "Brock and Rory gave her a ride."

"Thank God," Jesse says.

"What's that supposed to mean?" Don asks.

Donny and Jesse are still trying to irk each other. It's really time for both of them to grow up.

Callie darts them both an *Are we really going there again?* look.

"It means she didn't go into town with Jake and Cage and the town girls."

"I agree with you," Callie says. "That's good."

"Okay," Jesse says. "I'm beat. I'm going to head home."

"Night, Jess," Callie says and then elbows my brother.

"Good night, Pike," Donny says begrudgingly.

"Steel." Jesse turns and walks through the house.

The urge to follow him is so great, but what do I say? He's tired, and I have no reason to believe he's not going anywhere but home.

I should probably be more worried about my older sister

35

talking to Dragon Locke outside.

But what they're doing seems innocent enough. Sitting on Adirondack chairs over by the pool house, deep in conversation.

If Dragon even knows how to have a conversation.

I take a seat next to Donny. "What's up with you guys?"

"Nothing much." He grabs Callie's hand. "Just enjoying the night. We'll be heading out soon."

Donny and Callie live in the guesthouse behind my parents' house.

I feign a yawn. "I guess I should get to bed."

"So tomorrow is the day?" Donny says.

He's referring to me telling my parents I'm going on the tour, of course.

"I guess I've put it off long enough."

"They won't be happy," he says.

"Rub it in, why don't you?"

"Why do you want to do this again?" he asks. "I'm not quite clear on it."

I hold out my left hand. I need a manicure. "It's a chance to see Europe. I've never been."

"Then go for a couple of weeks with us," Callie says. "You don't have to go the whole time."

Callie clearly doesn't know I'm madly in love with her brother. No one does. Not even the rest of the awesome foursome.

I pause. Maybe I could tell Callie the truth, but not Donny. He'd freak.

"I just feel strongly that I want to do this," I finally say. "I'd still be in school anyway if I hadn't graduated early. Mom and Dad have no reason to need me here. They didn't know I'd be here until a couple of weeks ago."

"Yeah, but you're still their baby," Donny says.

I cross my arms. "I'm a grown woman capable of making my own decisions."

"You're a cowgirl through and through, Bree," Donny says. "The most of any of us. Even Dale, though he stayed on the ranch, is far from a cowboy. You're Dad's true progeny. The only one to share his interest."

I huff. "I'll still share his interest six months later. I just want to go."

"But once Callie and I leave," Donny says, "what will you do?"

I rise, pace across the deck and back. "I'll go with the band. I'll make myself useful. And if I can't, I'll stay out of their way. But I'll be at every concert cheering them on. Rory's going to be a Steel soon. Shouldn't a Steel be with her, cheering her on?"

Donny narrows his gaze at me. "A Steel *will* be. Brock will be there."

He's right. That argument doesn't hold any water.

"I mean a Steel who she's not going to marry."

Donny shakes his head. "For the life of me, I don't get what you're doing, sis. But I support you. I'll have your back. And I'm glad Brock will be there to keep his eye on you."

"No one needs to keep an eye on me," I say, my tone petulant.

"You're still my little sis. So yeah, I'm going to have Brock keep an eye on you."

I roll my eyes. "Whatever." Brock is only two years older than I am, but he's got a Y chromosome. I love my brothers and cousins, but they take this overprotective chivalry way too seriously.

"Give us a call tomorrow," Callie says. "After you tell your mom and dad."

"If they don't react well, I'll probably be on your doorstep."

"It won't be that bad." Donny rises and gives me a brotherly hug.

"I guess we'll see." I sigh. "I think I'm going to bed. Good night, you guys."

I head up to bed.

I didn't say good night to Mom and Dad or Aunt Marj and Uncle Bryce, who are all still sitting on the other side of the deck, deep in conversation.

Instead, I head straight for my room, take a quick shower, and then flop onto my bed wearing nothing but a pair of cotton panties.

And I dream about Jesse Pike.

★ ★ ★

The next morning, I get up early. Ranching work starts with the sun, sometimes before.

Mom and Dad are already at the breakfast table, and I don't know where Diana is. Probably still asleep. She gave up keeping ranching hours when she went off to college to study architecture.

In fact, she'll drive back to Denver today to continue her internship. Then she'll be back for the holidays.

"Good morning, Bree," Mom says. "Coffee's on."

"Where's Darla?" I ask.

"She's taking a few days off. Spending time with her family so she can be here for the holidays."

"You're not letting her go home for the holidays?"

"We offered, of course," Dad says. "But she wants to be here."

I shake my head. "I can't say I understand that decision, but whatever." I go to the cupboard, pull out my favorite coffee mug, and pour a healthy dose of coffee. Mom makes the best coffee—strong, black, and robust.

I take a sip, thinking. I'm going to work with Dad today, but Donny is right. I need to let him and Mom know my plans for the first of the year.

"We're going to the office today, Bree," Dad says. "I've got some work to do with Joe and Bryce on the financials. We have some new contracts coming in for fruit. You can help me with all of that. We're expanding the Granny Smith orchard. I know that's your favorite."

He's right. I do love the tangy tartness of the green Granny Smith. "I'll be glad to, Dad."

"I have to tell you that it works out really well that you were able to graduate early. I'll sure be able to use you come the first of the year. One of our best men is leaving, and I thought I'd have to replace him, but instead, you'll be able to fill the void."

Uh-oh . . .

"Something wrong, Brianna?" Mom asks.

I can almost feel the color drain from my face. "Why are you asking me that?"

"Because you frowned when Dad said he was happy that you're going to be here. That doesn't make any sense to me."

What an opener. Apparently I don't have a good game face.

I draw in a deep breath. "Well, Mom, Dad . . . It's just that . . . I've made some plans."

"Oh?" Dad raises his eyebrows. "What kind of plans?"

I clear my throat. "I've always wanted to see Europe, and I thought since Donny and Callie are going over to the UK when the band leaves after the first of the year . . . Well, I thought I'd go along."

"Have you talked to Donny and Callie about this?" Mom asks.

"Oh, yeah. They know."

"Are you sure they want you tagging along?" Mom wipes her lips with her napkin. "They may consider it a private trip. A romantic one."

"It's not like I'm going to be staying in the same room with them. I'll have my own room. But I figured it was a good time to go—you know, since they'll be there. And of course Brock and Rory will be there too."

"It does sound like a great opportunity, Talon," Mom says. "I would have loved to see Europe at Bree's age. I was so envious of Marj the summer she went while I had to stay at home and work for my father's company."

"Aunt Marjorie went to Europe?" I ask.

"Wouldn't know," Dad says gruffly. "I was overseas myself then."

Dad doesn't talk much about his time in the military, but he was a hero, according to the rest of the family. Weird that Aunt Marj went to Europe, but my generation of Steels are content to stay closer to home. That's how we were raised. Now that I know our full family history, I understand why.

"I think she should go," Mom says.

Dad nods. "I suppose it's not a big deal. Donny and Callie are only going to be gone for the two plus weeks the band is in the UK. You can start work after that."

I bite on my lower lip. Here goes . . .

"Actually . . . I'm going to be assisting Brock and Rory." Okay, that's not what I was supposed to say.

"What do you mean?" Mom asks.

Yeah, what *do* I mean? That just popped out of my mouth. "Rory's going to need an assistant."

"And what kind of experience do you have assisting a rock singer?" Dad asks, his voice a little rigid.

I open my mouth to speak, but—

"Talon," Mom says, "I think what she's trying to tell you is that she wants to go on tour with the band."

I heave a sigh of relief. Good old Mom.

I send her a *thank you* glance.

However, the look on her face doesn't readily say *you're welcome.*

"Is that true, Brianna?" Dad asks.

"Well . . . It's just such a good chance to see Europe. And not have to go alone."

"If you want to go to Europe," Dad says, "why didn't you take a semester abroad during college?"

"There aren't really any semesters abroad where you can study American agriculture in Europe."

"So? You could've left your major for a semester. You could've studied art history. Or environmental studies. Or any number of things that I know you're interested in."

"That ship has sailed, Dad. Now I want to go to Europe, and this is a great chance."

Dad takes a sip from his mug. Then he frowns. "I don't think it's a good idea."

"I have to agree with your father," Mom says. "Going to the UK for a few weeks with Donny and Callie is one thing, but—"

"Brock is going, and he's only two years older than I am."

"Yes, but he's going as Rory's fiancé. Plus . . . "

Mom stops talking.

I know exactly what she's going to say. He's a man. Men can take better care of themselves than women. Which is a crock of shit, and she knows it.

"I can take good care of myself, Mom. Hell, I handle a gun better than Brock does."

"Did I say you didn't?" Mom says. "But you know you can't take a gun with you on a plane."

I let out an exasperated sigh. "For God's sake, I'm not a moron. I don't plan on taking my gun with me."

"And how do you plan to take care of yourself?" Dad asks.

"By using my brain, Daddy. Jeez."

Mom takes a sip of her coffee and then clears her throat. "You're a grown woman, Brianna."

"Damned right I am. I'm not asking your permission. I'm telling you."

"A grown woman wouldn't take that tone of voice with her parents," Dad says calmly.

Yeah. He's got me there.

I inhale, exhale. "I apologize for my tone. And thank you, Daddy, for having the confidence in me to be your second-in-command with regard to the orchard. I've been looking forward to that my entire life, and that hasn't changed. I'll only be gone the first half of the year. I'll be back by the time the trees are in bloom. Everything will work out fine."

"But if you're following the band around," Mom says, "are you going to have the chance to see many of the sights? Going to Europe is an experience you should never forget. There's so much culture and so many things to see and do."

"I'll do that during the day."

"Not if Rory needs you as her assistant," Mom says.

Ugh, why did I lie? Mom will probably talk to Rory, and she's not going to know what the hell I'm talking about.

Better to lay my cards on the table now.

"I'm sorry, Mom, Dad. That wasn't true. I'm not going to be acting as Rory's assistant. The truth of the matter is that . . . I just want to go."

"Can you tell us why?" Dad asks.

"Because I want to. It's a wonderful opportunity to see Europe with members of my family already there."

"We can't force her to stay, Talon," Mom says. "She's twenty-two years old."

"How do you expect to pay for the trip?" Dad asks.

Really? Is he going to play that card? "The trip isn't going to cost all that much. I have more than enough in savings. And even if I didn't, I can't think of a better use of a withdrawal from my trust fund than international travel."

Dad sighs. "You're right, blue eyes. We can't stop her."

I lean toward Dad and grab his hand. "I *am* sorry to disappoint you both. But this is going to be an amazing experience for me. I'll text you every day. Call you when I can. Take lots of pictures."

"All right, sweetie," Mom says.

Dad still doesn't look happy, but he gives a reluctant nod.

I take a sip of my coffee.

One hurdle.

Now . . . to figure out how to get the band to make peace with my presence.

Time to talk to Brock and Rory.

CHAPTER EIGHT

Jesse

The next morning, Brock and Rory arrive, and the three of us sit down to go over the logistics of the tour.

Emerald Phoenix is starting in London, will do two performances there over the span of six days to allow for getting over jet lag, and then we head north for a performance in Edinburgh, and then one in Glasgow. Back to London for one more performance. Then we fly to Paris.

Two concerts in Paris, and then Brussels, Berlin, Munich, Vienna, Venice, Florence, Rome, Barcelona, Madrid, and then back to Paris for an encore performance, and then we'll fly home.

The entire tour will take nearly four months.

"Will there be any time for sightseeing?" Brock asks.

"Jett says there should be plenty," I tell him. "We'll have some full days off. But there will be a lot of rehearsal. He's going to send me a full itinerary within the next week. We'll have the days off on it by then, and you can schedule your sightseeing around the rehearsal blocks."

"Sounds good. Callie and Donny will be with us for the UK portion," Rory says.

"I know," I say. "Mom's sending Maddie along as well. That way all four of us can experience the UK together."

"That's a lovely idea," Rory says. "I don't know why one of us didn't think of it."

"Because we've been too busy thinking about the concert tour," I say. "I feel bad that I didn't think about it either. We can blame Callie. She doesn't have her head in rock and roll. Maybe *she* should've thought of it."

Rory laughs. "Good enough for me. Placing the blame on Callie it is."

I take a sip of coffee. "So, Brock, you said you were going to invest in our merch."

"Absolutely."

"I've got some quotes." I shove the paper toward him. "Let me know if you think this is reasonable. If we sell out, you'll be paid off and then some."

"All I need to do is recoup my investment. All the profits go to the band."

"You should get paid for your troubles, Brock," Rory says.

"All I want is my money back, but if it makes you feel better, baby, give me two percent or something."

I pull the paper back. "Two percent it is."

"All right," Rory says. "Now we have to figure out which numbers we're going to perform."

"I know," I say. "I've had that on my mind. We can't do any covers, obviously, because people are going to be paying to see this, and I don't want to mess with royalty payments. We can't afford them anyway. So we'll be doing all original tunes."

"We have to do 'Faint of Heart,'" Rory says.

"Absolutely. That's number one on my list. Cage thinks we should do 'Flyaway.'"

"Yeah, that's a good one. And how about that other one? 'Three's a Crowd'?"

"That's a solo for the male," I say.

"I know, but it's such a gorgeous song."

I shake my head. "Sis, Emerald Phoenix asked us to open for them because they like you *and* me singing together. We need songs that showcase both of us."

"Can you write a part for me?"

"Maybe . . . Time is running out, though."

Rory sighs. "Yeah, you're right. But I could sing a third above or a sixth below you. We could make it work."

"If it means that much to you."

Rory pauses a moment. "No. We have better songs that you and I sing together. Cross off 'Three's a Crowd.'"

I do exactly that, and I write down the names of a few more of our original songs that I think will work and hand the list to Rory.

She scans and nods. "That should do it. We only need five or six numbers. Really only three or four. We just need extra for encores."

"Which we may not get," I remind her.

Rory cocks her head. "When have we *not* gotten an encore?"

"These people are paying to see Emerald Phoenix. Every encore we do keeps them from seeing Emerald Phoenix, Ror. This is a different situation. I don't think we're going to be doing encores."

"Yeah, you're right," she says.

"Send me the final numbers for the merch—" Brock's phone buzzes in his hand. "Sorry. Just got a text." He scans his phone quickly. "It's from Bree. She says she needs to talk to us, Ror."

"We're almost done here," I say.

"How much longer do you think we'll be?" Rory asks.

"Not long. Tell her to come over here and meet you. We'll be done by the time she gets here."

"Sure, that works." Brock taps on his phone. "She says she'll be over in about twenty minutes."

"Great. The rest of the band is coming over in half an hour to practice music without vocals in the garage, so you don't need to be here, Rory."

"I'm happy to stay if you need me."

"Well . . . maybe. You and I are the only two of all of us who actually have degrees in music, and yours is advanced. Having you here might be good."

"Sure. Brock and I can see what Bree wants to talk to us about, and then I'll join you."

"Sounds good."

CHAPTER NINE

Brianna

I walk into the Pikes' family room. "I hope you don't mind. Your mom let me in."

"Not at all," Rory says.

"So what's up, baby cousin?" Brock asks jovially.

I scoff at him. "*Baby* cousin? I'm only two years younger than you are."

"Still, the four of you—the awesome foursome—are the babies of the family."

"Okay." Better not to give Brock too much crap. After all, I need his and Rory's support if I'm going to go on the tour.

"So, I was wondering..." I look around the Pikes' family room. A lot smaller than ours but homey. "You know I graduated early, right?"

"Yeah, that's amazing," Rory says with a smile. "Congratulations."

I return her smile with a broad one of my own. "Thanks. Anyway... I would love to see Europe. And you know I'm a big fan of your band, Rory." I pause for a split second but then decide to rip off the bandage. "I've already made arrangements to go to England with Donny and Callie for the two weeks that they're going to be there. But I'd like to stay on. Go with the band. So I was wondering if maybe you needed an assistant or something?"

Rory scrunches her forehead. "I haven't really thought about that. I'm not sure we have it in our budget to pay you."

I raise my hands in front of me. "Oh my God, you don't need to pay me. You know we all have plenty of money."

"Bree," Brock says, "if you want to go on the tour, just ask Rory. You don't have to make up some baloney about being her assistant."

"Well . . . I'd like to be helpful."

"Nonsense," Rory says. "We'd be thrilled to have you along. Maddie will be coming along with Donny and Callie as well. Mom thought it would be a great opportunity for the four of us siblings to see the UK together."

I clap my hands together. "That's wonderful. If Maddie goes, she and I can room together."

Except . . . then I won't have a place to be alone with Jesse. But I'll worry about that later. Having Maddie along on the tour will give me some leverage. She'll want someone her own age around to hang out with. Or she will, once I tell her how fun it will be.

"Yeah, of course you could." Rory smiles.

"But," Brock says, "Maddie didn't graduate early. She has to get back by the end of January to start her second semester of her last year of college."

"Right . . . Well, if you just tell me all the places you're staying while you're on tour, I'll book a room at the same places."

"You'll have to have your own room," Rory says. "I'm the only woman in the band, and of course I'll be bunking with Brock."

"Right." Brock gives her a sultry stare.

I hold back a sly smile. That works just perfectly for me.

"So you're okay with me coming along?" I ask.

"Sure I am," Rory says. "But I'll have to ask the guys."

An idea pops into my head. "What if I went along as an influencer? Or your social media manager? I have a pretty large following on Instagram and some of the other apps. I could take photos and give the band some great publicity."

"Brianna," Brock says, "the band is already getting great publicity. They're opening for Emerald Phoenix."

I sigh, biting my lip. I can't tell the truth—that I'm going on the tour to get Jesse Pike to fall in love with me.

What if he doesn't?

Well ... If he doesn't ... I come home. I come home, patch up my broken heart, and take my place at Dad's side in the orchard.

But I have to try. And if it doesn't work out, I get to see some amazing concerts and a lot of Europe.

"Brianna," Brock says, "why don't you just tell us the truth? You want to come along."

A chill hits the back of my neck. Does Brock know about my feelings for Jesse? Or does he suspect? I may as well just admit the truth—or part of it.

"All right. I give. I want to come along."

Rory smiles then. "I think it would be lovely for you to come along. In truth, I wish Maddie could come along with you for the whole tour. In fact, I wonder ... " She tilts her head.

"What are you thinking?" Brock asks.

Rory grabs Brock's hand. "It would be a really awesome opportunity for Maddie. I mean, when else could she see so much of Europe with her family? Maybe she'd be willing to put off her last semester of college. That way, she and Brianna could room together, and neither one of them would be alone."

Damn it. I like Maddie and all, but having a roommate wasn't in my plans. Still, I force a smile. "That's a perfect solution. I bet Maddie would love to come."

"It would entail her going back to school in the fall and then graduating in December," Rory says.

"I'm not sure she'd be up for it," I say.

Seriously, why would she want to miss her last semester? I may get my private room after all.

"Well, we can ask her."

"What if she doesn't want to come? Can I still go?"

Now I'm acting too eager. *Be cool, Bree.*

"I'll have an easier time selling it to the guys if Maddie comes along," Rory says. "But honestly, it's a free world, Bree. I can easily give you the names of our hotels, and you can book a room. No one's stopping you. I just can't guarantee you'd be able to ride with us to all the gigs and stuff."

"I never saw you as a groupie anyway, cuz." Brock laughs.

"Riding with the band would be fun," I say. "I'd love to be able to do that."

"Then to get Jesse and the guys on board with that, we probably need Maddie to come. Jesse's very protective, and he wouldn't want you going along with the band unchaperoned."

Ha! Jesse could be my chaperone. I'd love that. However, that's not the way to get him to agree. "But I wouldn't be unchaperoned, Rory. You'll both be there, and Brock is my cousin."

"She makes a good point," Brock says.

Rory scratches the side of her head. "Yeah... That unchaperoned argument wasn't really working with me anyway. The truth of the matter is, Brianna, I don't know how the guys are going to react to this. Let me talk to Jesse and bring the idea up to Maddie as well. We'll try to get it to work out."

"I would love it if it could. This is a perfect opportunity for me to see Europe before I start working full time on the ranch. I'm a huge fan of Emerald Phoenix, and an even bigger fan of Dragonlock. So please, please make this work out."

Damn, Bree. Don't be so over eager. Of course my advice to myself is too late.

"I'll do my best," Rory says.

"Thanks." I give her a hug.

"Tell you what," she says. "All the guys are coming over for rehearsal. In fact, they're probably already here. If you want, we can talk about it to them right now."

"Maybe we should talk to Maddie first. Is she home?"

"Yeah, she's home. I think she's up in her room reading."

I stop myself from jumping. "I'll go see her right now. I know I can talk her into this."

I race up the few steps to the main level, and then down the hallway to Maddie's room. I knock on the door.

"Yeah, come in."

I open the door. Maddie's lying on her bed on her stomach, her head hanging over the edge of the bed, a book on the floor before her. Her bed is adorned with pillows and a cozy leopard-print duvet. Her bedside table holds a stack of well-loved books, a reading lamp, and a small potted plant. It's some kind of cactus. Her walls are oddly bare except for a corkboard where she's pinned what appear to be inspirational quotes.

"I am an outsider looking in, absolutely." — David Bowie

"Why fit in when you were born to stand out?" — Dr. Seuss

"The worst part about feeling like you don't belong is trying to find a place to belong." — Trent Shelton

Interesting. My parents are big David Bowie fans, and of

course I know Dr. Seuss, but I've never heard of Trent Shelton.

"Hey, Mads."

She cocks her head toward my voice. "Brianna? What are you doing here?"

"Who's Trent Shelton?"

"What?"

"The quote on your board."

"Oh." Her cheeks redden. "He's a former NFL player. He's... He's a big name in motivation and personal development. That kind of stuff. What's up?"

"I was talking to Rory and Brock, and we had this fabulous idea. I want to run it by you."

"Yeah, okay. What?"

"How would you like to take next semester off?"

She moves into a sitting position on her bed. "Why would I do that? It's my senior year. I know you don't mind missing all the parties and fun, but I don't want to."

I walk toward Maddie and sit on the bed next to her. "Wouldn't it be more fun to go to Europe? With the band?"

She stares at me intently. "Why would I want to do that?"

"You're already going for a few weeks, to the UK with Donny and Callie."

"Yeah." She breathes in. "I am looking forward to that. But I'll be back in time to start second semester."

"Mads, think of it. Sure, you'll miss all the parties, but I'm missing them too."

"That was your choice, Bree."

"I know. But if we go on tour with the band, you'll be with me."

"The band is my brother. And sister. And cousin."

"But three members of Emerald Phoenix aren't spoken

for. And we'll be in Europe, meeting European men."

That gets her attention. "All right. Keep talking."

"I'd really like to go, but Brock and Rory think they'll be able to sell it to the guys better if you come along. The two of us could room together."

"I'm not a groupie, Bree."

"Neither am I."

She laughs then. A scoffing laugh. "Are you kidding me? I've seen how you hang around my brother and the guys over at Murphy's. You, Gina, and Sage are total groupies."

I'm not sure how I can retaliate on that one. She's completely right.

"Okay, so I'm a little bit of a groupie. But that's not why I want to go on this tour. This is a chance to see Europe, Maddie. I'll be paying for my own room, so you can stay there free of charge."

"My parents wouldn't like that."

I shrug. "Your parents don't have to know. As far as they're concerned, the band is paying for everything."

"They would know better than that."

I sigh. "All right, Mads. What will it take—right now—for you to do this? Anything within my power, and it's yours."

She closes her book and scrambles off her bed, standing.

"Tell me. Tell me right now. Are you after my brother?"

I blink. "Of course not."

That's a lie. But I said I'd do what's in my power. I didn't say I'd be completely truthful.

"Do you have any interest in him whatsoever?"

"I think he's good-looking. I think he's mega talented. But he's thirty-two years old, Mads."

I feel my nose growing by the second.

"What about my cousin?"

"Cage? Of course not."

No nose enlargement on that one. Cage is handsome, but Jesse is . . . out of this world.

Maddie sits back down on the bed next to me. She doesn't say anything for a few minutes.

I rack my brain, trying to come up with something else to nudge her—

"All right. I think it could be fun. Just you and me."

Yes!

I grab her hands to stop myself from jumping up from the bed in joy. "Absolutely. It'll be a blast."

She looks down at her lap. "To tell the truth, I've always felt kind of left out of the awesome foursome."

Hmm. Those inspirational quotes are making some more sense. How could I—and Angie, Sage, and Gina—be so obtuse? "You know you're an honorary member, Mads. If it weren't for you, there would *be* no awesome foursome. You came up with that term."

"I know. But you guys forget about me so much of the time. The four of you head out to Murphy's, and you don't think to invite me."

"But we won't have to worry about that if we're in Europe, will we?"

Maddie rolls her eyes. "You're not getting it."

She's right. I'm not approaching this well at all. If she feels left out, I need to show her she's important to me. It's not even a lie. She's very important to me. She always has been.

"I'm sorry. I didn't know you felt that way. I'll do better."

She huffs. "I need to get over it anyway. I'm twenty-two years old. A grown-up. Time to let go of this petty jealousy."

I squeeze her hand. "This is a perfect opportunity for you and me to do something together. Without the others. It would be a total blast for us to see Europe."

"Yeah. It might be. I still have to find money for a plane ticket."

"You don't need to find money for a plane ticket. You're already flying out with Donny and Callie. Just change the dates."

"It's more than the dates, Bree. I'd have to change the return plans. I think the tour ends in Paris."

"That's true. But you can still change it. I'll help. All we need is a computer and your confirmation code."

"And extra money. I can't ask my parents for anything extra. They're already strapped."

I can't offer to pay for any change fees. She'll take that the wrong way. But I'm going to make sure she goes. I feel terrible that she's felt left out of the awesome foursome. The four core members are all family, so we don't always think about outsiders.

I'll do better.

Perhaps she and I can become closer in Europe.

"Plus," she continues, "I have to check with the university. I'm on scholarship. What if they're not willing to extend it to the next semester?"

"Why wouldn't they be?"

"Because, Brianna, sometimes money doesn't grow on trees. Sometimes money is available for a specified time period, and that's it." She huffs, her shoulders stiff.

Uh-oh. I may have just blown it.

"I know that, Maddie." I push my hair behind my ear. "I'm sorry. You're right. Sometimes I don't think about money."

"You *never* think about money, Bree. None of the awesome foursome ever thinks about money. Right now, my family is in a bind. We lost most of our livelihood in that fire. Rory and Jesse are hoping to help out with the money they make from this tour."

"Callie and Rory are engaged to my brother and my cousin. You guys don't have to worry about money ever again."

She scoffs. "Brianna Steel, you just don't get it, and you never will."

Damn.

How can I make this happen?

I rise, walk to the doorway of her bedroom, and then turn. "I see. Well, it would've been fun, Maddie. Maybe we could have gotten closer if we went to Europe together."

Maddie claps her hands to the sides of her head. "For the love of God, Brianna, it's not that I don't want to go. There are just some things I have to look into. I'm not *you*. I can't just decide something and then snap my fingers."

"I can't decide by snapping my fingers either, Maddie. If you don't go, I'm not going to get to go."

She shakes her head. "I should've known. You just want to use me."

Now I feel lower than a sewer rat. "That's not true, and you know it. We've been friends forever."

"Yeah. Friends." Maddie crosses her arms and drops her gaze to her hardwood floor. "But not family."

I take a few steps back toward Maddie's bed. "We're *going* to be family. Callie's marrying my brother. Rory's marrying my cousin."

And I'll marry your brother someday.

"Yeah, right. That doesn't make all the times you and the

rest of the awesome foursome left me out of everything hurt any less."

"I've already explained. None of us *knew* that, Maddie. We would never hurt you intentionally."

"I'd like to think you wouldn't."

I sit back down next to Maddie. "Listen. How can I make this up to you? Even if you don't want to go to Europe, I want to make it up to you."

"The past is in the past," she says. "And you're not going back to school. It's probably up to the other three."

"Well… If you look into coming to Europe on the tour with me, I'll try to make it up to you there. I'll always ask you what you want to do."

Maddie shakes her head. "Bree, that's not what I want. It's not all about me. I just don't want to feel like the fifth wheel anymore."

"In Europe with me, you won't be the fifth wheel. You'll be the sister of the two lead singers in the band. *I'll* be the odd man out."

She cocks her head.

For God's sake… *That's* what's getting to her?

The Pikes are good people, and Madeline is a nice girl. I honestly always thought we were friends, and I never knew she felt so left out with Angie, Sage, Gina, and me. I vow right now to make it up to her, whether she goes to Europe or not.

"I *would* like to see Europe, and I know my parents would be much more comfortable if Rory and Jesse were there."

"See? It's a great idea all the way around."

"All right. I'll look into it. But I'm not making any promises."

"That's all I ask." I give her a quick hug. "I have to go.

Would you like to go get a drink later at Murphy's?"

"With everyone else?"

"No. I thought maybe you and I could get one together."

She cracks a small smile. "Yeah, Bree. I'd like that."

CHAPTER TEN

Jesse

"Great rehearsal, guys."

Rory clears her throat at me.

"Oh, *and* Rory."

"Rory is one of the guys," my cousin Cage says.

"She doesn't look like a guy from where I'm standing," Brock says, eyeing her.

Damn. The way the Steel men look at my sisters is enough to make insects crawl up my spine. First Donny with Callie and then Brock with Rory.

But Callie and Rory are both in love, and from what I can tell, Donny and Brock feel the same way about them.

My sisters could do worse, for sure.

Maddie comes traipsing into the garage. "You guys done?"

"Yeah, we are," Rory says.

"Good. I have something to ask you."

"What's that, sis?" I ask.

"Brianna Steel was just here, and she thought it would be fun if the two of us came on tour with you guys."

Rory and Brock exchange a glance.

Apparently they know something I don't.

"Don't you have another semester at school?" I ask.

"Yeah, but I only have one class I absolutely have to take.

For the rest, I was going to take some easy electives. In fact ... I could probably take an online class to satisfy requirements for graduation, and we'd be back in time for me to walk for spring commencement."

"But it's your last semester," I say. "I know Brianna decided to skip it, but you and the rest of the Steel girls were looking forward to your last semester with your sororities and all that other shit I don't understand."

Rory punches me in the arm. "That stuff is important to college girls, Jess."

"Then why are you willing to miss it?" I ask Maddie.

"It was just a thought." She turns. "If you don't want me there—"

I grab her arm so she turns back around to face me. "Maddie, it's not that I don't want you there. It's just that I'm surprised you want to go, given that it's your last hurrah at college. Plus ... since when are you and Brianna so close?"

"We've always been friends." Her gaze shifts. "I mean, out of the awesome foursome, I'm closest to Angie, the quietest of the four, but we're all friends."

I won't mention the fact that I've seen my little sister crying on more than one occasion because she got left out of some awesome foursome activity. Those were times I had to stop myself from pummeling a Steel man out of spite.

I tip her chin up to meet my gaze. "Is this something you want to do, Maddie, or is it something Brianna Steel is talking you into?"

She bites on her lip, not talking.

"Frankly, I think it's a wonderful idea," Rory pipes in. "It's a chance Maddie might not have otherwise. She'll see the sights of Europe, and you and I will be there to keep an eye on her, which will make Mom and Dad happy."

"Exactly," Maddie says.

"I wouldn't mind having you along," I say. "But you'd better fix it with your college."

"Oh, yeah, of course I would do that. I also won't go if Mom and Dad don't want me to. But I'm at least going with Callie, Donny, and Brianna for the first couple of weeks before school starts."

I sigh, relenting. "Okay. Check it out with Mom and Dad and the university. But only if everything's good with school. I'm not going to be responsible for you not getting your degree."

"You're the best, Jess." Maddie gives me a quick hug and runs back out.

I turn to Rory. "Exactly what was that about?"

"Why does it have to be about anything?" Rory asks innocently.

"Because of the look on your face, Ror. You're my sister, and while you used to have me wrapped around your little finger, those days are long over."

"Oh, yeah, they were over when Maddie was born." Rory gives me a playful grin. "Now *she's* the one who has you wrapped around her little finger, so I have no doubt that she's going to be coming to Europe with us."

"Only if Mom and Dad say it's okay."

"She's twenty-two years old, Jess. She doesn't need Mom and Dad's permission."

My sister's right.

"Fine. We'll make it work. But we're going to have to get her a room. I suppose she could stay with me, but then the guys would have to go three to a room."

"This is all a nonissue," Brock says. "Brianna's going to

have a room, and Maddie will stay with her."

I take a sharp turn and step toward Brock. "I'll pay my sister's way, Steel."

Rory punches my arm again. "Just stop it, Jess. Brock is my fiancé. He's going to be a member of our family, which means Brianna's going to be a member of our family, so just get off your stupid *I'm not taking any Steel money* high horse and accept this gift for your little sister. She deserves it."

Yeah, Rory has a way of making me feel like a dick.

"Fine." I let out a sigh. "But I want to make sure Mom and Dad are okay with it. I also want to make sure the university is okay with it."

Brock looks at me, grinning. "I have a feeling this is all going to work out splendidly."

I stare daggers at Brock. "What the hell, Steel?"

Brock raises his hands in mock surrender. "What do you mean?"

"You've got a big-ass grin on your face, and I want to know why."

"I'm just happy for your little sister. She's going to get a trip she'll never forget. And so will my cousin."

"Your cousin can afford to go to Europe whenever she wants to, first class all the way. We're not exactly going to be slumming it in hostels, but we won't be going to five-star places."

"We'll be staying at the same hotels as Emerald Phoenix, Jesse," Rory reminds me.

I really hate it when my sister's right.

"You've lived here for a while, Pike," Brock says. "When have you seen the Steels jetting off to Europe—with the exception of Rory and me going to England last month for family business?"

I shrug. "How the hell should I know? It's not like I keep track of you guys."

"We're homebodies, Jesse. We don't venture out of Colorado that often. My dad and I went to Wyoming last month, also on business. When we kids were little, we took family trips, but always in the US. Yes, international travel would be great for Brianna. And for Maddie. It's new to both of them."

"But this is a rock and roll tour," I say. "I'm sure Rory has told you that it's not going to be one big sightseeing trip."

"Not for you guys. Not for the band. But I'll be there, and I can keep an eye on both Brianna and Maddie. And if you want them to have a chaperone, I can take them sightseeing."

Rory smiles. "You'd do that, Brock?"

"Of course I would. As much as I'd love being your groupie the entire time, Ror, you don't need me hanging around underfoot."

I sigh, giving in. "All right, fine. If Maddie wants to go, and Brianna wants to go, that's fine. And Maddie can stay in Brianna's room. It will be a great opportunity for her. I just can't believe she's willing to miss her last semester of school."

"How often do you think of your last semester, Jess?" Rory asks me.

"Well . . ." I chuckle. "I'm not sure I've given it a thought in ten years."

"Exactly. Me neither. And I had a lot of fun in college. I did the whole sorority thing, just like Maddie. I sang Cherubino in *The Marriage of Figaro* and Maureen in *Rent*. It was an awesome year. But I don't give it a lot of thought."

"I have the feeling something else is going on here," I say.

"What in the world would be going on here, Jess? Maddie's

just a young woman who wants to experience Europe. There's nothing more to it than that."

I nod.

I have no reason to disbelieve my sister.

So I'm not sure why I do.

CHAPTER ELEVEN

Brianna

I meet Maddie at Murphy's at eight p.m. It's a weeknight, but the bar is hopping already. Most of the college students are home on break for the holidays, and because it's early yet, a lot of the townies are there as well. They'll all leave by eleven, and it'll be all college kids after that.

So I'm surprised—and excited—when I see Jesse, along with Cage and Dragon, in the back of the bar.

"You didn't tell me your brother was coming tonight," I say to Maddie.

Maddie shrugs. "I didn't know he was."

My cousin Ava, pink hair and all, with a gorgeous new diamond engagement ring on her left hand, approaches us from behind the bar. "What can I get you ladies tonight?"

"Since when do you tend bar?" I ask.

"Since Brendan needed my help when we were researching our families. He taught me the basics, and I picked up the rest on my own."

"Why tonight?"

"Laney called in sick because she caught a nasty cold. I'm filling in for a few hours, until eleven. Then I have to get some shut-eye. The bakery doesn't open itself."

I nod. I really respect Ava. She doesn't touch her Steel

money to run the bakery. And she's expecting a windfall of cash from her grandmother's estate, which she's going to share with her sister and half brothers. She also got some money from a trust, which she's using to help the community.

Totally unselfish, that one.

And then I think...

I want to be unselfish too. "Maddie," I say, "how would you like to go first class to Europe?"

Maddie laughs. "Are you kidding me? I'd love it. But we don't have the money. Although we may be able to change our tickets to first class after the tour, after the band gets paid."

"Brock mentioned that all the band members got a signing bonus."

She stiffens her shoulders. "Yeah, they did, but ten grand doesn't go far when your family lost everything in a fire."

Back to this again. She probably won't take kindly to me offering to pay for her to upgrade to first class.

I love having money—all the money in the world. I wish I could use it to help others in town the way Ava is. She's doing it anonymously, but how long will it stay anonymous? The family knows. Of course, as the members of my generation recently found out, my family is very good at keeping secrets.

Our parents kept some pretty treacherous ones from us our whole lives.

"All right, Maddie. But don't say anything until I'm done, all right?"

Maddie stares at me, her head cocked. "Okay."

"I want to upgrade you to first class. I want us to have this European experience together. We'll sit together, be comfortable in our lie-back seats. We're going to room together anyway. You've already agreed to stay in my room. I want you to share this with me too. Correction. *I* want to share this with *you*. Yes, I have the money to do this first class. I want to give this to you as a gift."

"For Christ's sake, Bree." She shakes her head and sighs. "I think my family has made it pretty clear on where they stand with taking Steel money."

"Brock is paying for Rory to go first class."

"Brock and Rory are engaged. You and I are . . . "

"Friends," I say. "The word you're looking for, Maddie, is *friends*."

She looks down at the bar. "*Are* we, though?"

"We've been through this, Mads. I wish I had known how uncomfortable you were feeling. How bad you were feeling about being left out. It's my fault. It's all our faults. We're a very close-knit family, and we didn't see outside our bubble. I'm so sorry for that."

Maddie lifts her gaze to mine. "You know? I actually believe you, Brianna."

"So you'll take the gift I'm offering you?"

She looks down at her drink—a sidecar—that Ava just slid in front of her. I can't personally stand sidecars. They're way too sour. I drink straight Peach Street bourbon, like my father.

Maddie sighs. "You don't know how much I want to take you up on your offer."

"Then do it, Mads. I want you to. I want to do this for you."

"My parents will hate it."

"Do your parents even have to know? They're not going."

"I know that. But I don't like keeping secrets from my parents. I don't like keeping secrets from family."

This time I sigh. "Maddie, I understand that more than you know."

She looks back to me. "I do know. I know what your family's been through the last several weeks. I'm sorry, Brianna. I'm sorry your family has such a spotted history."

"Me too. But at least it has nothing to do with my parents. They were the victims."

"I know."

"Uncle Joe and Uncle Bryce took a more active role in keeping all the secrets." I shake my head. "But I can't stay mad at either of them. I love all my uncles and aunts. They were only doing what they thought was best."

"Yeah. And my parents are doing what they think is best when they tell *me* not to accept handouts from the Steel family."

"This isn't a handout, Maddie. It's a gift. Let's do this. We're practically family already. Callie's going to marry my brother, and Rory's going to marry my cousin. How much closer do we have to be?" I hop off my stool and kneel in front of her. "Will you . . . travel first class with me?"

Her features soften then as she laughs. "Get up, you idiot."

I slide back onto my stool and look at Maddie. Really look at her. She's quite pretty. Beautiful, actually. Of all three of the Pike sisters, she looks the most like their mother, Maureen, who was a local and regional beauty queen in her youth. Maddie's nearly as beautiful as Rory with her dark hair and eyes, pink cheeks, and oval face.

It's funny that I never think of her that way. I've always been so involved with the awesome foursome.

"Tell me something, Maddie."

"What?"

"Why did you start calling us the awesome foursome?"

She absentmindedly swirls her sidecar in the glass.

"Because there are four of you and you're awesome."

"No. I'm being serious."

"And you think I'm *not* being serious?" She lifts the sidecar and takes a sip. "I've always envied you guys. You're gorgeous, talented, rich. Who *wouldn't* envy you?"

"But you're also gorgeous."

"Thank you," she murmurs. "But I'm no Rory. And then there's Callie, who's also gorgeous and has the brains of a scientist. I'm just the afterthought. How can I compete with a big brother who's got more talent in his little finger than I will ever have in my whole body, a sister who is widely considered the most beautiful woman in town, and another sister who has the brains to make something truly significant of herself? Not to mention that both of my sisters are engaged to Steels.

"And then there are the four of you. All cousins, all the same age as me. When did I stand a chance at standing out in high school or in college when I was in constant competition with the *awesome foursome*?"

"This has never been a competition," I say.

"You were homecoming queen our senior year in high school," she says.

"Yeah, I was, and you, as I recall, were on the court along with Angie, Sage, and Gina. Quite frankly, I'm not sure why I was crowned. Gina's way more beautiful than I am."

"But don't you get it? It was always going to be a Steel. It had to be."

I hold up a finger. "No, it didn't have to be. Rory was homecoming queen. Callie was on the court."

"There were no Steels in either of their classes. The next year, after Callie, Diana was homecoming queen."

"Diana is gorgeous."

"She is. But even she isn't as gorgeous as you are, Brianna. You look just like your father in female form, and your father's gorgeous."

"Well, Uncle Ryan is more handsome than my father, and Gina's more beautiful than I am, so how did I get to be queen?"

She huffs then. "Because you're Brianna fucking Steel. You're not quiet like Diana. You're boisterous and flamboyant in your own way. You draw people to you, Bree."

Do I? I never thought too much about myself and my own personality. Of all my aunts and uncles, Uncle Ryan is the most boisterous and jovial. My father's always been a bit brooding. Now that I know his history, I certainly understand why.

"All of you are. You, Sage, and Gina the most. But even Angie, when she comes out of her shell, can be just as much fun as the rest of you. I'm nothing compared to the four of you."

My heart breaks a little for Maddie. I want this trip for her. Almost even more than I want it for me.

In this moment, making Maddie feel beautiful—to see herself as she truly is—becomes even more important to me than being with her brother.

I've been worshiping him from afar for so long... What if it just isn't meant to be?

But you know what *is* meant to be? Getting Madeline Pike out of this depressing slump.

"All right, Maddie. I'm no longer taking no for an answer. I'm going to get you the first-class ticket. In fact, I'm going to get the entire rest of the band first-class tickets. We're all going to be in first class together, and you are going to start thinking of yourself the way everyone else sees you. Beautiful, talented, worthy. Every bit as much as I am or the rest of the awesome foursome is. Even more so. You got it?"

She gives me a shy smile. "All this time, I never really thought the rest of you liked me."

"We've always loved you, Maddie. You've always been welcome in our group. You have to know that."

"Yeah. I mean, when all five of us are together, I don't feel left out."

"It's just when we make plans that don't include you."

"Right." She crosses her arms and looks to her feet. "And when you say it that way, I feel like I'm being an immature little brat."

"You're not. From now on, we're the . . . jivesome fivesome."

She laughs then. "That doesn't make any sense."

I take a sip of my bourbon, let the smoke and caramel taste float over my tongue and down my throat, warming me. "Then we won't be a fivesome at all. We'll all be individuals in our own right. Because honestly, Maddie, that's what we all deserve."

I take a look toward the back, where Jesse and Cage are playing pool. Though I'm tempted to go back there and flirt with Jesse just a little bit, I don't.

I'm still wildly attracted to him, and I really want things to work between us. But frankly, he doesn't know I'm alive, and right now his sister needs me.

I gesture to Ava. "Two more here, on my tab."

"You got it, Bree."

Ava gets busy on her drinks, and I pat Maddie's arm and pick up my nearly empty drink. "To a renewed friendship. And to our amazing trip that's going to make some awesome memories."

She clinks her sidecar glass to mine. "Yes, to all of that."

CHAPTER TWELVE

Jesse

I usually beat Cage at pool, but I'm off tonight.

For some reason, I can't keep my eyes off Brianna Steel, who's sitting at the bar with my sister Maddie.

Apparently they're both going on tour with us, which isn't necessarily a bad thing. I never thought of Brianna Steel as anything more than an honorary little sister—at least not consciously—but right now?

I'm kind of missing her watching me play pool.

Normally when the guys and I are here, the awesome foursome, as Maddie calls them, can't stay away from us. They usually get their own table and then bother us to help them with their shots, which in itself is ridiculous, because all the Steels are great pool players.

"Having trouble keeping your head in the game?" Dragon says to me.

He's standing, waiting for his turn to play the winner, with a Fat Tire in his hand.

He's not high, which is good. I told him to lay off the weed in preparation for the tour, and so far, he's doing it.

Of course, it's only been a day or two.

"I'm good." I take a sip of my beer and ready myself for a tough shot.

Which I blow.

Because I'm thinking about Brianna Steel.

Which is strange.

She's beautiful. She's always been beautiful. Ever since she was a kid. She looks a lot like her father—tall, dark hair, dark eyes—but she's got the voluptuous body of her mother, Jade Steel, the daughter of a supermodel.

Luscious tits on Brianna.

But because I remember her as a flat-chested little eight-year-old, I feel very uncomfortable thinking of her the way I'm thinking of her right now.

I actually miss her following us around in the back of the bar where the pool tables are.

"That's a wrap," Cage says. "I guess you're playing me, Dragon."

"Yeah. God, I suck." I look at my pool cue, deriding it in my mind as if it's the reason why my game is off.

"You don't suck." Dragon grabs a cue from the wall. "Your mind is elsewhere. What's eating you? The tour?"

"Hell no." I look away from Dragon. "I mean, sure. I'm nervous about the tour. But we'll do our best, give a great performance like we always do. And either Emerald Phoenix's fans will love us or they won't. I can't get bogged down in that shit."

Dragon chalks his cue. "Then what's the problem?"

"Hell if I know." I drain the last of my Fat Tire and head to the bar. "You all enjoy your game."

Ava Steel is tending bar tonight. She's as gorgeous as all the Steels are. Of course, people say the Pikes are gorgeous too. Hell, our mother was a beauty queen.

"You need something, Jesse?" Ava asks.

I gesture to the guys in the back playing pool. "I'm switching to water. My pool playing sucks tonight. I'm not sure why. I've only had one beer."

Ava grabs a glass filled with ice and squirts water into it. "Here you go."

"Thanks."

Maddie turns around on her stool. "Hey, Jess."

"Hey, Maddie." I look beyond her to Brianna. "Hey, Bree."

Brianna smiles. "Jesse."

"So I hear the two of you are going to be on tour with us," I say.

"It was all Brianna's idea," Maddie says.

I raise my eyebrows. News to me. "It was?"

"Well . . ." Brianna's cheeks redden. "I want to see Europe, and I thought it would be a great idea for Maddie to come along."

"Except you're already done with school, and she's not."

"I talked to Mom and Dad," Maddie says, "and they said as long as the university's good with me finishing online, I have their blessing."

"We're going to have the most fun." Brianna sips what appears to be bourbon. "Just you and me—a couple of women seeing Europe for the first time."

"Along with Brock," I say dryly.

Brianna twists her full lips into a frown. "What's that supposed to mean?"

I squeeze the lemon wedge from my glass into my water and take a sip. "Your good cousin Brock offered to chaperone you while the rest of us are doing band stuff."

Brianna's jaw drops. "Maddie and I are twenty-two years old. We don't need a chaperone around Europe."

"All right," I say. "Then don't think of him as a chaperone. Think of him as your cousin who's going to Europe with you."

"But Maddie and I—"

"If Maddie's going, someone's going to keep an eye on her. End of story."

"Oh, for God's sake, Jess"—this from Maddie—"will I always be a baby to you?"

"Yes," I say succinctly, turning to Brianna. "And I'm sure Dale and Donny feel the same way about you."

Brianna rolls her eyes.

Her very beautiful dark-brown and long-lashed eyes.

Damn.

What am I thinking?

She's ten years younger than I am.

Shit. Now she's going to Europe with us.

I didn't really need these feelings to sprout now.

Hell, I've spent the last ten years consciously ignoring her. No reason to stop, no matter what my dick thinks of the situation. It's stiffening in my jeans.

"Not only that, but Brianna's going to—"

Brianna nudges Maddie.

"Oh." From Maddie.

"What the hell is that about?" I ask.

"Nothing," Maddie says. "Just something between Bree and me. I misspoke."

I stifle my eye roll. "Good enough." I take a long drink of my water. "I guess I'll go back and play the winner of the next game. Man, I suck tonight."

"You?" Brianna asks. "The king of pool? The guy who can even beat Donny? Which he hates, by the way."

"Don and I are good."

76

It's not a lie. At least it's not supposed to be. Callie made us kiss and make up when she and Don got engaged.

Brianna smiles. "I'm glad to hear that. The two of you are more alike than different."

I look to the doorway. "You all know what my beef is."

"Yes, you think that he got most valuable player your senior year because he's a Steel. And he agrees that the choice between you and him was impossible. You probably should've both been chosen."

"But we both *weren't* chosen. That's a fact."

Maddie interjects. "You know how tired I am of hearing about this? It was fourteen years ago, Jesse. Get over it."

"Yeah, sis. You're right." I drain the rest of my glass of water. "Back to the salt mines for me."

"Salt mines?" Brianna asks. "The pool tables are salt mines?"

"Yeah, they are. The way I'm playing tonight, anyway." I set my empty water glass down on the table more harshly than I mean to. "Ciao."

I walk back, resisting the urge to look at Brianna again.

Damn.

What the hell is getting into me?

That fact that it's been so long since I've been laid is part of the problem. I don't particularly like indiscriminate sex, but tonight?

If someone comes my way, I'll be biting.

CHAPTER THIRTEEN

Brianna

Maddie finishes her drink.

"You want another?" I ask.

She shakes her head. "How about a game of pool?"

I promised myself I wouldn't go to the pool tables and flirt with Jesse Pike. I promised myself that tonight was about kindling my friendship with Maddie.

But... this is her idea, right?

"Sure." I gesture to Ava. "I'll have another."

"You got it, cuz." Ava gives me a thumbs-up, her diamond sparkling on her left hand.

"Where's Brendan?"

She motions toward the back of the bar. "He's doing some inventory. He'll be out in a little while."

I nod and follow Maddie back to the pool tables. Just our luck. The one next to where Jesse and the two others are playing is free.

"You want to rack?" Maddie asks.

"Sure." I grab the triangle and rack the balls quickly. My pool cue of choice is being used by another person, so I grab a different one.

"I rack, you break." I nod to Maddie.

Jesse's standing, drinking another glass of water, watching

HELEN HARDT

Dragon and Cage finish their game. Cage is beating Dragon.

Maddie takes a perfect shot, and the three ball hits one of the side pockets. "Looks like I'm solids." She takes another shot, missing.

I'm good at pool, and I always hope that Jesse is watching me when I win a game.

He's usually not.

I have a perfectly lined-up shot to land two balls into one of the corner pockets. I breathe in, out, line up my shot, and shoot.

"Yes!" I make the shot.

"Was this my idea?" Maddie asks. "I forgot how good you are."

"I can give you some pointers," I say.

"I get all the pointers I need from Jesse."

Jesse's eyebrows rise at the sound of his name.

"You need something, sis?" he asks.

"Nope." Maddie scans the remaining balls on the felt. "I'm just gearing up to get my ass kicked by Bree here."

"You want to bring in a ringer?" Jesse asks.

"A pinch hitter?" Maddie shakes her head, chuckling. "Hell no."

"Tell you what, Jesse," I say. "If you're that into this game, you can play the winner."

Maddie laughs. "We already know who that's going to be."

I seriously *did* want this night to be about Maddie and me, but now I'm determined. I line up my next shot, sink my ball into the side pocket.

Again. Again. Until I'm down to one ball … and I miss.

"Ha! You mean I get a turn?" Maddie says.

"Looks that way," I say dryly.

79

Maddie makes her shot and then...to my ultimate surprise...every shot after that, until she downs all her balls, and then the eight ball.

I stand, hands on my hips, my mouth dropped open. "Wow."

"Right?" Maddie shrugs. "I didn't know I had it in me. I guess I get to play my big brother now."

Jesse walks over. "Since Cage and Dragon are still fighting it out, sure, sis, I'll play you."

"And you'll kick my ass," Maddie says. "But since that's what I was expecting from Bree, it won't be so bad coming from a family member."

Watching Jesse Pike play pool is a turn-on.

Usually.

He is *way* off his game tonight. Even his form is suffering. I'm not sure what's going on with him.

He ends up beating Maddie, but only because she missed an easy shot.

"I guess you're mine now," I say to him.

He looks me over in a way I've never seen a guy look at me before.

My nipples harden.

"You're up, Jess," Cage says from the next pool table over.

"Sorry. I'm up over there." Jesse gestures to his sister. "You all play together."

My heart drops. Oh, well. This night was supposed to be about Maddie and me getting closer anyway.

"Okay, Mads." I chalk up my cue. "I racked the last game. You rack this time, and I'll shoot first."

"Good enough." Maddie racks the balls, and I do a really lousy break.

What is wrong with me?

I sigh. "Your shot, Mads."

She shoots, sinking the three ball. "I'm solids."

She continues shooting until the game is over before I even have a shot.

Damn. She *has* gotten better. Jesse must be giving her pointers.

I look over at his table, where Cage is beating him again.

Man, the planets must be out of alignment tonight.

I take a sip of my drink. Peach Street is my father's favorite bourbon. It's made here on the western slope. And I have to say, it's delicious.

Despite the fact that our family owns a winery and we all like alcohol, rarely do we ever drink to excess. Sure, we've all been known to tie one on occasionally, but it's not the norm for us. Four drinks is my limit when I'm eating. Three when I'm not. I have a high tolerance.

"You want to play again?" Maddie asks.

"I do need to redeem myself," I say, "but I guess I'm not really into it tonight. But if you want to play another game, I will."

Maddie places her cue on the rack. "No, I'm done. There's a table available over there. We can watch the guys play."

I nod and follow Maddie to the table.

Angie and Sage walk into the bar. I wave them over.

"No Gina tonight?" Maddie asks.

"No." Sage takes a seat, her gaze wandering to Jesse, Cage, and Dragon.

"She's hurting," Angie says. "All the stuff she just learned about her dad and her grandmother. She's having a hard time with it."

"Is there anything I can do?" Maddie asks.

"No," Angie says. "She just needs to accept it and get through it on her own."

Maddie glances at the bar. "Ava seems to be doing okay."

"Ava's been dealing with it for a while now," I tell Maddie. "Apparently Wendy Madigan, her grandmother, reached out to her and Brendan. It's all a very strange story, but Gina's having a hard time finding out she's not related to our grandmother, Daphne Steel, who she always thought she looked like."

"From the pictures I've seen," Angie says, "you're the one who looks like Grandma Steel, Bree."

"Yeah, I'm kind of a dead ringer for sure." I scan the twins' faces. "Though the two of you kind of look like her, and so does Aunt Marjorie."

"Yeah, but you . . ." Angie shakes her head. "I mean, if you look at Grandma's senior picture from high school and then put yours next to it, it's almost like you're looking at twins."

"I know. Gina looks like Uncle Ryan."

"She does," Maddie says. "And that's certainly not a bad thing. He's the handsomest of all the Steel Brothers."

"That's what everyone has always said," Sage agrees.

"It's going to take Gina a while to deal with this," I say. "We just need to give her some time and space. Be there if she needs us but leave her alone to deal with it until she asks for help."

Maddie nods. "Okay. That's all I'll say. You all know her better than I do."

"Excuse me." Sage rises and walks over to where Jesse, Cage, and Dragon are playing.

"I'm surprised you're not over there, Bree," Angie says.

I steal a quick glance at Jesse. "For some reason, I'm

playing like complete crap tonight. Even though I started out strong, Maddie beat me twice."

Angie nearly drops her jaw to the table. "You're kidding me."

"Thank you for the vote of confidence," Maddie says dryly.

"I don't mean it that way, Mads. But since when have you ever beaten Brianna?"

Maddie gives a smug grin. "Since tonight, apparently."

"We have some great news," I say. "Maddie's coming with me on the tour."

Angie grabs Maddie's forearm. "Maddie! What about our plans for our last semester?"

"I decided a trip to Europe would be more fun. More memorable."

Angie widens her eyes. "How can you say that? It's bad enough Brianna is deserting us. We need you there for the sorority."

"Her mind's made up, I'm afraid." I smile at Angie.

"So it's just going to be the three of us?" Angie glances around the bar and lowers her voice. "And who knows what Gina is going to be like if she doesn't snap out of this funk she's in."

"You and Sage will have the time of your lives, and so will Gina. She's strong. She'll get through this."

"Yeah, but we're sure going to miss you guys." Angie pouts.

"The parties will be the same without us," I say. "And there will be two fewer people to compete with you over the guys."

Angie frowns. "That's supposed to make me feel better?"

I shrug. "Well, not *you* maybe. It might make Sage feel better. She's the party animal who likes to ... You know."

Angie rolls her eyes. "Do I ever. Sometimes I wonder how two twins can be so different."

"Well, you're fraternal, not identical," I say. "Though sometimes it is hard to tell you apart physically."

"But not mentally for sure." Angie glances over at Sage, who's hanging onto Jesse's arm.

A spear of jealousy lances through me.

What the hell is she thinking?

Of course, while the rest of the awesome foursome has seen me flirt relentlessly with Jesse, they don't actually know how I feel about him.

Maddie seems to have a little bit of a clue, though. I hated lying to her, but I'm not ready for anyone to know my real reason for going on the tour yet.

If it doesn't work out, at least I'll have a wonderful trip to remember for the rest of my life.

But already my feelings trump my thoughts.

Jesse Pike is *mine*.

CHAPTER FOURTEEN

Jesse

Man, I'm still playing like shit.

And Sage Simpson yanking on my arm every other second isn't doing me any favors.

Sage is the biggest flirt of the awesome foursome. Whenever the guys and I are here at the same time as her, she never leaves us alone.

I glance over to the table where Brianna sits with Maddie and Angie Simpson.

The fourth, Gina Steel, doesn't appear to be here tonight.

Can't say that I blame her. Some shit just came down about her family, and it's rocked the entire town.

The Steels can handle it.

They can handle fucking anything.

They can buy their way out of emotional trauma.

"Your shot, Jess," Cage says.

I take a look at the table. There are no clear shots. None at all.

Fuck.

I line up a shot that I have about a one percent chance of making. I do the geometry in my head. It could happen, and on another night when I'm playing well? I might have a better chance of making it. Tonight? I may as well bow out now.

I take the shot . . .

And to my surprise, my ball hits the pocket.

"You redeemed yourself." Cage pats me on the back. "Jesse's back."

Except I'm not back. My next shot is an easy one . . . and I manage to miss it.

Cage takes his final couple shots, winning the game.

"All right, Dragon," Cage says. "You and me again."

Jesus.

"Anyone could miss that." Sage gloms onto my arm again.

"Are you kidding me? I made one of the most difficult shots I've ever made, and then I miss an easy one. So no, anyone could *not* have missed that."

"Come on." She yanks on my arm. "Let me get you a drink."

"No thanks," I say. "I mean, thanks for the offer, Sage. But I'll pass."

She eyes my empty glass of water sitting on the cocktail table by the cue rack. "You're empty."

"I am. And I'm going to call it a night." I replace my cue on the wall and walk to the bar to take care of my tab, leaving Sage at the pool table with Cage and Dragon.

Brendan Murphy has replaced Ava at the bar.

"Hey, Jesse."

"Just want to close out my tab," I say.

He heads over to the cash register. "Not a problem." He hands me a receipt.

I sign. "I noticed that Gina isn't here tonight with the rest of the awesome foursome," I say. "Is she okay?"

"Thanks for asking." Brendan shoves my signed receipt into his register. "She's having a hard time. I mean, anyone would."

"Ava seems to be at peace."

"Yeah, but it was a while coming. Ava has a different way of looking at things than most people."

I nod. "Well, give Gina my best if you see her. So long."

"See you, Jesse."

I head to the door, and then I look back at the table.

And there's Brianna Steel.

Staring straight at me.

And *damn*.

Why am I feeling these sparks? I don't have time to get involved with anyone, and certainly not a woman ten years my junior. I need to give my all to the band right now. To this tour. We have to kill this thing. Our family needs it.

So I leave.

I leave the bar.

And I try to leave Brianna Steel there.

But a piece of her comes with me, in my head. In my groin.

I have to make peace with her being on the tour. She's a part of my circle now. My sister is engaged to her brother. My other sister is engaged to her cousin.

One thing's for sure, though.

I'm going to have to keep my hands to myself.

I reach for my phone in my pocket—

"For the love—" I say out loud. I must've left my phone in the bar. In fact, I can see it in my mind, sitting on that cocktail table right next to where the pool cues are.

I was looking at my phone when I put my cue on the rack, and I set it down.

So back into the bar I go, jingling the bells on the door.

And as I walk in—

Brianna is walking out, and we collide, her own phone clattering to the wood floor.

My whole body reacts to her presence.

She's so tall. Perfect for a guy my height.

She drops her jaw. "Oh, Jesse! I'm so sorry." She reaches down to retrieve her phone.

And I take a good look at her ass. I should have picked up the phone for her. Some gentleman I am.

"Are you leaving?" I ask.

"No. I just wanted to get some air. I thought you left."

"My phone's still in there."

She nods and walks past me out the door.

I head back into the bar, where Sage is now hanging on Dragon.

Dragon, who I've told in no uncertain terms to stay away from the awesome foursome.

But . . . I'm not here to enforce that rule.

Do I need to stay?

My head's not here, though, so I find my phone, wave bye to the guys again, and leave the bar.

Brianna's standing outside the bar, leaning on the brick building.

She looks amazing in her Levi's and cowboy boots. A black leather jacket covers her long-sleeved tee.

She nods at me. "Hi again."

"Hi."

"So you're heading out?"

"I am. I'm playing like crap tonight."

She sighs. "I know. So am I. Maddie beat me twice."

"Maddie isn't bad."

Brianna shrugs. "No, she's not bad at all. She's good, actually. But of all of us, including Maddie, I'm the best at pool. Apparently not tonight."

"Yeah, I hear you."

Then something comes out of my mouth that I'm not expecting. "You want to take a walk?"

Her cheeks go rosy. "Hmm . . . Yes and no."

I step closer to her. "What's that supposed to mean?"

"It means on another night, yes, I'd love to take a walk with you. But I invited Maddie here for a drink, so I can't just ditch her."

"True." I glance inside the bar. "I don't want you ditching my sister."

She fidgets with her phone. "I suppose I could go in there and ask if she minds if I take off for a few minutes."

"It's okay. Don't bother. I'm out of here."

"Jesse?"

I turn, look over my shoulder.

"Yeah?"

She pauses, as if she's thinking about what to say. Then, "Nothing. See you around."

"Yeah. See you around."

But my pulse goes into overdrive, and my already hard dick takes the lead. I take a step and then another. One more, and then I turn around, stalk back toward Brianna, and glare at her.

"Why are you doing this to me?"

"Doing what?"

"Making me . . . " I shake my head, rake my fingers through my long hair. "Making me *want* you, for God's sake."

"Jesse, I—"

I grab her then, stare into her eyes. They're wide, but not in fright or anger. It's been a while for me, but I still know how to read a woman. Anticipation builds from my pounding heart to my throbbing groin through every inch of my body. Excitement. Nerves. Curiosity.

And again her dark and smoldering eyes.

They're wide in want.

"Jesus Christ."

She says nothing, but her lips are slightly parted, and they're glistening.

God, yes. Those full red lips . . .

"No." I let her go. "I apologize."

"You don't have to apologize, Jesse."

"Yeah, I do." I brush my arms off, as if I'm dusting her off me. "I'm a rocker, but I'm not that kind of rocker. I don't take advantage of young women."

She closes the short distance between us. "I know you don't. Please. If you want to kiss me, just do it."

Fuck. She knows. How can she not? I all but said it. "No."

"Please."

God, her lips are still parted, so sexy and shining, so I grab her again, and I crush my mouth to hers.

I slide my tongue between her lips, and she meets it with her own.

She tastes like smoky bourbon mingled with the sweetness of fresh strawberries.

How long has it been since I've kissed a woman?

Too damned long, and even longer since I've taken one into my bed.

But what the hell am I doing?

I break the kiss, let her go. Then I walk away.

CHAPTER FIFTEEN

Brianna

My lips . . . Stinging, tingling, and I can't catch my breath.

I want to yell to Jesse, tell him to come back, but my vocal cords are paralyzed—paralyzed by the arousal and need that has taken me over.

I lean against the brick wall of the bar, steady myself.

The kiss . . .

It was better than I've ever imagined—and I've imagined a lot. So many times in dreams and in waking hours.

I always wondered what those full Jesse Pike lips would feel like against my own.

It was so much more than a kiss. It was a moment filled with possibility and vulnerability, where the outside world dissolved away and gave rise to pure sensation.

Absently, I bring my fingers to my bottom lip, touch it lightly.

God, the prickles, the tingles, the sizzles.

This from a kiss.

I've been kissed before. Many times, in fact.

And I've done . . . a lot.

But never the actual deed.

Not because I didn't have the chance. Not because I didn't want to.

But something always held me back.

It was a gift I could only give once, and I've dreamed so long about giving it to Jesse.

Could my dream actually come true?

I inhale, exhale, inhale, exhale, and when I finally think I can walk, I make my way back into the bar.

Maddie and Angie are still sitting at our small table, and Sage is still flirting relentlessly with Cage and Dragon.

I sit back down.

"Are you okay?" Maddie asks. "You were gone quite a while."

I put on my best smile. "I'm fine. Just needed some air."

Angie raises an eyebrow at me. "You look . . ."

"I look what?" I ask as innocently as I can muster.

She cocks her head. "Nothing. Just a little frazzled."

I pause a moment to gather my thoughts into something coherent. "Well, who wouldn't be? I'm about to embark on an amazing adventure. With this girl here." I squeeze Maddie's arm.

"I have to say, now that you've talked me into the whole thing, I'm really looking forward to it." Maddie beams. "I mean, seriously, when else would I be able to see Europe? Both my brother and sister will be there. And Callie, for part of it. It'll be like a Pike sibling adventure."

"Yeah. It'll be great." I grin, my lips still reeling from Jesse's kiss.

"I suppose a Steel cousin adventure for you," Angie says. "With Donny and Brock there."

"Yeah, Brock has offered to *hang out* with us." I roll my eyes.

"I know," Maddie says, "but maybe it's a good idea. Is he familiar with Europe?"

"Not really, but he feels a sense of duty. I'm sure my mom and dad have already told him to keep an eye on me."

"We're grown women," Maddie says. "But Jesse feels the same way."

"Yes, I know. To all of them, we're still babies."

"I don't mind Brock joining us," she says. "Since he and Rory have been together, I've grown to like him quite a lot."

"Yeah. Brock is a lot of fun."

He is. I love my cousin. I love all my cousins. But with him watching over me, I won't be able to get near Jesse.

And now? After that kiss?

I might have a shot.

But I can't get ahead of myself. I can't throw myself at him. My God, I actually begged him to kiss me tonight.

And he did.

Then he left.

Maybe the kiss wasn't good for him. But how could it not have been? It was an amazing kiss, and I've done a fair amount of kissing.

Of course . . . he's probably done much more kissing than I have. He's a rocker. He probably has groupies in the other towns where the band plays.

I can't even think about it.

All the Emerald Phoenix fans are going to see him up there and fall madly in love with him when they hear him sing.

How am I going to deal with this?

Maybe going on this tour wasn't such a good idea.

No.

I will *not* second-guess myself.

This is my chance. My chance to try to get close to Jesse. After all, he won't be rehearsing and performing the *whole* time. He'll have a chance to do some sightseeing himself, and somehow, I will finagle a way to go with him.

Without Brock, and without Rory, and without Maddie.

Jesse and me.

I will find a way.

★ ★ ★

The next day, I drive into Grand Junction alone for some shopping. I want to find the perfect holiday gift for Jesse.

I'll give it to him anonymously—figure out a way to sneak it under the Pikes' tree. Probably during a visit to Maddie.

If only I could give him money. It's what he needs, but he wouldn't take it.

I'll find something. Something that will have meaning to him. Meaning to both of us.

I stop at a mall, wander around. I don't have any idea what I'm looking for, until I see it in the window of a small shop called Yesterday's Treasures.

It's a brass belt buckle with a dragon etched on it.

A dragon for Dragonlock.

I walk into the shop, and I feel like I've stepped out of a time machine. The decor is an intriguing blend of history and charm, and I inhale the scent of lavender and parchment.

The walls are lined with wooden shelves, showcasing an eclectic assortment of iconic items. Each shelf is a visual feast—vintage vinyl records, classic movie posters, porcelain figurines, leather-bound books, and myriad vintage jewelry.

I'm drawn to the rack of retro sunglasses. I can't help myself. I choose a pair of round frames, put them on, and view myself in the mirror.

Yeah, I could have lived in the sixties. I rock these frames. But I'm not here to buy for me.

At the center of the store, a young man sits behind the counter. "May I help you?" he asks when I approach him.

"I'd like to buy that dragon belt buckle in the window," I say.

He smiles. "You got here just in time. That's our last one."

I frown. "It's not vintage?"

"Not that piece. Most of our figurines and a lot of our jewelry are new."

Bummer. It's not one of a kind. But on Jesse it will be.

"I'll take it."

"Would you like to have it engraved?"

Hmm. I tilt my head. That way I can make it one of a kind for a one-of-a-kind man. "Yeah. Maybe."

"It's an extra twenty-five dollars."

"Sounds great. Let's engrave it."

The clerk steps out from behind his counter, walks to the window, grabs the belt buckle, and brings it back.

"What would you like it to say?"

"On the front, I want it to say Jesse. J-E-S-S-E."

He makes some notes. "And anything on the back?"

"I don't know . . ."

"Is it a gift?"

"It is. Let's see . . ." I tap my fingers on the counter. "Engrave it to say *With lots of love* on the back."

"Perfect. What's your name?"

"Brianna."

"All right, Brianna. I'll have this ready in about an hour if you want to pick it up today." He rings up my purchase.

I slide my credit card through the reader. "Good enough.

I'll be back in an hour. Thank you so much."

I grab a light lunch and then peruse a few more shops. Most of my holiday shopping is already done, but I can't resist grabbing a little something for Maddie—a guidebook for the UK and continental Europe. I purchase one for myself as well.

The clerk at Yesterday's Treasures smiles when he sees me. "I've got it ready for you."

"Thanks so much. Can I take a look?"

"I took the liberty of giftwrapping it for you, but I'm happy to unwrap it and then rewrap it." He hands me a small box.

It's beautifully wrapped in shiny red paper with gold dragons and holly. "This is so perfect. I don't want to disturb it. Thanks for the wrapping."

"You're very welcome. Happy holidays to you." He places the wrapped box into a black gift bag.

"You as well." I take the bag and leave the mall to drive back to Snow Creek.

Once home, I print *Jesse* on the tag that's tied to the gift.

Then I change my mind. I remove the tag from the gift. This way, if they find it, they won't know who it's for. When someone opens it, they'll find out it's for Jesse. That way, if someone catches me with a gift before I have a chance to slide it under the tree, no one will know who it's for.

Good thinking, Bree.

Now…to figure out how to slide it under the Pikes' Christmas tree without anyone knowing.

I'll go over to the house under the pretense of visiting Maddie. I've even got the guidebook to give her as an early Christmas gift.

Perfect.

I slide the small gift into my purse, grab both guidebooks,

and return to my car to drive to the Pikes'.

"Brianna," Maureen Pike says when she opens the door. "How nice to see you."

"Nice to see you too, Mrs. Pike. Is Maddie home?" I glance over Maureen's shoulder to regard their tree.

"I think she's up in her room. I'll go see."

The Pikes' Christmas tree is in the living room, next to the foyer where I'm standing.

I look around, making sure there's no one here. I hear some clanking in the kitchen, but if I act quickly...

A moment later, the gift is under the tree, hidden in the back.

Perfect.

Maddie comes out from the hallway. "Hey, Bree. What's up?"

"I was out shopping, and I picked up European guidebooks for us. I wanted to drop yours by." I hold up the books.

"Sure. That sounds like fun. Come up to my room."

Maddie fires up her laptop, I grab one of the guidebooks, and we both sit on her bed, our backs against the headboard, the laptop sitting between us so we can both see.

"So we'll be in London for the first six days," Maddie says. "I want to see Buckingham Palace, of course. Westminster Abbey. And Rory says we have to go to Fleet Street and have a meat pie."

I wrinkle my nose. "What?"

"It's a reference to the urban legend of Sweeney Todd. You know, the demon barber of Fleet Street?"

"You mean the musical?"

"Yeah, *Sweeney Todd* by Sondheim. But it started as an urban legend. Rory says Brock took her to this amazing pie place on Fleet Street."

"Meat pies?"

Maddie taps on her keyboard, and a photo of a giant pie emerges. "You know, like potpies. Don't you like potpies?"

"Sure I do. I guess I just thought that we'd be eating something more . . . elaborate."

Maddie laughs. "British food is anything but elaborate," she says. "I've been doing some research. Lots of meat and potatoes. Sausages."

I'm used to a lot of meat. But I was hoping to eat some gourmet cuisine. I guess we'll save that for Paris. "Okay. If it's important to you, Mads, we'll have a meat pie. Let's see a show too. In the West End."

"Brianna . . . "

"My treat. We'll get Brock to go with us. And Callie and Donny. And Rory."

"Rory may not have a lot of time."

"But it's a West End show! Rory of all people will want to do that."

"That's a good point." Maddie scratches her head. "Let's see what's playing."

We narrow it down to a couple of shows that we think everyone will like, but we don't know when Rory will have time off from the band.

"I guess we need the entire schedule before we can make these decisions," I say.

"Yeah. I'll text Rory and see if she has it." Maddie grabs her phone, taps on it. "She's not responding. She and Brock are probably doing the deed."

"Oh my God . . . " I've always known Brock was a player, but I don't like to think about it.

"I know. She's living with Brock in the guesthouse behind

Joe and Melanie's. And Callie is living with Donny in the guesthouse behind your parents' place."

I nod. "Oh, I know. Their houses are being built. Both of them."

Maddie sighs. "It's all so foreign to me. Having the resources to just build a house whenever you want, and the land to build it on."

"You guys have quite a bit of land here." I rise from the bed and look out Maddie's window that faces the backyard. Beyond the vast yard lie the charred remains of the Pike vineyards.

"True. Jesse talks about building a house on our property, but he hasn't been able to afford it yet."

A house on our land or on the Pike land—doesn't matter which—for Jesse and me. He may not be able to afford it, but I can.

"Anyway," Maddie continues, "we'll have to table the discussion on the show until we have the schedule from the band."

"Is Jesse here?" I sit back down on the bed.

"I think he's in his room, working on lyrics."

"He'd have the schedule, right?"

"Yeah. But I don't like to bother him when he's working."

"All right." I let out a sigh. "On to the next thing, then. So we're going to do all the touristy things, the palaces, the abbeys, Big Ben. We'll eat pies on Fleet Street and see a show in the West End. What else?"

"We have to have a pint."

"A pint of what?"

"Of beer, silly." She punches my arm. "When they order an ale, they ask for a pint. Didn't you do any research before deciding to go on this trip?"

Uh ... no, I sure didn't. I'm going because Jesse is going. I can't say that to Maddie, though, so I settle on, "I'm not a big beer drinker, Mads."

"Okay. You can have whatever you want, but I'm having a pint."

I pause a moment. "You know what? We're going for the experience. I'll have a pint too."

"Good. That's what it's all about, after all. The experience."

I smile at my friend. "We both gave up our last semester of college, which was going to be full of parties. So yes, Maddie, we're going to make this an experience neither one of us will ever forget."

I plan to make it an experience her brother will never forget too.

CHAPTER SIXTEEN

Jesse

Christmas Day...

A modest number of wrapped gifts sit under our decorated tree. We didn't have a lot of money to spend on shopping. Rory and I got our signing bonus for the band, ten thousand dollars each, but we gave most of that to our parents to help with expenses.

They didn't like taking it, but they did it anyway.

Because that's what families do. They take care of each other.

Still, we each managed to get one gift for each family member.

We all open our gifts, with Maddie playing Santa, handing them out.

She's done that since she was old enough to, and since she's the baby, none of us have ever challenged her on it.

Mom takes a giant trash bag and starts picking up discarded boxes and wrappings.

Brock and Donny are both here, doing Christmas with us this morning. The Steels celebrated on Christmas Eve.

Maddie picks up a small box wrapped in bright-red wrapping with gold dragons and holly etched on it. "Here's one more gift, but it doesn't have a tag."

"That's strange," Rory says. "Why don't you open it, Mads? Maybe we'll be able to tell who it's for."

"Works for me." Maddie rips the paper from it, and inside is a white rectangular box, like the kind that would hold large jewelry. "Here goes." She takes off the lid.

Then she gasps.

"What is it?" Callie asks.

"It's beautiful." Then she hands it to me. "It's for you, Jess."

I raise my eyebrows. "It is? Okay, which one of you forgot to put a tag on your gift?"

"You got all our gifts." Callie grins. "This must be from a secret admirer."

I look inside the box. Nestled on cotton is a brass belt buckle with a dragon—one that looks a lot like our Dragonlock logo—etched on it.

"I think this might be for Dragon," I say, but then I notice the engraving below the dragon.

In block letters. J E S S E.

"Why would anyone leave a present for Dragon here?" Rory asks.

I shake my head. "Never mind. I was wrong. It's for me."

"Are you going to show us what it is?" Brock asks.

I pass it around, the buckle still lying on the cotton. My family oohs and aahs over it.

"It's perfect for you, Jess," Dad says.

"Yeah. I love it. But who's it from?"

The box goes to Donny, and he lifts the belt buckle. "May I?"

"I think you already did."

He turns it over, and then his jaw drops.

"What?"

Don pauses a second before he says, "There's engraving on the back too."

He puts it back in the box and hands it to me.

He doesn't look happy.

I take the belt buckle, turn it over, and—

Now *my* jaw drops.

With lots of love, Brianna

"You want to explain that, Pike?" Donny demands.

I open my mouth, but words don't form, until finally, "I don't have an explanation."

"Something going on with you and my sister?"

This time, the whole family's jaws drop in unison. It's almost comical.

"What's it say on the back?" Maddie grabs it from me, and her eyebrows shoot right off her forehead. "Oh my God . . . "

Mom grabs it from her then. "Brianna? Brianna Steel?"

None of us know any other Briannas.

"Jesse . . . " Dad says. "She's so young."

I shake my head vehemently. "You guys are all looking at me like you think I know what this is about."

Except for that one kiss we shared . . . That was over a week ago. I haven't seen Brianna since then. Rory and I have been busy working with the band, coming up with our repertoire, and making tweaks in the music and choreography.

Donny is glowering at me.

"Give it a rest, Steel," I finally say. "That's *my* sister you put a ring on."

He says nothing. How can he? I'm a hundred percent right.

MELODY

"When was she over here?" Donny says finally. "Someone had to leave it."

"She's been here several times." Maddie rubs her jaw. "We've been talking about the trip. But I've always been with her. I would have seen her put it under the tree."

Donny rises. "I'll find out what's going on."

Callie pulls on his hand. "Donny, no. This isn't your business."

"The hell it's not."

Callie pulls Donny back down beside her on the sofa. "It's not. Your sister's a grown woman. This may not even be from her."

"You know another Brianna?"

"Does that even matter?" Callie asks. "You guys are assuming this gift has some hidden meaning. It could just be a thank-you gift from Brianna to Jesse for agreeing to let her come on the tour."

Yeah. That must be what it is.

Except... If that's the case... "Then why didn't she get *you* anything, Ror?"

"Everybody knows you're the leader of the band," Rory says.

But from the looks on their faces, not one of them is buying that explanation either.

Only one thing to do. I'll have to go see Brianna. I can't do it today. It's Christmas Day. Family day.

But then I see Donny still glaring at me, and I know I have to go see Brianna and question her about this. Because if I don't? Donny will do it for me, and that won't be pretty.

"Nothing will be solved in the next half hour," Mom says. "So everybody get in the kitchen. I've got our breakfast all fixed."

HELEN HARDT

Mom makes us eggs Benedict every Christmas. Something her mom used to do, and it's a tradition that I'm sure Callie and Rory will continue with their families.

Fine. But this afternoon—once I'm positive all the Steels are up, dressed, and showered—I'm paying Brianna a visit.

I'm not sure what this is about, but one kiss doesn't mean anything.

Even if her lips *were* the sweetest I've ever tasted.

CHAPTER SEVENTEEN

Brianna

"What do you think?" I ask Diana as I twirl around my bedroom in the dark-red pleated halter dress she got me.

My sister's eyes beam. "I think it looks amazing on you, just like I knew it would."

"You're one of the only people who knows how to pick out clothes for others," I say. "I was always surprised when you went into architecture. I figured you'd be some kind of fashion designer or something."

Diana shrugs. "I considered it, but fashion is so fleeting, you know? If I want to be remembered, I need to design something that will be around for a long time."

"Buildings will be around for a long time, for sure."

"Yes, if they're designed and built right. Which mine will be."

I have no doubt of that. My sister's a genius. She always got the best marks of all four of us kids. Straight As all the way for Diana Steel.

Everyone's always had a soft spot for Diana. She was the first girl born into this generation of Steels. My parents adopted Dale and Donny first, and when Aunt Marj married Uncle Bryce, she adopted Henry. Then Uncle Joe and Aunt Melanie had Bradley. So four boys, and then Diana.

She was doted on for sure.

Then came Brock, Ava, and Dave, all in a row. My parents and aunts and uncles used to call them Huey, Dewey, and Louie because they were the same age and always together.

Then the awesome foursome, again, nearly all in a row. Gina, the twins, and me.

That's the end of this generation of Steels.

It's amazing that we're going to have a new generation soon, with Dale married and Donny, Brock, and Ava well on their way.

"I'm going to take this dress to Europe."

"Are you sure?" Diana touches the fabric of the skirt. "It's more of a summer dress. The UK in January can be vicious, I've heard."

"So I'll wear a coat." I twirl around and watch the skirt flow gracefully, accentuating my hips and legs. The silky fabric gently billows and catches the light as I move. The halter neckline frames my straight shoulders and emphasizes my neck, while the bodice fits snugly, highlighting my curves before flaring out into a full, pleated skirt. "This dress looks dazzling on me. You have a good eye, Dee."

"Why is it so important that you look dazzling in the UK?"

I stop twirling. "You know I always like to look my best."

Diana tilts her head. "Brianna, I got you that dress because you don't have anything like it. You wear jeans and cowboy boots all the time."

She's not wrong. Diana has always been more feminine than I am. But if I'm going to catch Jesse Pike's eye ...

"Brianna, look at me."

I take my gaze away from my own reflection and turn to my sister. "What?"

"You look beautiful. But I get the feeling..."

"Yeah?"

"Don't try to be someone you're not, Bree. It never works."

Not only is Diana the smartest of all the Steel kids, she's also the most intuitive. She always seems to know what I'm thinking before I do.

"Don't be silly. I can enjoy a dress every now and then."

"Of course you can. Why else would I have bought it for you? But my point is that you don't have to be someone you're not to impress anyone."

"Who says I'm trying to impress anyone?" I ask innocently.

"No one's saying that." This time Diana's feigning innocence.

I let out a heavy sigh. Diana's the closest person in the world to me, and I have to confide in someone. "Listen, Dee, let me tell you a little secret."

She smiles then. "I'm listening—"

A knock on the door interrupts us.

For crying out loud...

"Yeah? Come on in," I say with exasperation.

Mom enters, wearing leggings and a sweatshirt. Our mother is still so beautiful, even nearing fifty-one. There's hardly a wrinkle on her face, and only a few streaks of silver in her hair, which she keeps covered with hair color. Her figure is still stunning, and her eyes are magnificent. No wonder Dad calls her blue eyes.

"Bree, there's someone here to see you." Then she looks at me. "Is that the dress from Diana? You look amazing."

"Thank you," I say. "I absolutely love it."

"Certainly not your usual style," Mom says.

"Which is why I bought it for her," Diana says. "She may

only wear it once or twice a year, but it's perfect for her body type."

"Indeed it is," Mom agrees. Then, "It's Jesse Pike. He wants to see you for some reason. He wouldn't say why."

I widen my eyes, my heart pounding. "He's *here*?"

"Yeah. He wants to see you. I assume it has something to do with the tour."

"Yeah, that must be it." I turn to Diana. "Unzip me, will you?"

Diana turns me around, makes me face her. "Why don't you keep it on?"

I look down at my legs. I haven't shaved in a few days, and dark stubble is starting to erupt.

"Oh, hell no. Unzip me."

"I'll tell him you'll be right down." Mom leaves, closing the door behind her.

Diana helps me out of the dress, and I throw on a pair of jeans and a sleeveless T-shirt. I keep my feet bare. My bronze polished toes still look good from my pedicure a few days ago.

"You seem nervous," Diana says.

I try to still my fidgeting body. "Why would I be nervous?"

Diana curls her lips into a surly grin. "I don't know, baby sis. Why don't you tell *me*?"

"There's nothing to tell."

"You may as well tell me now," she says. "I'm pretty sure you were going to before Mom interrupted us. We both know you're going to tell me at some point, and I have to leave soon. I'm meeting Ashley over at her and Dale's house for dinner tonight."

"Oh, she invited you?"

"Yeah. Since we had a big dinner on Christmas Eve,

Ashley decided to do dinner tonight with just Dale and her mom, Willow. Since Ash and I are friends, she invited me."

"Okay, sounds fun." I attempt to look my sister in her eyes, even though I'm pretty sure I'm not fooling her. "But there's nothing to tell, Diana. I swear."

Lying to my sister is never a good look. She already knows it's a big fake.

But I scurry down the hallway to the foyer where Jesse Pike stands, looking more handsome than ever.

"Jesse," I gasp. "Did you cut your hair?"

His hair is normally around the same length as my brother Dale's, but now it's been cut and layered so it sits right above his shoulders.

And damn . . . he looks even better.

"It was time," he says in his rich drawl.

"Why?"

"Easier to manage for the tour."

"Right. That makes sense." I clear my throat. "You wanted to see me?"

He points to the belt buckle that he's wearing. It looks great against his medium-blue jeans.

"Is this from you?"

I blink, my heart pounding like the hooves of a wild mustang, unconstrained and free. "Of course not. What would make you think that?"

He removes the buckle, hands it to me.

"It's really beautiful."

"It is."

"Whoever bought it has exquisite taste," I say, "but why do you think it's from me?"

"Turn it over."

Right. I had it engraved *With lots of love*. That was it.

I turn it over and—

"Oh my God!"

"See what I mean?"

That stupid clerk. I told him to engrave *With lots of love*. Not *With lots of love, Brianna*.

Damn it all to hell! I knew I should have unwrapped it and looked at it before I put it under the Pikes' Christmas tree.

What was I thinking?

"That right there is why I think it's from you," he says.

Embarrassment wells through me. My cheeks are burning. "It was meant to be anonymous."

He frowns. "Why?"

"I don't know." I drop my gaze to the floor and then wander around the living room aimlessly. "I saw it and I thought of you. Every time I see you, you seem to have a different belt buckle on. This one was beautiful."

He closes the distance between us and takes the buckle from me, the warmth of his hand making my stallion heartbeat turn to wild antelope. "If it was supposed to be anonymous, why is your name on it?"

I sigh. "Tell me and we'll both know. The clerk fucked up."

His gaze softens then, and his dark eyes burn into me. "Brianna, I'm not looking for—"

I hold up a hand to stop him. "That's not what this is about, Jesse. I just wanted you to have it."

He places his hand on my shoulder—my bare shoulder—making my flesh burn. "Good. Then we have an understanding?"

"Of course. I mean, it was only one—"

He touches his fingers to my lips. "That never happened."

My heart cracks a little then. He truly isn't interested.

Perhaps he's attracted to me—I mean, you can't kiss a person like that if you're not—but he's not interested in me in *that* way.

Maybe I shouldn't go on this tour after all.

"Well, thank you for the gift."

"You're welcome. I guess I'll see you at the airport."

"Yeah. See you then." He turns, walks out the door.

Damn that clerk. I'm going to have him fired. First thing tomorrow I'm going back to that mall and—

A tear wells in my eye.

No, I'm not going to have him fired. He's a clerk at a small shop. He probably needs that job. Maybe he's the owner of the shop, in which case I can't have him fired anyway.

He screwed up.

Who the hell hasn't screwed up in life?

I sure did. I should've opened the package and made sure the engraving was right.

This is no one's fault but my own.

And now?

I no longer want to go on the tour.

But I already talked Maddie into going, and I can't disappoint her. Not after she's already been disappointed by my cousins and me on so many occasions.

I walk down the hallway to my bedroom, flop on my bed—right on top of the gorgeous dress from Diana—and the tears come.

CHAPTER EIGHTEEN

Jesse

Two weeks later...

My pulse is hammering in my neck. We're ready to leave for the UK.

Brianna Steel is here, waiting for the plane with us. She and Maddie are in first class, along with Brock, Rory, Donny, and Callie.

Brock tried to pay for the rest of us to go first class, but the only one to take him up on it was Dragon.

I wanted to.

The thought of this eight-hour flight in those ninety-degree seats kind of makes me sick.

But I'm not taking any more Steel money.

"Ladies and gentlemen, we're now ready to board Flight 756 with nonstop service to London. We'd like to offer pre-boarding to any of our active military passengers, as well as any passengers traveling with small children. You're welcome to board now."

A few guys in fatigues—Cage and I thanked them for their service when we got to the gate—along with one family with a toddler and a baby—*that's* going to be fun—head toward the gate for boarding.

A few moments later—"Ladies and gentlemen, if you are in our first-class cabin, you're welcome to board now."

Brianna rises, along with Maddie, Donny, Callie, Brock, Rory, and Dragon. They head through the gate with their carry-ons.

"We're idiots," Cage says to me.

"Why do you say that?"

Cage eyes the line of people boarding the large plane. "Because we could be going into that posh first-class area right now."

"There was nothing stopping you from taking Brock up on his offer."

"No," Jake says, "only you and your fucking glare."

I shake my head, snarling. "For Christ's sake. See if there are seats available then. Change it."

"Not a bad idea," Cage says to Jake.

Jake rises. "I'm with you, buddy." They head to the counter.

A few minutes later, just as the first-class passengers are done boarding, they trail off to the end of the line.

Looks like they got seats.

For the love of . . .

I walk to the counter.

"Good afternoon, sir," the young man at the counter says. "What can I help you with?"

"My friends just got upgraded to first-class seating. I'd like to do the same."

He taps on his computer. Then he frowns. "I'm sorry, sir, but those two got the last two seats available."

"You've got to be kidding me."

"I'm afraid not, sir." He peers at the screen again. "We

do have one first-class passenger who's checked in but hasn't arrived yet. Once everyone else is on board, if he hasn't arrived when we're ready to close the doors, you can get the seat then." He taps his computer again.

A passenger comes running, racing toward the gate. He holds his phone to the reader and gets on the plane.

My heart sinks to my feet. "Don't tell me. That was him."

"I'm afraid so. I can offer you a seat closer to the first-class cabin."

"Would it be any better than the seat I'm in?"

He types some more and then wrinkles his nose. "No. In fact, I'd advise you to keep your current seat. It's on the aisle, and you're obviously very tall. You'll be more comfortable with a little more room to stretch out your legs."

"Yeah. Got it." I sigh, grab my carry-on, and stand near the gate to wait for my section to be called.

Sometimes pride has its downfall.

The rest of my party will be in lie-back seats, enjoying the flight with gourmet food, free booze, and the ability to sleep.

Jesus Fuck.

Two more groups of passengers board before my group is called.

The only consolation is that I board through a different door on the airplane, so I don't have to walk past the rest of my group as I head to my seat in steerage.

I find my aisle seat. The plane has rows of three seats, four seats, and then three more seats. My seat is on the end of a row of the middle four, and the rest of the row is occupied by three college-aged girls. They're already laughing and squealing about how much they're going to drink on the plane.

Dear Lord, kill me now.

I arrange my carry-on in the overhead compartment and take my seat, fastening my seat belt.

"Hi there," the girl sitting next to me says. "I'm Lexi. This is Barb and Chris."

I shake her hand. "Nice to meet you."

"What's your name?"

"Jesse."

"It's great to meet you." She giggles. "Isn't this exciting? Going to London?"

"Yeah."

"What are you going to London for?"

"A concert."

Lexi drops her mouth open. "Really? Us too! We're going to see Ed Sheeran. Are you going to see him too?"

"No. I'm actually performing in a concert."

"Are you in a band?"

"Yeah."

Her eyes widen. "Where are you playing?"

"We're opening for Emerald Phoenix in London and then going on tour with them."

Lexi gasps. "Emerald Phoenix? I love them! Maybe we can get tickets."

"They're sold out," I say.

"Oh my God." She gestures to the others. "Do you hear that? Jesse here's a rock star."

I chuckle softly. "I wouldn't go that far."

"Are you kidding me? If you're opening for Emerald Phoe—"

"Ladies and gentlemen," a voice over the speaker says, "please take a look at your monitors for our safety video."

Thank God. I stick my AirPods in my ears and glue my

gaze to the monitor on the back of the seat in front of me.

Headphones. The universal symbol for *leave me alone*.

I hope Lexi and her friends understand that.

The plane begins taxiing toward the runway as the video begins.

I close my eyes.

This is a new form of hell.

CHAPTER NINETEEN

Brianna

I couldn't help noticing at the gate that Jesse's *not* wearing his belt buckle.

I also couldn't help noticing that Jake and Cage are here in first class with us.

And Jesse's not.

Maddie and I are next to each other, and these are cushy seats. A menu is in the pocket, detailing our dinner and breakfast choices plus specialty cocktails.

No Peach Street bourbon, but I'll make do.

Maddie has a smile on her face, a giddy smile. I'm happy. Happy that I could do this for her.

"Are you reading this cocktail menu, Bree?" She giggles. "Mile-high margarita, aviator's old-fashioned, winged sunset. That one sounds delish. Rum with passionfruit and pineapple juices. Or maybe the first-class fizz. This is the only time I'll be in first class. I want the whole experience!"

I smile. I'll be having Buffalo Trace. Fruity cocktails don't do much for me, but Donny will be in his element with the mile-high margarita. This will be a trip we'll all remember.

Not for the reasons I want to remember it—meaning Jesse and me—but it will still be wonderful. I'll be with my brother for the first couple of weeks, and then with Brock and Maddie for the rest.

I may not even go to any of the concerts.

Except I already know I will. Brock and Maddie will go, so I'll go too. We have front-row seats reserved for all of them.

And I love Dragonlock, and I love Emerald Phoenix.

So why would I not go?

Just because I have to watch the man I've been infatuated with for the last eight years of my life sing on stage with his sister, make beautiful music that speaks to my heart?

Not a problem, right?

The plane increases its speed, ready for takeoff.

I turn to Maddie and smile. "Here we go!"

"This is so exciting!"

A few moments later, we're airborne, and about twenty minutes after that, one of the flight attendants announces that the seat belt signs have been turned off.

I'm scanning the menu when a flight attendant interrupts. "Can I get you anything to drink, ma'am?"

"Yes, I'll have Buffalo Trace neat."

"And for you, ma'am?" To Maddie.

"The winged sunset, please."

Seeing Maddie so happy makes my heart sing. For a moment, I almost forget that her brother broke my heart.

Serves him right to be back there in economy with no legroom.

And with his long legs, that's got to be torture.

Good.

Hey, Brock offered. Pride goeth before the fall, Jesse.

A few moments later, the flight attendant returns with our drinks.

I take a sip. Buffalo Trace is good stuff. Not Peach Street, for sure, but it has a subtle sweetness with notes of caramel and honey with a rich apple undertone. And I do love apples.

Maddie tentatively takes a sip of hers.

"What do you think?" I ask.

"It's so good!" She lifts her glass. "Do you want to try it?"

"No thanks. You enjoy."

"How's yours?" she asks.

"It's no Peach Street, but it does hit the spot."

"I don't know anything about bourbon," Maddie says. "The only one I know is Jack Daniels."

I take another sip. "Technically Jack Daniels isn't bourbon. It's Tennessee mash whiskey. But technically, Peach Street isn't bourbon either, even though its label says otherwise. Real bourbon comes from Kentucky."

Maddie takes another sip of her cocktail. "You Steels know a lot about alcohol."

I shrug. "Not really. I know a little bit from my dad. The ones who really know about alcohol are Uncle Ryan and Dale, but that's mostly limited to wine."

Maddie nods. "You think Dale would've enjoyed this trip?"

"Are you kidding me?" I can't help a laugh. "Dale would hate it. Being cooped up on a plane for eight hours? Then being in a foreign country that he doesn't know? Dale is an outdoor homebody if there ever was one. Ashley, on the other hand, would probably love it. I'm sure she'll drag Dale to Europe at some point."

"At least you have Donny. It's so amazing that all my siblings are here. We're going to have the experience of a lifetime together, something Mom and Dad could never give us. Mom and Dad weren't thrilled about me missing my last semester, but they realized this is a once-in-a-lifetime opportunity for all of us."

Crap. Here comes the guilt.

The only reason I initially invited Maddie on this trip was to get Jesse to agree to let us come. I knew he wouldn't be able to say no to his sister.

Now?

Jesse and I aren't going to happen. He's made that abundantly clear.

The only way I know how to assuage my guilt is to make sure Maddie has a wonderful time. Especially since she's always felt so left out among the four of us. I'm going to make sure she gets a trip she'll never forget.

"So," she says, taking another drink, "when do you think these weddings are going to be? I can't get anything out of Callie or Rory."

"I haven't really thought about it," I say truthfully. "You think they'll want a double wedding?"

"I don't know. That would sure make it easier on Mom and Dad. Only paying for one wedding instead of two."

"Oh, your parents don't need to—" I stop. "Sorry."

"Thank you," Maddie says, smiling.

"No problem. Sometimes I forget to think, you know? I was born into this fortune. I didn't ask to be, but I was, and I'm grateful. I want to spread it around, Mads. I'm glad you're letting me help with this trip."

"Actually... Rory and Callie talked me into that. Since they're both engaged to Steels, and they can go first class, they wanted me to have the same experience. That's why I took you up on the offer."

"Whatever the reason, Maddie, I'm glad you did. I wish

Jesse would have taken Brock's offer."

Maddie frowns. "Me too. It looks like Cage and Jake caved at the last minute." Maddie steals a glance backward to the curtain dividing first class and coach. "Jesse's going to be so tired when we land. There's no way he's going to be able to sleep in one of those uncomfortable seats with his long legs."

"Well"—I take a drink of my bourbon—"he had his chance."

"True. At least we'll have two days before he has to sing. He'll need to get over his jet lag." She plays with the button on her seat. "I can't believe these things actually lie flat. It won't be like my own bed, but it's going to be great."

"It's not bedtime yet, Mads. We have a gourmet dinner to look forward to." I leaf through the menu. "Did you choose the beef, chicken, or vegetarian?"

"Beef. You?"

"Chicken. The beef would just disappoint me because it won't be nearly as good as anything my mom can make out of our own beef."

Maddie wrinkles her nose. "Yeah, maybe I should've thought of that. But that's okay. It's beef with a balsamic reduction, with asparagus spears and potatoes au gratin. Seriously, like restaurant food on the plane. What do you think Jesse will get to eat?"

"Honestly, I don't know. But it won't be this good."

"Yeah, he probably won't get alcohol either."

"Oh yeah, he will. Alcohol is always available on international flights. Sometimes for free, I think. Or he can buy a drink."

"That's good. At least he'll have something."

"Yeah. Something."

He could have had me.
But I'm going to have to let him go.

CHAPTER TWENTY

Jesse

Kudos to the pilot. That was one smooth landing.

I'm still uncomfortable as all hell. My back aches, my knees ache, and my head aches. My shoulders are knotted, and so is my neck.

To top all that off, the three girls in the row with me seemed to sleep like babies. At least that meant they were quiet, but now they're chatting uncontrollably about how excited they are to see London.

"It was amazing meeting you," Lexi says. "I'll see if we can get tickets."

"Like I said, I think everything is sold out. But good luck."

"Have you been to London before?" she asks.

"Afraid not."

"Oh." She pouts, sticking her bottom lip out. "That's such a shame. I was hoping maybe we would meet someone who could show us around."

"Listen," I say, "I have a sister your age, and I'm going to give you the same advice I would give her. Don't go looking for some strange guy in a foreign country to show you around."

She laughs dismissively. "This is England. It's not really a foreign country."

I resist an eye roll. I could give her a geography lesson, but we'll be deplaning soon. "Do you have an older brother, Lexi?"

"No, I don't."

"That's becoming pretty clear. For the next minute, think of me as your older brother, and listen carefully. If you want to see London, join a guided tour. Do not go up to some good-looking guy and ask him to show you around."

"That takes all the fun out of it."

I hold up my hands. "Suit yourself. I hereby resign as your honorary brother. You have my advice. Whether you take it is up to you."

The plane stops taxiing, and the bells ring, indicating the doors are being opened.

I take off my seat belt and stand, stretching my legs. I used the bathroom a couple of times during the flight, but other than that, I've been stuck in the seat. It will be good to do some walking, even though I'm exhausted because I didn't sleep a wink.

I pull down my carry-on and grab Lexi's for her. Her other two friends have their stuff in the overhead compartment on the other side.

No one moves. I'm far in the back and have to wait for all the people ahead of me to get off the plane, but standing feels damned good.

I rub the crick in my neck, massaging it, finding knot after knot after knot.

Damn. Maybe I can get a massage tomorrow or something. I can't have all this muscle tension if I'm going to perform.

Finally, the people ahead of me begin to walk. I advance forward, finally making it off the plane and into the gate.

The rest of my group stands there, looking rested and refreshed.

And Brianna looks the best of all of them. Her long hair is pulled up in a high ponytail, and it looks freshly brushed. Her cheeks are pink, and her lips glossy.

"Bye, Jesse!" Lexi calls. "I hope we can get tickets for your concert."

"Bye, ladies." I wave.

Cage, Jake, and Dragon all look well rested as well. They may not look perfect like Brianna, but their eyes are bright.

"I see you made some friends, Jess," Cage says.

"Just some college girls in my row. I didn't talk that much during the flight. Kept my headphones in."

"You mean you didn't join the mile-high club?" Jake gibes me.

"Uh . . . no."

Brock and Donny are walking ahead with my two older sisters. Behind them are Brianna and Maddie.

The guys and I bring up the rear.

"To baggage claim," Cage says. "And then customs and all. I have to say, Jess, I'm really glad I changed my mind and went first class. I got a good night's sleep, and I'm feeling great. You doing okay?"

"Oh, yeah," I lie. "Slept like a fucking baby."

He cocks his head at me. "Great."

Sarcasm is totally lost on my cousin.

My gaze is drawn to Brianna's long and shapely legs encased in black leggings.

On her feet are sneakers of some sort, and she's wearing a hoodie that unfortunately covers the beautiful curve of her ass.

And still . . . she looks amazing. The most beautiful of all the Steels. I've always thought so. Some give it to Gina, the daughter of Ruby and Ryan, but I'm team Brianna all the way.

Not that I've ever thought of her that way—except for that one kiss.

I'm not wearing the belt buckle she gave me for Christmas, but I did bring it with me. It felt wrong to leave it at home. For some reason, I want it near me.

We make it to baggage claim, and I take a seat.

Even though my back, legs, and knees are killing me and are begging me to remain standing, my exhaustion has weighed me down so much that I have to sit.

The rest of my group is standing by the baggage claim carousel, chatting animatedly.

I mean really animatedly. Even Dragon seems excited.

Christ.

I jerk when the light flashes and buzzes, indicating our bags have arrived. I groan as I push myself up from my chair and walk toward the carousel, looking for my bag.

First to grab her bag is Maddie. She squeals in delight. "I don't fly a lot, but I'm always a little bit nervous until I see my bag come down the carousel."

"There's no reason to be nervous this time." Brianna squeezes her hand. "Oh! There's mine."

Donny pulls Brianna's bag off the carousel for her, and soon after, his own and Callie's arrive. Dragon's is next, and then Cage's, Rory's, Brock's, and Jake's.

Leave it to me to be the last man standing.

Suitcases, bags, and duffels slide down the carousel, making their way toward me.

My bag is a hard shell and basic gray. I bought it especially for this trip with some of my bonus money. Inside are my clothes, personal grooming items, and most importantly, Brianna's belt buckle.

"For Christ's sake." I rake my fingers through my hair.

"Don't worry, Jess," Rory says. "It's coming. Many are still sliding down."

Bag after bag after bag . . .

A hot pink hard-sided. A bright-orange duffel. But mostly black and gray hard and soft sides. I tied a bright-green tag on my bag so I'd be able to see it easily.

Bags and bags continue . . . and no green tag.

And then . . . the bags stop coming.

"Oh my God," I groan.

"Jesse, bags get lost all the time," Rory says. "We'll go talk to the guy from the airline and figure it out."

Rory accompanies me to the tiny office in the baggage area where reps from our airline sit.

"Yes, may we help you two?" one man says.

"My bag is lost."

"I'm sorry to hear that, sir. We're here to help. May I see your claim check?"

I pull my wallet out of my back pocket, grab the claim check, and hand it to him.

He scans the code.

"Oh, goodness. It appears your bag is still in Denver."

"You mean it didn't even get on the flight?"

"I'm afraid not. I apologize for this inconvenience, but sometimes these things happen." He taps on his computer. "Looks like it's on the next flight out, which will arrive the same time tomorrow."

"Twenty-four hours? I have to go twenty-four hours without my bag?"

"Again, we apologize. But this does happen. In the contract for your e-ticket, it states—"

I hold my hands up. "I'm too damn tired to listen to the jargon. Yes, I'm sure it's some kind of contract that I have to agree to in order to buy a ticket. Whatever. What happens now?"

"I just need the address of where you're staying, and your bag will be delivered to you as soon as it's here."

Fine. I rattle off the name of the hotel. "Good?"

"Yes, excellent." He reaches under his desk and then hands me what looks like a cosmetic bag. "In the meantime, there's a toothbrush, toothpaste, some lotion, and antibacterial wipes in here along with a sleeping mask. We regret the error, and we hope this helps."

"That's just like the ones we got on the plane," Rory says.

I unzip the small pouch and inspect the contents. "You got these on the plane?"

"Yeah. In first class." Rory reddens a bit.

I roll my eyes. "Thank you," I say, and we leave the tiny office.

"Jess, you could have—"

"Save it. I tried. Cage and Jake got the last two seats in first class."

Rory frowns. "Oh my God. I'm sorry."

"I hope this isn't some indicator of how the rest of this trip is going to go," I say.

Rory grabs my arm. "Jesse, bags get lost all the time."

"My bag's never been lost."

Rory doesn't reply. Sure, we don't fly a lot, but this just sucks.

We return to the others, where they're standing with a tall gentleman dressed all in black holding a sign that says *Steel*.

"What's all that?" I ask Rory.

"Brock rented a limo to get us to the hotel. Isn't that great?"

I roll my eyes again. "Yeah. Great."

CHAPTER TWENTY-ONE

Brianna

I should feel sorry for Jesse. He has dark circles under his eyes, and the whites are bloodshot. He keeps rubbing at the back of his neck, which means it's probably aching.

And the airline lost his luggage.

What a shitty trip so far.

But I don't feel too bad for him.

He could've flown first class with the rest of us. He just had to get over himself. Cage and Jake finally got over themselves, and the two of them are bright and jovial, enjoying a beer in the limo that Brock ordered.

Maddie and I aren't drinking. We decided only to drink in the evenings during this trip, and even then to keep it to a small amount. We want to soak in every bit of culture and enjoy every minute of being here without any interference from alcohol.

Brock is also having a drink. Other than him, Cage, and Jake, no one else is drinking.

Not even Jesse, who looks like he could use one.

He's sucking down a bottle of water.

Flying does dry you out, but the flight attendants in first class kept us well hydrated, refilling our waters practically every five minutes while we were awake.

I got four and a half hours of uninterrupted sleep, and

then the flight attendants served us an amazing breakfast of bacon, eggs, and oatmeal. Plus I had a few cups of coffee, so I'm feeling great.

Maddie and I are determined to stay awake until the actual bedtime here in London. That's the best way to get over jet lag.

Looking at Jesse, though? He's going to crash as soon as he hits his room.

Jeez ... here I go.

I *am* feeling bad for him. It's kind of like a little ache at the back of my neck.

I don't want Jesse to be uncomfortable.

I want him to have a good time.

I'd love it if he were going to have a good time with me, but apparently that won't happen.

The limo stops in front of an ornate building.

"Is this our hotel?" Maddie gasps, gaping out the window.

"Yes, it is, Maddie," Brock says. "This is where Emerald Phoenix is staying at this very moment. They arrived a week ago."

"They flew on New Year's Eve?" Maddie asks.

"Yeah," Rory says. "Apparently they wanted to be sure they were over any jet lag by the time the tour started."

"Jet lag? Surely they all flew first class," I say.

"Jet lag is still a thing, Bree," Brock says. "We all got some sleep, but not the normal amount. Be sure to stay awake until at least nine o'clock tonight. That'll get you over the hump quickly."

"Yeah, but it's more important that you guys get over the hump quickly. You're the ones who are performing."

"Very true," Rory says. "I'll be hitting the sheets at nine

o'clock sharp tonight. But before that, we have reservations at a pub."

"What do we do between now and then?"

"Settle into your room," Rory says. "Take a little walk if you want to do some sightseeing, but under no circumstances should you take a nap."

Maddie and I nod.

"That goes double for you, Jess," Rory says to her brother. "You look like you just got run over by a truck."

"I'm fine," Jesse grumbles.

"I'm sorry about your luggage," I say to him.

He simply rolls his eyes and doesn't give me the courtesy of an answer.

Fine. He wants to be like that? He wants to forget the best kiss either of us has ever had?

I don't know if it's the best kiss he's ever had. I only know it's the best one I've had. I've been saving myself for him all this time, but maybe . . .

Here I am in a foreign country. Maybe I need some fun.

We get out of the limo, and a bellhop takes our bags.

Once Maddie and I are inside our room, I strike. "I think I might want to have some sex on this trip."

Maddie gasps. "Bree!"

I shrug. "Yeah. I mean, why not have some fun? I'm on the pill. I'll make sure the guy uses a condom. What do you think?"

"I think you're letting your libido do the talking. Let's just have fun."

I sit on the edge of one of the beds. They're full beds, not queens—apparently the standard in the UK. "What better way to have fun than to have *fun*?"

"I'd like to be able to talk you out of this. I won't be having any sex here."

"Why not? Are you seeing someone?"

"If I were seeing someone, I doubt I would have hopped on a plane to be gone for four months."

"True."

Maddie was in a long-term relationship the first couple years of college with a guy from Wyoming. They called it off about a year ago.

"Have you dated anybody since you and Lance broke up?"

Maddie pulls her carry-on onto the bed and unzips it. "Every so often, but I never got intimate."

"So was Lance your first?"

Maddie's cheeks burn. "Yeah. My first and only. Who was *your* first?"

Now *my* cheeks burn. The awesome foursome—plus Maddie—are sorority sisters and besties . . . but we don't talk about our sex lives very often. Except for Sage. She loves telling us about her exploits.

I've dated a lot. Had a couple of steady boyfriends in college, the longest for about four months. We did a lot of things together, but we never did the actual deed.

"You're kidding me," Maddie says.

"Kidding about what?"

Maddie pulls her laptop out of her carry-on and plugs it in. "You're a virgin, Brianna."

How could she tell? She simply stares at me, her eyes gleaming.

I scoff. "Okay. I'm a virgin. Don't you think it's time I got my cherry popped?"

"All this time and I never knew."

"If it makes you feel any better, I never told Angie, Sage, or Gina either."

"You mean you have a secret from the rest of the awesome foursome?"

"Yeah. It's kind of private. So...you're on your honor, Mads."

"Thanks for trusting me with this secret."

"Well, *you* figured it out."

"I did, but you have nothing to fear from me. I'll take it to my grave."

I smile. "Thanks."

Maddie finishes with her carry-on. "Do you want to take a walk? I feel great."

"Yeah. Should we ask any of the others if they want to go?"

"Maybe Donny and Callie. The band members probably have something going on."

Then I jerk at a knock on the door.

"Speak of the devil," I say when I open it. Donny and Callie stand there, along with Brock.

"We've got the afternoon free, ladies," Brock says. "Rory and the others are having a meeting to make sure Jesse doesn't fall asleep."

"I wish he had—"

Brock puts a hand up. "We all do, Bree. But you know Jesse Pike."

Callie and Maddie both nod.

"We do for sure," Callie says. "I've had to deal with this rivalry since Donny and I got together."

"It's over, Cal," Donny says.

"I think it is...on your side." Callie frowns. "I'm not so sure about my brother's."

"True," Maddie says. "If he had any brains at all, he would've taken that first-class seat."

"Actually," Callie says, "Rory told me he tried to get a seat, but Cage and Jake took the last two."

"Oh my God," Maddie says. "That plus losing his luggage? He must be so upset."

"Our brother's a trouper," Callie says. "He'll be fine. So let's go. We can take a walk, check out what's around here. Maybe do a little shopping or something. We'll save the big sightseeing spree for tomorrow."

"Sounds great. You ready, Maddie?" I ask.

Maddie grabs her purse. "Absolutely. Let's go."

CHAPTER TWENTY-TWO

Jesse

I'm the leader of the band, and I can't keep my fucking eyes open.

"Jess"—Rory nudges me—"you didn't answer the question."

I force my eyelids to stay up. "What was it again?"

"What time rehearsal will be tomorrow. We've got a location that's reserved all day. Personally, I think morning would be good. It'll force us out of our jet lag."

"The rest of you don't have any fucking jet lag," I say crossly.

"For Christ's sake, Jesse," Rory admonishes. "Stop feeling sorry for yourself and man up."

I can't help a chuckle. "Man up? I can't believe those words just came out of your mouth, sis."

"I mean it, Jess. I'm sorry there were no more first-class seats available. I'm sorry they lost your luggage. It will be here tomorrow, and everything will be better."

"I'd feel better if I could have a nap."

"No way. If you nap now, you'll never get over jet lag, and your performing won't be up to par. You and I both know that." She punches my upper arm. "This is important, Jesse."

"Fine." I rub the spot she hit.

She's right, of course. This is our big chance, and if I blow it because of self-pity, I'll never forgive myself.

Rory and the others will never forgive me either.

We go through the rest of the business, and then Rory grabs my arm. "Brock and the others are out walking around, sightseeing and exploring. You and I are going on a walk."

"I just want to go to my room, sis. I won't fall asleep. I promise."

"I respect your good intentions, Jess. But you and I both know that if you go to that room, you *will* fall asleep."

"I can make sure he doesn't," Dragon says.

"No, you can't," Rory says. "No one can. So you're walking it off, and then we're going to dinner at the pub, and after *that*, you can go to sleep."

"Fine," I say again, this time with more exasperation.

"Let's take a walk. The rest of you are on your own."

"Good enough for us," Cage says. "Where's the bar?"

The three of them are laughing—well, two of them, Dragon doesn't laugh—as they walk through the lobby of the building.

"Let's go to the pharmacy," Rory says. "There's one about a block away. I looked it up."

"What for?"

"You can get the stuff you need."

"There's shampoo in my room."

"Yes, and the airline gave you toothpaste and a toothbrush. But they didn't give you any deodorant."

She has a point. If I don't use deodorant every day, watch out. "All right. Let's go."

★ ★ ★

A few hours later, when I'm literally on my last legs—seriously, they want to give out—Rory and I meet the others at the pub for dinner.

Emerald Phoenix isn't with us. They're keeping to themselves, doing some kind of meditation they do before concerts. Maybe I should look into something like that for our band.

I'm too tired to think about it now.

The pub and restaurant are housed in a quaint building, with wooden beams, brickwork, and whitewashed walls. The centerpiece is its well-stocked bar, boasting an array of spirits, ales, and wines. Behind the bar, shelves showcase rows of whiskey bottles and a collection of local and international beverages. The bar counter is made of dark wood, like Murphy's back home.

The remainder of the restaurant consists of wooden tables and chairs scattered throughout the space. Our group fills a big round table in the back of the pub. I take a seat and then slog my elbows onto the table and stick my head in them.

"Oh, no." Rory yanks one elbow off the table. "No falling asleep here. We'll get through the next couple hours of dinner, and then you can crash."

"Fine."

I'm beginning to think that's the only word in my vocabulary now.

Our server comes, and Brock orders pints for everyone who wants one. If I drink a pint of beer right now, I'll pass out before dinner is over.

"Not me," I say, raising my hand, which drains the remaining energy I have left.

"Good enough. Anyone want anything else?" the server asks.

"Water," I say.

"Gas or no gas?"

"Huh?"

"He means sparkling or still, Jess," Rory says.

"Oh. Nonsparkling, please."

A few moments later, our drinks arrive, mine without ice.

"Could I get some ice, please?"

Our waiter, whose name is Snod—seriously—furrows his British brow. "We don't serve water with ice, but I'll see what I can do."

"Right," Rory says. "I remember that from my reading."

"Whatever. I just need the water." I take a big gulp. It's . . . cold. Just not icy cold. Yuck.

"This place is known for its fish and chips," Brock says.

"Along with every other pub across London," Brianna gibes. "Didn't you read your guidebook, cuz?"

I can't help but raise my head to look her way. Fuck. She looks gorgeous, her cheeks rosy, her eyes shining . . . and awake.

"Fish and chips sounds amazing." Maddie smiles.

"I think I'll have the chicken pasty," Brianna says.

"That sounds good to me too," Rory says. "How about you, Jess?"

"My God, I don't care." I scan the menu quickly. "I'll try the meat pie."

"No, Jesse," Rory says. "We're all going for meat pies later on Fleet Street. Have something else."

"For the love of God, Rory. What does it matter whether I eat a meat pie tonight?" I close my menu and place it on top of my plate.

I will eat what I want.

Brianna is sitting next to Dragon, and I don't like how he's looking at her and her shining brown eyes.

I clench my jaw.

Brianna is not mine. Brianna will *never* be mine. But she won't be Dragon's either. Or Cage's or Jake's, for that matter.

Or any randy Englishman who comes across her.

Jesus Christ. I've got to get a grip.

The server comes around to take orders, and I order the meat pie while Rory scowls at me. I down all my water and then signal to our server that I need more.

I've got a headache from dehydration—or exhaustion or whatever. Who knows? All I know is a hammer is pounding nails in my head and I really want to find my pillow.

But no... I have to sit through dinner with a bunch of people who got to sleep on the plane, whose luggage didn't get lost, and who don't seem to care that Dragon is looking at Brianna as if she's his next meal.

This day can't end soon enough.

CHAPTER TWENTY-THREE

Brianna

After dinner, and once we're back at the hotel, Maddie goes up to bed, but I stay down in the bar with Donny and Callie for a nightcap.

We find seats at a high bar table and sit down. A giant yawn splits Callie's pretty face.

"Did you get to sleep on the plane?" I ask.

"Oh yeah, I did. I'm just a little tired, though."

"If you want to, go on up to the room," Donny says.

"You know, if you don't mind, I think it will." She kisses Donny's lips. "Night, baby. Night, Bree."

"Good night." I turn to my brother. "You can go with her if you want."

"No, that's okay. I need to talk to you."

"What about?"

Donny leans toward me. "Remember back in November when Brock and Rory came over here to see Ennis Ainsley? To get information about his girlfriend of ages ago, Patty Watson?"

"Right, the first Steel winemaker. A friend of our grandparents."

"Yeah. Well, Brock emailed him to let him know we were coming back, and he invited us to tea tomorrow. Rory won't be able to go because she'll be working with the band, and Callie booked a spa day. But Brock and I are going to go, and we thought you might like to join us."

"Yeah, sure. High tea served by an actual Englishman sounds awesome. Count me in."

"It'll be afternoon tea, not high tea like you get at the Brown Palace in Denver."

I frown. "You mean I'm not going to get scones and clotted cream?"

"You might. I don't know. But you love tea."

"I do, and I'd love to meet him. I kind of remember him."

"Yeah, he lived on the ranch after Uncle Ryan took over the winemaking, and then he moved back to England a couple of years later. So you may have some memories of him."

"I remember he was nice-looking. I liked his accent."

"Right."

"So he wants to see us? How come?"

"Well, our family was a big part of his life for a long time. So we have to tell him . . ."

I swallow. "I suppose you're right. You have to tell him what really happened to Patty Watson."

He nods. "I know. Brock's not looking forward to it."

I bite my lip, thinking. "Maybe I shouldn't go. Maybe it should just be you and Brock."

"Don't be silly. He's going to want to see you."

"We'll be here for the next several days, and then we'll be back after Scotland. I can see him then."

"No, I'd like you to come along." He wrinkles his forehead. "Or did you and Maddie already make plans for tomorrow?"

"Brock was going to take us sightseeing in the morning. Is it okay if Maddie comes along?"

"Callie isn't going. Would she feel uncomfortable?"

"I don't think so."

"All right. I'm sure it'll be fine."

A server comes and asks what we'd like to drink.

"Just a Coke for me," I say. "Make it Diet Coke."

"I'll have the same," Donny says.

I give my brother a punch in the arm. "You're not going to have another pint?"

He laughs. "I don't like beer that much, and I'm not sure if they serve margaritas on this side of the pond."

"They probably do, Don. Just order what you want."

He shakes his head. "I've had enough alcohol for the night. I need to get a good night's rest. We all do. Jesse may be jet lagging worse than the rest of us, but it's going to hit all of us soon. That's why Callie's tired."

"I'm not tired at all," I say. "I'm just so excited to be here."

"Yeah, this can be a fun time for all of us. Especially you and Maddie. You're going to get to go on the whole tour, see so much of Europe."

"You could do that too, you know. You and Callie both."

"The city of Snow Creek needs its attorney," he says. "I can't be away for that long. Besides, I already promised Callie an amazing honeymoon wherever she wants to go once we get married."

I stifle a yawn. "So...when *are* you guys going to get married? And what about Brock and Rory?"

"They're talking about a double wedding, which Brock and I are fine with. They think it will be easier on their parents. Of course, Brock and I have told both Rory and Callie not to worry about expenses, but they're worried about what their parents will think. And I get it. So if they're willing to have a double wedding, Brock and I are in."

"Actually, a double wedding could be really fun." I pull my phone out of my purse and tap the calendar. "What about dates, Donny?"

"Rory has to get through the tour first. Then we'll see what happens next. Rory and Jesse are hoping that the band gets more popular, and maybe they'll be able to open for some other big names, or maybe even get asked to tour themselves. Once we know what's going on after that, we'll set a date."

"Oh, sure. I see. You don't want Rory to miss out on any band stuff."

"Of course not. Rory's a big part of the band now. Emerald Phoenix wouldn't have asked Dragonlock to open for them if not for her."

I smile. "It's so great that she's finally found her true calling. She has a beautiful operatic voice, but boy, she can rock too."

"You don't have to tell me. She's awesome. It's funny how Rory and Jesse got so much musical talent, but Callie and Maddie don't seem to have any."

"Callie's got the brains, though."

"True enough."

"It all kind of bothers Maddie," I say quietly. "Jesse and Rory are so talented, and Callie's so smart. Maddie feels really...ordinary."

Donny frowns. "Really? She's beautiful, and I've never really talked to her, but I assume she's as smart as the rest of the family."

"She is. She's gotten straight As all through college. But she's in the shadow of three amazing older siblings."

Donny laughs. "That's silly. I suppose you never had that feeling, huh?"

"What feeling?"

He chuckles. "Being in the shadow of three amazing older siblings?"

I give him a good-natured swat. "You guys *are* all amazing. You know what I think of you. But we're all so different. I don't know how we could ever be in competition with each other. You've got reclusive Dale, with his gift for winemaking. Then you, such a big personality who followed Mom into law. Quiet and brainy Diana, who completely does her own thing with architecture. And then you have me. The only one who's really interested in what Dad does."

"You *are* the cowgirl of the bunch," Donny agrees.

"And damned proud of it." I smile for a moment but then sigh.

"What's wrong?"

"Dad wasn't happy when I decided to go on this tour. He was excited that I was going to be able to start working with him right away since I graduated early."

"You'll be able to do that when the tour is over."

"Yeah, that's what I told him. Both he and Mom agreed that this would be a wonderful time for me to see Europe, especially since you were going to be here for part of it and Brock for the rest of it. But you know Mom and Dad. I'm their baby, so they think I need to be looked after all the time."

"I suppose we all kind of feel that way about you, Bree."

"You don't have to. I'm perfectly capable of taking care of myself."

"Callie and Rory are thrilled that you're doing this for Maddie. This is huge for her. The fact that you're letting her stay in your room, and that Brock paid for her flight. They worry about her a bit."

"Why?"

"Because she feels left out so much."

"Angie, Sage, Gina, and I don't mean to leave her out. It's just that we're all family. We've known each other, well, since we were born."

"I know, but like you said, she feels like she's overshadowed by her siblings too. She seems a little depressed lately."

"She won't be depressed for long." I glance around the hotel bar. The UK flag is displayed proudly on one wall. "We're in England, Donny. Can you believe it?"

"I know. It's going to be great."

Our Diet Cokes arrive . . . without ice.

"I guess we have to get used to no ice," Donny says.

I pour some soda from the can into the glass it was served with. "I guess so. But isn't it cool? To see how other people live?"

"It's very cool."

I take a drink of my Diet Coke, let the fizz slide down my throat. It's good and refreshing. I just feel . . .

I feel like I'm about to embark on an amazing adventure.

If it doesn't include Jesse Pike? Oh, well. I'll get over it.

But I still haven't ruled it out.

"Jesse was in a bad mood this evening, wasn't he?" I say to Donny.

"Yeah. You know how tall he is, and he was stuck back in economy in one of those uncomfortable seats. Then they lost his luggage. I'd probably be in a foul mood if it were me."

"You think he's okay?" I ask.

"Callie says he'll be fine. It's just how he is. Jesse's an artist. He can be moody. Though not as moody as that Dragon guy." Donny's handsome face goes rigid as he leans toward me.

"What were you two talking about at dinner?"

"Nothing much. Small talk mostly."

"I didn't know Dragon Locke could make small talk."

"He's actually a good guy. Sage and Gina think he's the hottest of all the band members."

Donny rolls his eyes. "You've got to be kidding me."

"Come on, Donny. You've seen them hang all over him at the bar at home."

"I try not to think of you, Sage, and Gina doing anything of the sort. To me you're still little girls holding on to your teddy bears."

I give him another swat. "Sorry, big brother. Those years are long gone."

Donny takes a drink. "Well, I'm just glad that once I leave, Brock will be here for the duration of the trip. Somebody needs to keep an eye on you and Maddie."

I hold back a scoff. "Are we back to that again?"

And then I drop my jaw.

Jesse Pike just walked into the bar.

"What is it?" Donny asks.

Then he follows my gaze. "Jesse!" He gestures him over.

"Hi," Jesse says.

"Thought you were heading to bed," Donny says.

"Yeah. I was looking forward to it, but then I hit the pillow and was wide awake. Thought I'd get a nightcap."

"That's what we're doing. You can join us if you'd like," I say brightly.

I'm still a little embarrassed about the whole belt buckle thing, and Jesse and I haven't really talked since then. But my God, even exhausted, with bags under his eyes, Jesse Pike is the most amazing man I've ever looked at. No one wears washed-out jeans quite like he does.

Jesse takes a seat. "Where's Callie?"

"She went up to bed." Donny yawns. "I think I'll join her. Come on, Brianna."

I hold up my can. "Not quite done yet."

"All right. I'll text you with the details for tomorrow." Donny throws a twenty-pound note on the table, rises, and walks away, leaving me alone with Jesse.

"What details about tomorrow?" he asks.

"We're going to go see this old guy, Ennis Ainsley. He was the first winemaker for our vineyards. He still lived there when we were little kids, but I don't really remember much about him."

"Oh, right. Rory told me about him. She and Brock came over to see him a couple of months ago."

"Yeah." I take a tiny sip of my Diet Coke. I have to make it last. "I'm sorry you can't sleep."

"I'll be fine." He signals to a server. "I need a shot of scotch please."

The server nods.

"I'm also really sorry about your luggage."

Jesse shrugs, not meeting my gaze. "It happens."

"Yeah. And I'm sorry you couldn't get that upgrade to first class."

"My own fault. I waited too long."

I'm not sure what to say to that, so I take another very tiny sip of my drink.

The server comes with Jesse's scotch, nods to my can. "You want another?"

"Yeah, thank you."

"You sure you want to drink all that caffeine?" Jesse says.

"We need to sleep if we're going to get on London time."

"The caffeine in Diet Coke never bothers me," I say. "When you've been raised on strong coffee like I have, this is nothing."

He doesn't say anything. Simply nods.

Then he downs a scotch in one gulp.

"Good night." He rises, pulls some bills out of his wallet.

"I can get that," I say. "If it's more than Donny's money, I'll just charge it to the room."

"I pay my own way." He leaves the bills, turns to walk away, but then he looks over his shoulder.

My heart races.

"You want to get out of here?"

"And go where?"

"I don't know. But there's one thing that I know will help me sleep tonight."

CHAPTER TWENTY-FOUR

Jesse

I tried.

I fucking tried.

How am I *not* supposed to look at her?

Brianna Steel is fucking beautiful.

She looks better now than she did at dinner tonight, but at dinner, I was trying not to fall asleep.

Then of course when I finally get back to my room, threw myself onto the bed—sleep didn't come.

And now?

Brianna—her long dark hair like a curtain around her shoulders and over her breasts, her long-sleeved Dragonlock T-shirt that hugs her figure, and her tight boot-cut jeans and cowboy boots.

Her whole look screams American cowgirl.

All I can think about is what she might look like naked. Naked and underneath my body.

This is not a good thing.

I know how she feels about me. Why else would she have bought me that belt buckle?

It's a crush, and I shouldn't lead her on.

But I'm running on no sleep, and my dick is hard in her presence.

Where would we go?

Dragon's in my room, and Maddie's in hers.

"Where?" she asks.

"What?"

"You asked if I want to get out of here."

Yeah, I did. "Come with me."

She stands, and I rake my gaze over her entire body.

My God, her nipples are hard. They're protruding right between the D and the O in Dragon.

Fuck. Me.

"Do you remember our kiss, Brianna?"

She swallows. "Yes."

"It was amazing."

"It was," she agrees, her lips trembling.

I close in on her, caress her cheek. God, it's like silk. "I want you. I need you, right now. Just tonight. I can't make any promises other than tonight."

She swallows again, and this time I hear her soft gulp. "What are you saying, Jesse?"

"Do I have to spell it out for you? If that's the case, I'm going to need to rethink this."

"Of course you don't have to spell it out for me. I'm a grown woman." She crosses her arms, covering up those luscious nipples. "If you're asking to take me to bed, just where and how do you think we're going to do that?"

There's her fire. That beautiful fire of the Steel women. But not just any Steel woman. The most beautiful of all of them.

"I don't know. I have to think."

She raises her eyebrows. "Maybe the hotel has extra rooms available."

"Right. Let's go." I grab her hand, walk swiftly out of the bar and through the lobby to guest services. "We need a room."

"Let me see what we have." The attendant taps on his computer. "I'm afraid we're booked except for a suite on the top floor."

A suite? That's going to cost way too much.

"We'll take it," Brianna says quickly, throwing her credit card on the counter.

"Oh no," I say.

"We can argue about who pays later."

Ten minutes later, after Brianna shows her passport and signs her name, we're on the elevator, propelling upward to the top floor.

And all that exhaustion that's been weighing on me since the plane landed?

It's gone.

I have the energy of an eighteen-year-old, and I plan to use every bit of it.

I take the key card from Brianna, hover it over the reader, and the door clicks open.

We walk in and—

I hold back a gasp.

We're in a hallway. A freaking hallway in a hotel room, and the tile under my feet is black polished marble. The lighting is soft and welcoming, and it makes Brianna look even more beautiful—as if she's almost ethereal.

The living area boasts plush leather sofas and armchairs are arranged around a coffee table, and floor-to-ceiling windows showcase London at night.

Jesus Christ. How much is she paying for this?

In the next moment, I don't care anymore. I close the

door, grab her, push her against the wall, and crush our mouths together.

She opens for me instantly, and oh my God—the same velvety smooth tongue, the same sweet strawberry taste—this time accented with Diet Coke, the same perfect sliding of our lips together.

An amazing kiss.

A prelude of the things to come.

I want to take my time. I want to go slowly and savor every bit of her body.

But already my dick is aching. Bulging against my jeans, and—

I break the kiss. "Bedroom," I rasp out.

She gasps softly, nodding. Her body trembles.

"You sure?" I ask.

She nods.

"I need to hear you say it, Brianna. I need to hear you say 'yes, Jesse, I'm sure. I want this as much as you do.'"

She nods again. "Yes, Jesse. I want this as much as you do."

My dick hardens further.

So beautiful. I need to get inside her. I like to savor a woman. I'm not a wham, bam, thank you ma'am kind of guy, but it's been a damned long time since I've been laid, and I know once I get inside her tight little cunt and fuck her silly, I'll be able to sleep.

I pull her toward the bedroom and then—

I stop.

What the fuck am I doing? I'm being so selfish.

I can't use Brianna Steel to get sleep, no matter how much I want her. No matter how much she appears to want me.

It won't be fair. She'll be on the tour with us the whole

damned time, and there will be this thing between us. This thing we don't speak of. Discomfort.

I rake my hands through my hair and turn to her before we go through the door to the bedroom. "I'm sorry."

"For what?"

"I want you. I want you more than I can even comprehend at the moment. But I can't do this. It's not right."

She grabs my hands. "It's okay, Jesse. I said I want to."

"I know, but I'm not being fair." I place my hands on either side of the doorframe leading to the bedroom. "I'm attracted to you, for sure. But I don't feel *that* way about you."

She blinks a moment, and her eyes glaze over, but no tears fall, thank God. "I didn't ask how you felt about me."

"You're young. Impressionable. I don't think you can handle a onetime fuck."

"You don't know anything about me. You have no idea how many onetime fucks I've had. I can handle anything you throw at me, Jesse Pike. I can handle you and more." She stands tall, shoulders back, chest forward, her soft jawline hard.

And all I can think about is getting into those pants.

God, give me strength.

"I've already paid for this room," she says.

"And I will pay you back."

"It'd be a shame to let it go to waste," she says.

My God, she's trying to kill me.

I cup both her cheeks, rub my thumb over her full lower lip. "You have the sweetest lips I've ever tasted, Brianna Steel."

A soft sigh comes from her throat.

"I can't promise you anything past tonight. I'll be busy with the tour, and I'm not looking for a relationship. I'm looking for a fuck, Brianna. Can you handle that?"

MELODY

She nods, her lips trembling under my touch.

"You sure?"

"Jesse, I don't think I've ever been more sure of anything."

I slam my lips onto hers again, still holding her face.

She opens for me, and the kiss is more feral than before. It's a raw and animalistic kiss because that's what I am right now. A fucking animal. A fucking stag who needs to rut, who needs to let out his aggressions so he can sleep.

She kisses me back, sliding her tongue between my lips.

She's an aggressive kisser. Most women keep their tongues in their own mouths, but not Brianna Steel. She shoves hers past my lips and is an active participant in this kiss.

And it makes me want her all the more.

If she's this aggressive at kissing…

Oh. My. God.

I wish I could take my time with her. Savor this beautiful body of hers.

But that's not to be.

That's not what this night is about.

This night is about a fuck, about relieving tension, about being able to sleep.

Again guilt consumes me. This young lady deserves better than what I'm about to give her.

But who am I to tell her what to do?

Besides, Donny Steel took my sister. It would serve him—

I break the kiss.

What is wrong with me?

This is not a competition between Donny Steel and me. He and Callie are in love.

As much as I want Brianna Steel, I'm not in love with her.

But God, I want her.

156

In fact, in my entire sexual life, which began at sixteen, I can't recall wanting a woman more than I do right now.

So I kiss her again, plunder her lips, push her through the door into the bedroom.

I break the kiss quickly. "Take off your clothes," I grit out.

"Only if you take off yours," she says.

"I wasn't planning on doing this with my clothes on." I kick off my shoes, unbutton my wrinkled shirt, fumbling, trying to do it quickly.

All the time watching her.

She sits down on the bed and pulls off her cowboy boots first, and then she pulls that tight black Dragonlock T-shirt over her head.

I suck in a breath.

She's wearing a lace bra, no padding, so that's why I could see her nipples sticking out earlier. She moves her hand behind her back, unclasps it, and then shimmies out of it, tossing it to the floor along with the shirt.

She has the most gorgeous set of tits I've ever seen. Big, pert, and bouncy, with brownish-pink nipples that are sticking straight out.

I quickly remove my shirt from my shoulders and toss it next to hers.

She gapes at me.

"My God, Jesse."

"I'm glad you like what you see, because I sure like what I see as well."

She cups her breasts then, as if she's holding them out in offering.

My dick grows harder.

"Stand up," I say. "Take off your jeans. Take off your

underwear. I need to see that pussy."

She stands, her legs trembling a bit, but she steadies herself. She unbuttons her jeans, unbuckles the belt, unzips, and slides them over her hips, down her thighs to her feet, exposing her beautiful long legs. She steps out of them. Only a lacy pink thong separates me from heaven.

"Take it off," I growl.

CHAPTER TWENTY-FIVE

Brianna

Part of me can't believe what's happening.

This must all be a dream.

I am alone with Jesse Pike in a hotel suite. Naked, my nipples pebbled into hard berries, my pussy already throbbing.

I stand here in a thong.

I wasn't even going to wear a thong today, but when I changed out of my traveling clothes, I wanted to feel sexy, so why not?

Thongs make me feel sexy. Panty lines don't.

Even though Jesse Pike has been clear that nothing will ever happen between us, I'm glad I wore it.

This thong is apparently my good luck charm.

So it's a onetime thing. My heart will be broken, but at least I'll have Jesse one time. I'll have given my virginity to the man I've worshiped for so long.

Is that fair to him? He has no idea I'm a virgin. If he knew, he would probably run away screaming. Or would he? Some men like taking a woman's virginity. God . . . I don't know . . .

"Do I have to repeat myself?" he growls.

I slowly slide my thumbs into the waistband of the thong and glide it down over my thighs until it ends up around my ankles, and I kick it off.

He sucks in a breath.

I'm not shaved down there, only trimmed. Doesn't seem to matter to him. Thank God I shaved my armpits and my legs before we left Denver.

He's still wearing his jeans, but the bulge beneath them is apparent.

This may be only physical for him, but at least he wants me.

I want to tell him to finish undressing, but I can't speak because I can't stop staring at his perfectly sculpted chest. Black hair in just the right amount scatters over his pecs. His shoulders are broad and golden. And his abs. God, his abs... firm and perfect with that sexy V that points to his cock. Again, I want to tell him to finish undressing. To take off those jeans so I can see as much of him as he's seeing of me.

But the words are caught in my throat.

My entire body is on fire, yet goose bumps erupt. How can that be?

My nerves skitter underneath my flesh, and flames ignite between my legs.

I'm wet. So wet.

Will it hurt?

After all my years of horseback riding, I can't have much of a hymen left.

And already I know Jesse Pike's going to be huge.

I've seen men's dicks before. Handled them, sucked them. I just never let one inside me.

That ends tonight.

Jesse unhooks his belt, discards his belt buckle—which is not the one I gave him.

Did he bring it with him? Does he even care?

I should stop this.

I should stop this before I let him take my virginity. He may never forgive me.

But I can't stop it.

I'm powerless against my aching need for him.

In slow motion, he slides the leather of his belt out of the buckle, unsnaps, unzips his jeans.

He slides them over his hips, steps out of them.

He's wearing gray boxer briefs that cling to his muscular thighs, and the bulge . . .

My God, the bulge.

Already, a tiny drop of liquid is apparent on the fabric of his boxer briefs.

"You sure about this?" he growls. "The condoms I brought are in my lost bag. I swear I'm clean, though, and it's been a while for me."

"I'm on birth control, and I'm clean."

Of course I'm clean. I've never done this.

He slides the boxer briefs over his perfectly formed ass, and his cock springs out, giant and hard and beautiful.

I gape at him. At the black bush that surrounds it, at the twin veins marbling over the granitelike surface.

"I'd like to take you slowly," he says. "But I can't. I need to get inside you, Brianna. I need to—"

He turns me around, bends me over the bed, and I feel his cock dangling between my ass cheeks.

No. Not like this. I want to be looking into his beautiful dark eyes.

I nudge him backward.

"Yeah, I'm coming."

No. He thinks that means I want him to do it this way. "No, not like this," I say.

He moves backward. "What do you mean?"

"I want you facing me. I want to see you. See what you're doing to me." I turn around, gaze into his smoldering dark eyes.

He doesn't smile. He sits down on the bed next to me and scoots us up toward the head of the bed.

Then he kisses me, a quick kiss with minimal tongue.

He cups my breasts, squeezes them, and then he climbs on top of me and hovers over me, his dick dangling between my legs.

God, I want more. I want his lips on my nipples. His mouth between my legs. I want to touch his cock, suck the pearly drop off its head.

So much I want to do to him, so much I want him to do to me.

"You ready?" he growls.

I gulp. "Yes, Jesse. I'm ready."

He thrusts into me swiftly, and I gasp.

It's not painful exactly, just... I'm not sure what. I'm full, so full. Can he tell? Can he tell no man has ever been here before?

"Damn it." He pulls out as swiftly as he went in. "Why didn't you tell me?"

"Tell you what?"

"That you're a goddamned virgin, Brianna."

I clasp my hand to my lips. "How could you tell?"

"By the way your body reacted. You're tense as a board."

He rises from the bed, his cock still hard, goes into the bathroom, and then he returns with a wet rag. He wipes it over me and then shows it to me. On the white hotel washcloth are streaks of blood. "This is not the way any woman should lose her virginity."

I sniff back tears, cross my legs over the ache between them. "What if it's how I *wanted* to lose my virginity?"

"With a quick fuck? A quick fuck from a man who only needs a release so he can get to sleep?" Jesse buries his face in his hands. "You're better than that, Brianna. Fuck. Your brothers will never forgive me for this."

"It may interest you to know, Jesse, that I don't talk about my sex life with my brothers."

He moves his hands from his eyes and looks at me. Glares at me. "What sex life? This is your first experience."

I huff. "Maybe it's my first experience of the act itself, but I assure you I'm not some untried little kid. I've had plenty of experience. I've given hand jobs, blow jobs. I've had men go down on me. I even messed around with another woman once. I've done—"

"Stop it," he commands. "Just stop it right there. This is all so wrong."

"I never thought you were the kind of guy who would start something and not finish," I say in a daring tone.

"Are you crazy?" He waves the washcloth in my face. "This is your virgin's blood, Brianna."

"Exactly. And I'm no longer a virgin, so why don't you finish?"

He stares at me, dropping the cloth onto the floor. "You have no idea how tempting you are. No idea how beautiful you are, what a tight little pussy you have. How much I want to get back in there."

"What's stopping you?" I uncross my legs, move onto all fours, and crawl sexily—I hope—down the bed, closer to him. "You've already taken my virginity. That can't be changed. Not now. So take what you need from me, Jesse. This one night.

You gave me what I wanted. I wanted to lose my virginity. Now I want to give you what *you* want."

He looks away from me. "You should've told me."

"Well, I didn't. So now what do you want to do about it?"

He sits down on the foot of the bed. "Nothing. I'm going to do absolutely fucking nothing."

I crawl to him and sit next to him. "Let me take care of you. Maybe I'm a virgin, but I'm not a virgin in other ways. I've had many cocks in my mouth, Jesse. I can take care of you that way."

He shakes his head, rises. His dick is still hard.

"This is my own fault. I'm sorry, Brianna. This should have never happened." He rises, walks into the bathroom, closes the door.

I know what he's going to do in there. And he's going to be doing it without me.

I scurry to the bathroom and knock. "Jesse, please. What's done is done. At least give me what I deserve."

He opens the door then. "Are you crazy? What you deserve is way more than I can give you."

"That's not what I mean. What's done is done. But don't I deserve a little better? I wanted you to take my virginity, which you did—"

"I didn't mean to."

"I know that. And you're right—I probably should've told you. But I wanted it so badly. Now the deed is done. You want me as much as I want you. Don't try to deny it."

"Have I denied it?"

I open my arms to him. "So take it. Take it from me and give me a night to remember. Even if it's just one night, Jesse. I want to remember the loss of my virginity as something special."

164

He looks at me then—really looks at me, staring into my eyes. He cups one cheek, thumbs my lower lip. "I can do that much."

My heart pops up from my stomach as he takes my hand, leads me back to the bed.

He's still so hard, he must be aching inside. But he's willing to give me a night.

I lie down, and I expect him to climb back on top of me, finish what he started, but he doesn't.

Instead—

"Close your eyes," he says.

I obey.

And then I gasp as his lips close around one nipple.

Sweet suction. He sucks lightly at first, making me want him even more, while he plays with the other, rolling it lightly between his thumb and forefinger.

So gentle, and so erotic.

He lets the first nipple drop from his lips. "You have the most beautiful breasts I've ever seen," he murmurs.

I smile, still keeping my eyes closed, even though I want more than anything to watch him.

He told me to keep my eyes closed, and that's what I'll do. I've done enough to him already tonight. I was dishonest with him by omission. I won't disobey him again.

He plays with my nipples a while longer, and I move instinctively beneath him, my hips undulating and rising from the bed.

He drops the nipple again, kisses the top of my breasts, shoulders, my neck, my cheek, going to my ear and nibbling on the lobe.

"You should be against the law, Brianna Steel," he

whispers, his hot breath erotically massaging my neck. "You're lethal. Like a fucking drug."

I sigh softly, still not opening my eyes.

He trails his lips over my cheek to my own lips, and he slides his tongue between them.

We kiss for a few moments—timeless amazing moments— our lips sliding together and my heart rate increasing exponentially.

He breaks the kiss and draws in a deep breath.

Then he kisses me on the top of my chest, my breasts, and he sucks on each nipple for another minute, and then he kisses from my belly down to my abdomen, spreading my legs and kissing my inner thighs.

"You're beautiful," he says.

How I want to open my eyes, to see his head between my legs. But I keep them shut.

Then I gasp softly when his lips close around my clit and he sucks gently.

I'm about ready to come. I've come before when a guy eats me, but never this quickly.

He moves his lips away from my clit, slides his tongue over the entrance to my pussy. And then he swirls around my clit again.

I can't help myself—

I jump off the cliff and soar into an orgasm.

"Fuck, yeah, baby. You come."

"Please, may I open my eyes now?"

"Yeah, open them."

I shoot them open, and the image of Jesse's handsome face between my legs nearly sets me on another climax.

"Watch what I do to you, Brianna Steel. Watch me make you come again."

He never wavers from my gaze as he slides his tongue over and around my clit again.

I arch my back, raise my hips, sliding my pussy over his chin, the stubble making me insane.

"God, you're hot," he growls.

Then he sucks my entire labia into his mouth, pulling and tugging.

I'm about ready to come again, all I need is just—

His lips on my clit! And I soar off into the horizon once more.

My entire body throbs, and those contractions in my pussy radiate outward, making my fingers and toes tingle.

"God, you're gushing," he says against me.

"Do it, Jesse. Fuck me now. I'm wet. I promise it won't hurt. And I'll—"

"Not yet," he growls. "You've got a few more orgasms left in you, and I'm going to pull them out."

No. I can't take any more orgasms. I just want him inside me. I need that aching feel of completion.

He tongues my pussy again, and then he pushes my thighs forward, slides his tongue over my most forbidden place.

A place no one has been, ever. Not a tongue, a finger, anything else.

I gasp out.

He seems to understand, moves his tongue back to my pussy, licks my clit. As I begin to soar into another orgasm, he inserts one finger into me.

That's all it takes.

Orgasm number three.

This one's even better than the first two. He massages the inside of my pussy, pressing against the anterior, and the penetration—the penetration while he licks my clit—is so good, so freaking good.

"Please, Jesse," I rasp out. "Get inside me. Please."

"You owe me one more orgasm, Brianna. And I'm not going inside until I get it."

I'm still tingling from the last one. I've never had more than one orgasm at a time with a guy. This is crazy. Insane.

And oh so good.

He slides his tongue over my inner thighs. "God, you're fucking wet."

Then he comes back between my legs, licks my clit, placing his finger inside me once more, teasing.

My God, it's better than I ever imagined. I always knew Jesse Pike could take me places I've never been, but even *I* hadn't imagined this amount of paradise.

He nips at my clit while massaging the inside my pussy with his finger, and when he adds another—

"Jesse!" I scream out.

He groans against my pussy, still eating me as I give him that last orgasm he demanded.

"Please," I beg. "Inside me. Now."

This time he gives me what I yearn for. While I'm still coming, he removes his fingers, crawls slowly toward me, and slides his cock inside me.

"Fuck," he growls.

He stays inside me for a moment, and then he kisses me, sliding his tongue between my lips and letting me taste myself. I've tasted myself after oral sex, but never has it tasted this wonderful, mingled with the beautiful flavor of Jesse himself.

We kiss, we kiss, and we kiss, and finally he pulls out and thrusts back in me.

One more thrust, and then another, and—

"Fuck me," he grits out, sliding his tongue over my neck.

I feel every pulse of his cock as my walls clench around him.

"You're so fucking tight," he growls against my neck.

"Feels so good," I say.

I'm still reeling from four orgasms, but nothing feels quite as good as Jesse Pike inside me.

I've dreamed about it for so long, and I don't ever want this night to end.

He stays inside me for a few moments, and he turns us on our sides so we're facing each other.

He meets my gaze. "I hope that was good for you."

I wipe a bead of sweat from my forehead. "It was perfect."

"Good. I didn't mean to take your virginity, but I hope it was memorable."

"I'll never forget it."

Then he pulls out, rolls off the bed, and heads to the bathroom. He comes back with the warm washcloth again and gently cleans me.

"No more blood this time," he says. "That's good."

"I don't care."

He looks at me sternly. "I do. You tricked me."

"No."

"Don't even bother lying to me, Brianna. You tricked me into taking your virginity, and we both know it. It was already done, so I decided to give you a night you would never forget. I want the night you lost your virginity to be memorable for you. But know this." He burns me with his gaze. "It will *never* happen again."

CHAPTER TWENTY-SIX

Jesse

I am the worst sort of lowlife scum.

I at least hope I gave her a good memory. No woman should lose her virginity to a man who's only after one thing.

I was looking for a release tonight. Release so I could sleep. I've had it, and it was fucking great, but I won't be able to sleep anyway, knowing what I did to Brianna.

I defiled a young woman, took her virginity, for a completely selfish reason.

It's something most other guys might not think much about, but I'm not most other guys.

Brianna Steel deserves better.

Which is why I *will* stay away from her from now on.

"Jesse, I—"

I hold up a hand. "Please. Don't say anything, Bree. I feel terrible enough about this as it is."

"I don't want you to feel terrible," she says, sniffling a bit.

My God . . . Please do not let her cry.

She sniffs again and seems to stop whatever sobs might have been coming. Thank God.

"You didn't do anything wrong."

"Are you kidding me? I took your virginity. I never meant to do that, Brianna."

"I told you that you could."

"You told me I could fuck you. There's a difference."

She shakes her head, her lips swollen and so pretty. Her hair a mass of dark brown around her milky shoulders. "There's no difference from where I'm standing. When I said you could have me tonight, I knew I was a virgin. I knew what I was getting into."

"*I* didn't," I say. "You kept an integral fact from me, and that was unfair."

"Do you ask all the women you sleep with whether they're virgins?" she demands haughtily.

"For God's sake, Bree." I rub my forehead. "Admit it. You should've told me."

"But if I told you, you might not have done it."

I let out an exasperated sigh. "Isn't that the damned point? Of *course* I wouldn't have done it. I can't offer you anything beyond tonight. If I knew you were a virgin ... "

Would I have done anything differently?

I wanted her so badly.

But once I found out, I withdrew and went to the bathroom to take care of things myself. I only returned at her urging.

After all, she was right. The deed was already done at that point.

I still feel like a fucking heel.

What I really need is sleep. I have rehearsal tomorrow. I've got a tour to do—a tour that could make or break the band's career.

The last thing I need is to get involved with a woman, especially Brianna Steel.

But I took her virginity.

There's no escaping that now.

We're both still naked, and she looks so sweet and innocent, gazing up at me.

There's something in her eyes. Is it love?

Not that I would recognize love, but clearly she feels something for me. She bought me that belt buckle, and now . . . *this*.

She gave me her virginity of her own free will. I gave her multiple chances to change her mind, and she didn't.

Here comes the overwhelming guilt, like a freaking anvil strapped to my back.

Because I'm *not* in love with this woman. I'm not in love with any woman.

This isn't even me.

I don't do indiscriminate fucks. Which is part of the problem. I was horny, needed release, and I wanted to get laid.

She was here, offering herself up on a platter.

Would I have stopped if I'd known she was a virgin?

I'd like to think I would have.

But fuck . . .

The way her pussy held my cock.

So tight—a tightness that had nothing to do with her virginity. I could fuck her again tomorrow and she'd still be just as tight. Just as perfectly tight . . .

Damn, tomorrow . . .

She's going to be sore. Does she know that?

I slide the cloth over her once more. It's a bit cooler now but still warm enough to be a little soothing.

I sigh. "You're going to be sore."

"Maybe not."

"You bled a little. Trust me. You're going to be sore."

"But it didn't hurt that much, Jesse."

172

"Some girls hurt more than others after their first time. You're still going to be sore."

She closes her eyes, sighs. "Whatever. It was worth it."

God . . . The guilt just went from an anvil to a ton of bricks. I don't have indiscriminate sex, despite my decision to screw around during this trip if it was offered. I sure as hell don't have indiscriminate sex with young and impressionable women.

How could I have done this to such a sweet girl?

Except Brianna is no girl. I may remember when she was eight years old, but the woman lying before me is a fully grown, fully developed woman.

Any man would want her.

"Look," I say. "You and Maddie are going to be here the whole time with us on this tour. We're going to have to come to some kind of an understanding."

She opens her eyes and meets my gaze, her head still on the pillow. "All right, Jesse. Whatever you want, I will agree to."

"Seriously?"

"Yes, because you're right. I did deceive you. I shouldn't have done that. I don't want this to change things between us."

"There was never anything between us, Brianna."

"That's what I mean." She rises and heads toward the bathroom. "I suppose we can't call ourselves friends. We certainly don't run in the same circles. But I am friends with Maddie, and I don't want what happened to change that. I promised Maddie a wonderful trip, and I aim to keep that promise."

My heart softens a bit. She *is* doing a lot for Maddie. Maddie wouldn't have this experience if not for Brianna.

A sliver of emotion coils in my belly.

I nip it in the bud, though. I don't have time to get involved. Especially not with Brianna Steel.

"We're friends," I say. "But you have to understand, Brianna. When I look at you, I see—" I stop myself abruptly.

Because I was about to lie to her, to tell her I see that pretty little eight-year-old girl in cowboy boots following after her father.

But it's a lie.

That's *not* what I see when I look at her. If it were, I should probably go to jail. What I see is a beautiful, seductive, passionate woman.

A woman who—

I shake my head to clear it.

I will *not* go there. I will not develop feelings for her.

"You see what?"

I sigh and look to the floor. "I see…a woman whose virginity I just stole."

"You didn't steal it. I gave it to you."

She's right. "But I didn't mean to take it," I say. "So that makes me feel like I stole it. I know that doesn't make any sense, but it's how I feel."

"I don't want you to feel that way, Jesse. I've wanted to be with you for a long time."

Oh God. Just cut my heart in two, why don't you? I've seen how Brianna and the rest of the awesome foursome hang around the band. They're all pretty, sweet young women. But the other band members and I have never thought of them in that way. Mostly because they're all the same age as Maddie.

A ten-year age gap isn't a bad thing. I might be fine with it if she weren't so darned young. Even if she were twenty-five and I was thirty-five, things would be different.

But twenty-two...

"I'm flattered," I tell her. "But you deserved something better."

"Did I? You made it wonderful for me, Jesse. Even after you were angry because you felt I deceived you. You still gave me four orgasms and a night I'll never forget."

I did, but I wasn't being altruistic. Sure, there was a part of me that felt guilty and wanted to give her a better loss of her virginity than a quickie. But another part of me? I did it because I wanted to. Pure and simple. Sure, my first instinct was for a hookup, to get the release I so craved. But making *love* to Brianna, giving her orgasms, was absolutely no hardship at all.

I grab my jeans and shirt, begin to dress. "I'm glad you enjoyed yourself. But I have a job to do on this trip. The future of the band hinges on our success on this tour. So this thing—whatever it is—between us? It's over, Brianna. It's over."

CHAPTER TWENTY-SEVEN

Brianna

I will *not* cry.

I've been kicked in the shins hard by a balking steer, and I swallowed the pain. Never cried.

I never cried when I was learning to ride a horse as a kid and got thrown onto the hard Colorado clay dirt.

Never cried.

But the pain I feel now is nothing like the physical pain I subject myself to working daily on the ranch.

It's like Jesse opened up my chest, took my heart in his hands, and squeezed the life out of it.

I can't make him feel something for me.

But I did get what I wanted out of this.

I'm no longer a virgin.

I was the last of the awesome foursome to succumb, even though they don't know that. They always assumed I'd slept with previous boyfriends, and I just let them believe it. It was easier that way.

I lie back down on the bed, still naked.

Jesse walks to the bathroom, picking up his shoes on the way. I hear the water running. Then I hear the toilet flush. He emerges from the bathroom fully clothed, his eyes sunken, dark circles still surrounding them.

I didn't think I could possibly feel worse after his rejection, but I do. I did this to him. He needs sleep, but he's not going to get any. Now he feels this overwhelming guilt, and that is all my fault.

He's feeling like he's the worst person who's ever lived, but that's not true. *I'm* the worst person who's ever lived.

I got what I wanted, but now I've given us both so much guilt—so much guilt, right as we're about to embark on a months-long tour together.

A tour that could make or break Jesse's career.

I gulp. "Jesse..."

"Good night, Brianna."

He walks out of the bedroom, and I hear the door to the suite close.

"I'm sorry," I finish.

Then I let the tears come.

★ ★ ★

I wake up to my phone buzzing. For a moment I don't know where I am, until I remember...

The ache between my legs reminds me.

Jesse was right. I'm sore.

Where the hell is my phone? Probably in my purse. I dart my gaze around the room and find it sitting on the floor near the door of the bedroom.

It has stopped buzzing by then, and I have a voicemail. From Maddie.

"Oh my God, Brianna, where are you? I woke up and you're not here. Please call me as soon as you get this. In the meantime, I'm throwing on some clothes, and I'm going to look for you."

What am I going to tell Maddie? I sure as hell can't tell her I spent the night in a suite with her brother. That's not even true. Jesse left in the middle of the night.

But I can't let her go on being frantic. I call her back.

"Oh my God, Bree!" she gasps into the phone.

"Hi, Mads. I'm okay."

"Where the heck are you?"

"I . . . got up early. Came down for coffee."

"Your bed is still made."

"I know. I made it."

She huffs into my ear. "Brianna, why are you lying to me?"

"Oh, Maddie . . ." The lump in my throat grows larger. "Please don't push me on this. My heart's not in it. All you need to know is that I'm okay, and I'm coming back right now."

"Brianna . . ."

"Please, Maddie. I'll tell you everything when I'm ready. Just please . . . Don't push this right now." I choke back a sob. "I just can't."

"Oh my God. Are you crying?"

"No," I lie. "I'll be back in a moment."

I get my clothes on, go into the bathroom, wash my face, getting rid of the raccoon eyes leftover from my mascara. I don't bother fixing my makeup after I wash it off because I don't really care. I run a comb through my hair. I'll take a shower in my own room, where all my products are.

I leave the bathroom, the bedroom, and the suite. I gaze back into the large living area before I close the door for good.

Somehow I get to the elevator and push the right button to take me to the floor where Maddie and I have a room.

I slowly shamble to the room and get the key card to unlock the door with a click.

When I walk in, Maddie grabs me, hugging me. "Don't ever do that to me again."

"Don't worry. I won't."

She doesn't know how true my words are, because if her brother doesn't want me, I don't want anyone else.

I'm only twenty-two. Chances are I'll meet someone else eventually. But right now, I imagine myself as a spinster living on the ranch, working alongside my father . . . for the rest of my life.

★ ★ ★

I convinced Maddie to continue her sightseeing plans with Brock, Callie, and Donny this morning. I convinced her to tell them that I was a little nauseated from something I ate last night. I stayed back in the room, took a shower, and then sat around feeling miserable.

They pick me up at lunchtime.

"You feeling better?" Maddie asks.

"Hey, sis." Donny says. "I'm sorry you ate something bad."

"Yeah, I'm fine now, though."

Maddie gives me a sympathetic gaze.

She wouldn't tell any of them that I was gone all night. I know I can trust her to be discreet and keep my secrets.

We end up at a small sandwich shop for lunch, where I order a curried chicken sandwich called coronation chicken. The bread is white and moist, but it tastes dry like sawdust against my tongue.

I have to snap out of this. We're going to afternoon tea to meet Ennis Ainsley. I force my lips to curve into a smile.

I gather all my strength to engage in the conversation

among the rest of our party.

By the end of the meal, after my sandwich—which turned out to be delicious—and a lot of water, I feel somewhat better.

Not great, but I'll deal.

We walk around London for the next hour until it's time for tea. Because of our time constraint, Brock suggests the Tower Bridge, a suspension bridge that crosses the River Thames. It's striking—two towers are connected by a walkway and drawbridge.

The Tower of London and St. Katharine Docks are nearby, but unfortunately we don't have the time to visit them today. We admire the majestic bridge and take lots of photos. Then we take a cab to Ennis Ainsley's house.

We're on the outskirts of London, near the countryside. The house is a gorgeous stone mansion, and I wish Diana were here to see it. It's stately, with an imposing facade and meticulous architectural details—including majestic columns and arched windows—that she would appreciate. The gray stone appears to be granite, though I can't tell for sure. The expansive grounds are beautifully landscaped and feature lush gardens, a manicured lawn, and a cobblestone driveway leading to the main entrance.

"Wow." Maddie's eyes go wide.

"Yeah, our family paid Ennis really well," Brock says. "Rory and I were amazed at this place when we came. Wait until you meet his British butler, Havisham."

"I know," Maddie says. "Rory told me all about him. A real British gentleman's gentleman."

We exit the cab, and I steel myself. I've managed to keep from crying all day, and my eyes are finally looking somewhat normal. I skipped the mascara this morning after my shower. I didn't want raccoon eyes again.

"You're going to love Ennis," Brock says, knocking on the door. "He's awesome."

CHAPTER TWENTY-EIGHT

Jesse

"Damn it, Cage," I yell. "Could you fucking keep up?"

Rory and the guys all drop their jaws and stare at me.

Of course they do.

I never yell during rehearsal. Okay . . . maybe *never* is too harsh a word, but rarely.

"Jess, what's your problem?" Rory demands.

"My problem is our cousin has been late on his entrance each time we've played the damned song, Ror."

"He hasn't," Rory says.

I turn to face my sister. "You questioning my ear?"

"Yeah," Rory says. "I am. You were supposed to go right back to your room and get some sleep last night. Did you?"

"No, he didn't."

I glare at Dragon sitting behind his drum set. "Thanks a lot."

"Listen, Jess," Dragon says. "This tour means everything to all of us. Not just you. We need you at the top of your game. Right now you're not. I don't know what the hell you were doing until one in the morning when you finally came back to our room, but whatever it was, you need to fucking move past it and get on board here."

I glare at Dragon again. These are the most words he's

ever said at one time.

At least in front of the whole band.

"You stayed out late?" Cage says. "What the hell is wrong with you?"

"I don't owe any of you an explanation."

"Fine," Rory says, "but if it were any of the rest of us who were fucking up today, you'd demand an explanation."

She's not wrong.

I've always been the de facto leader of this band.

"Still none of your business," I say dryly. "Could we please try this again?"

I nod to Jake, who begins on the guitar, and then Cage, who comes in on point this time.

Yeah, he was probably doing fine. I think I'm just . . .

I don't fucking know. I tossed and turned all night. Dragon must not have noticed, or if he did, he hasn't mentioned it to me.

"Stop, stop, stop . . . " Rory says.

"What is it now?" I say.

"*You* didn't start that time, Jesse." She huffs.

"What the fuck is wrong with you, man?" This from Jake, who doesn't talk much more than Dragon.

"Exhausted. I'm fucking exhausted," I grit out. "But we have to get through this rehearsal. Let's just get it done."

"To do it, we need to get you to come in on time," Rory says.

"Sis, I fucking know that. Jesus Christ." I nod to Dragon. "Let's start again."

This time I manage to come in on cue, and we get through the song. Rory sounds great, of course, and the others do their job well.

My voice sounds like a croaking frog.

"Good job," I say when we're done.

"You call that good?" Cage asks. "What the hell is wrong with your voice, Jess?"

"A little bit of a dry throat. Dehydration from yesterday. The traveling and all."

Rory shakes her head at me. "You'd better get it together before the concert in two days."

"Yeah. I will. Don't worry." I take a long drink from my water bottle. My throat is still parched. "All right. Let's run through it again."

★ ★ ★

After rehearsal, Cage, Jake, and Dragon go out for a pint, but Rory grabs my arm.

"You're with me, Jess." She drags me up to the hotel suite she shares with Brock, which is a carbon copy of the one Brianna and I . . .

Fuck.

"Where's your other half?" I ask.

"Sightseeing. Then they're going to Ennis Ainsley's for tea."

"Who?"

"The original Steel winemaker."

I plunk down on the leather sofa. "Who cares?"

"I care," she says. "I'm missing tea with Ennis Ainsley, who I like, for rehearsal. Only to have you be a complete asshole." She sits next to me. "You better level with me now, Jesse. Because if you and I aren't at our best for this tour, we can forget ever being asked to tour with any big name again."

My sister's right. The sound of our voices together is what made Jett Draconis and Zane Michaels notice us, think we were something special.

"Don't screw this up for us," she continues. "The guys will never forgive you."

"And you?"

"I want this chance as much as they do," she says, "but you're my brother. I will always forgive you."

She doesn't need the money, though. She's marrying Brock Steel. The other guys? I can't let them down.

I sigh. "I'm fine. I just didn't get any sleep last night, and I really needed it."

She rubs her forehead, as if to ease an ache. "Why were you out past midnight? You were supposed to go straight home after dinner and go to bed."

"Who are you now, my mommy?"

"Be serious for a minute, Jesse. You know what jet lag does. You didn't sleep on the plane, mostly because of your own stubbornness."

I open my mouth to argue, but she holds up a hand.

"Don't. I heard you the first time. You tried, but all the first-class seats were taken. If you'd gotten over your stubborn pride in the beginning, we would've all been in first class from the outset."

Again, she's right.

I don't bother opening my mouth to argue this time.

Besides, she keeps chattering.

"This is our one shot, Jesse. Sometimes you only get one, and we'd better not blow it."

"I—"

"Shut up. I'm not finished yet." She shakes her head.

"This isn't just your shot. It's mine. All those years I thought a performance career wasn't in the cards for me. The opera industry rejected me. So I was teaching the students of Snow Creek how to play piano and sing. I thought that was all I was good enough for until now. I've been given a second chance at a performance career, and no one—especially not my big brother—is going to screw this up for me."

As if I couldn't feel like more of a dick ...

Not only did I take a young woman's virginity, but now my sister and the rest of the band think I'm destroying their chance at the big time.

"Rory ..."

"Not finished yet."

I sigh. "Fine. Let me have it."

"Callie texted me."

"Oh?"

"She told me you were down at the bar last night. That you were with Brianna Steel when she and Donny went to bed."

"So?"

Rory digs her phone out of her back pocket and scrolls through her texts. "Maddie texted me this morning. Frantic. Brianna didn't come back to the room last night."

"You heard Dragon. I got back at one."

"Which leaves several hours for you and Brianna unaccounted for. What the hell, Jesse?"

"Nothing."

Rory holds up her hand. "Don't you give me that. Brianna Steel is Maddie's age. She's young and impressionable."

I rise and head for the door. "This is none of your business, Rory."

Rory stands and blocks my path. "You're right. It's not.

Except when it affects the band. Whatever the hell is going on with you, Jesse, you need to nip it in the bud right now. And if you did anything..." She shakes her head. "My God, I've been at Murphy's bar back home. I've seen how the awesome foursome hangs around the band. I swear to God..."

"I'm handling it," I say.

"And then that belt buckle she gave you for Christmas. What are you thinking, Jess?"

I rise, pace around Rory's suite, rake my fingers through my hair. "I'm *not* thinking, Rory. Isn't that obvious?"

She crosses her arms. "Yeah, it *is* obvious. This is our one shot, damn it. Why is your head not in the game?"

"Rory, for God's sake. You and I have never talked about this kind of shit."

"Yeah, you're right. And I don't really want to start now."

"Then don't."

"Fine." She raises a finger. "I'll just say this. Whatever is eating at you, fix it. If it's Brianna Steel? Fix it." She shakes her head. "You'd better be damned happy Callie and Donny don't know about any of this. They're with Maddie and Brianna right now, so you'd better hope your little sister doesn't start talking about the fact that her roomie didn't come home last night."

"Christ." I rub my eyes, and my face splits into a yawn. "I'm just so fucking tired, Ror. I got back after dinner last night, and sleep wouldn't come. So I went down for a drink."

"Which is where you found Brianna Steel, and you figured out a way to make sleep come."

I feel woozy, as if all my blood is rushing to my head. "I suppose so. At least I thought I did. But then sleep didn't come anyway, because I felt so..." I sigh.

Rory slaps the back of my head. "Guilty? Stupid? Like this

is the dumbest thing you could've ever done?"

"Ow!" I rub my head. "And yeah. Among other things."

"Jesse, this is a complication we did not need on this trip. You know that."

"I know. I was thinking with the wrong head."

Rory sits back down. "God, you men are idiots. To think I could have had a woman as my life partner."

I open my mouth, but no words come out. I'd like to defend my sex, but at the moment, I'm just too damned tired.

"You do whatever you have to do to sleep tonight. Something besides fucking Brianna Steel. Go to a pharmacy, see if you can find an over-the-counter sleep aid. But get some fucking sleep tonight, Jesse Pike, or I swear to God I will kick your ass."

I scoff.

"Fine. I'll get my fiancé to kick your ass."

"Like he could."

She laughs as she rakes her gaze over me. "Yeah, he could, especially with the shape you're in right now."

"Stop it with your empty threats, Rory," I say. "I know this is a problem, and I'll fix it."

"You'd better hope Brianna doesn't go running to Donny about this. Or Brock, for that matter."

"Don't you think I've already thought of all that?" I close my eyes, inhale slowly. "I've gone over every scenario in my head. Every single one points to one conclusion. I fucked up."

"Damned right you fucked up."

Rory doesn't even know how badly I fucked up. She doesn't know Brianna was a virgin.

I'm not about to enlighten her.

"I don't want to take some pill, even if it's over the counter.

I've never needed anything like that before."

"Then get on your phone and do a search. Find out how to overcome jet lag. Whatever it is, you fucking do it."

"Yeah. But with Dragon in the room—"

"That's a nonissue." She taps on her phone. "The hotel was fully booked, but a room became available this morning. I booked it for you. It happens to be right next to mine . . . and you'd better be the only one in it." She eyes me, glaring.

"We've been through this. The band has expenses. We can't afford our own rooms." I grab her phone and read the confirmation email. "Five hundred pounds a night? You're kidding, right?"

She yanks her phone back from me. "That's why *I* booked it. I'm paying for it. It's my gift to you, Jesse. Use it. Get in your room, take a long bath if you have to."

I grimace. "I don't take baths. I feel like I'm stewing in my own filth."

Rory's features finally soften. "You are. But they help. They help you relax. I've also booked you a massage this evening. Go to it. When you're done, take a warm bath in your private room to get rid of all the toxins that work their way to the surface from the massage."

"Yes, ma'am," I say dryly.

She stands and pokes me in the chest. "And no alcohol for you tonight."

"Are you kidding me?"

"Alcohol doesn't help you sleep, Jesse. It may help you pass out, but then you wake up. I want you to get at least eight hours of uninterrupted sleep. Ten or twelve would be even better."

"Fine."

She hands me a small folder. "Here's the key to your room. I'll be keeping an eye on you. I'd better not see anyone go out that door."

"Like you'd see me all the time."

"You are allowed to go out at five p.m. for your massage."

I roll my eyes.

"I'd better see you back in that room no later than six thirty this evening. Then you take your bath, order your dinner from room service. And you'd better be bright-eyed and bushy-tailed tomorrow morning at eight o'clock."

"Eight o'clock? Rehearsal doesn't start until one."

"You're meeting Brock and me for breakfast at eight in the morning. You're going to get on London time if it kills me."

"If it kills *you*?"

"You think this is fun for me? Watching my big brother fuck up this one opportunity? I'm not going to let that happen." She curls her hands into fists. "The spa's on the second floor. Your appointment's at five."

I sigh and shove the key card in my pocket. "You already told me that." I look at my watch. Four o'clock now. I have an hour to kill before my massage. "I'll go down to the spa now. They probably have a steam room or hot tub or something. It'll help me relax."

She smiles. Finally. "Jesse, that is the most coherent thing you've said all day."

CHAPTER TWENTY-NINE

Brianna

"Good afternoon," the tuxedo-clad butler says to us. He's tall, with a receding blond hairline, piercing blue eyes, and slightly crooked teeth.

"Hello, Havisham," Brock says. "Remember me? Brock Steel?"

"Yes, of course I do, sir. Mr. Ainsley is expecting you. Please come in."

Brock holds his hand out, letting the rest of us go first. "Let me introduce you to my companions. This is Maddie Pike. She's Rory's sister. You remember Rory, my fiancée?"

"Yes, of course I do. Lovely woman."

Maddie holds out her hand. "Great to meet you, Mr. Havisham."

Havisham doesn't take her hand, simply bows. "It's my pleasure, Ms. Pike."

"And this is my cousin Donny Steel. He's engaged to Callie, Rory and Maddie's sister."

Havisham bows. "Mr. Steel."

"And this is my cousin Brianna Steel, Donny's sister."

"Such a pleasure to meet all of you. Please follow me into the drawing room. Mr. Ainsley will be in shortly." He walks the length of the grand foyer, and I glance around at the soaring ceilings, intricate moldings, and a sweeping staircase. A few steps later, we enter an elegant living room.

I gape. This place is so...English. The furnishings are dark wood—cherry, I think—and look antique, though I wouldn't know. The sofas and chairs are upholstered in lavender and blue brocade.

I've fallen in love with England already.

Or maybe I've just fallen in love with what England has given me so far.

The loss of my virginity to the man I adore.

Who can't stand the sight of me now.

Nope. Can't go there. I need to enjoy this experience of afternoon tea. Besides, I don't want all eyes on me while I'm sniffling.

We all take a seat, and I nearly slide off the silky brocade. I push my feet into the elegant carpet to save face.

Havisham bows. "I'll go prepare your tea. As I said, Mr. Ainsley will be in shortly."

"Right behind you, Havisham," a low voice says.

An elderly gentleman enters the room. He has a shock of silvery-white hair, and he walks upright without the help of a cane. Ennis Ainsley is eighty-eight years old. This gentleman doesn't look a day over seventy. He wears a blazer with leather patches on the elbows, blue jeans, and brown leather loafers.

"Here you all are," he says.

Brock stands, walks to him, and shakes his hand. "It's so good to see you again, Mr. Ainsley."

"Yes, Brock. You too. Have you forgotten to call me Ennis?"

"As you wish, Ennis." Brock introduces us all, and Mr. Ainsley comes to me first.

"Goodness, Brianna. You look exactly like your father."

"That's the same thing he said to *me* when we met." Brock laughs. "About my father."

"I'll take that as a compliment," I say.

"As it was meant." He continues to gaze at me, squinting his eyes. "But my God... No, it's not Talon you resemble. It's your grandmother. Daphne Wade." He widens his eyes then. "I feel like I've gone back in time. She was such a beauty."

I'm not sure what to say. Luckily, he keeps speaking.

"I think you weren't but two the last time I saw you."

"That would've been twenty years ago, then," I say.

"Yes, the timing is about right. Havisham will be in with the tea in a moment."

Less than thirty seconds pass before Havisham comes back, pulling a trolley along.

"I asked Havisham to prepare two types of tea today." He gestures to two ornate porcelain teapots, both depicting what I assume are English landscapes. "I of course prefer a basic black afternoon tea. I didn't know if all of you are tea drinkers, so he also prepared a nice herbal infusion of hibiscus and chamomile as well. Ladies first, of course."

Havisham approaches me. "Miss?"

"Thank you. I'll have the black tea."

He pours tea into a china cup with a less detailed etching of the landscape from the teapot. "Milk or sugar?"

"No, thank you."

Havisham hands the cup to me on a saucer, along with a plate that contains a scone and a small sandwich.

"What is this?" I ask.

"A cream scone and a cucumber sandwich with a bit of watercress."

"Thank you. I'm sure it will be delicious."

"Ma'am?" Havisham says to Maddie.

"I think I'll try the herbal. Thank you."

The rest of our party chooses the black tea, and when Havisham is done serving, he bows and exits, leaving the trolley.

Ennis takes a bite of his scone, chews, and swallows. "I know you Yanks probably had a large lunch, so I didn't have Havisham prepare a full tea."

"What is a full tea?" Maddie asks.

"A very good question, lovely lady. A full afternoon tea consists of cucumber sandwiches, of course, scones with clotted cream, but also something hot and savory, such as a mini quiche, and something sweet, perhaps a cupcake or tart."

"That sounds great," Maddie gushes.

"I would love for you to join me here tomorrow for afternoon tea."

"That's kind of you," I say. "Can we, Donny? What's on our schedule tomorrow?"

"More sightseeing. The first concert isn't until the day after."

"Then it's settled," Ennis says. "Tea tomorrow here at my house. I promise you a better tea than you'll get anywhere else in London. Be sure to bring the rest of your companions if they're available."

"That sounds exciting, doesn't it, Brianna?" Maddie says.

"Sure, Maddie." I give her a weak smile.

As much as I'm trying not to think about Jesse, he keeps creeping into my head. How can't he? His sister is right next to me.

It's slowly driving me insane.

We finish our tea, and Brock stands. "Ennis, I need to speak with you in private, if I may."

"Yes, of course."

The two of them leave us in the living room with the tea service. Havisham returns and cleans it up.

I look at Donny as a brick hits my gut. Brock is telling Ennis about Patty Watson, who was my grandmother's best friend in college and Ennis's girlfriend, until she disappeared. Donny and Brock found some of her bones on our property, and then Uncle Ryan's birth mother, Wendy Madigan, admitted to being behind the deaths of both Patty Watson and Brendan Murphy's great-uncle, the original Sean Murphy, who was my grandfather's best friend.

That woman was evil.

I can't even imagine what Ennis is going through. She was his one and only love, according to Brock and Rory, who visited him several weeks ago.

"That poor old guy," Maddie says.

"I can't believe he never got married," I say.

"Sometimes you only find it once," Maddie says. "It's sad."

"I think there probably could've been someone else for him," Donny offers. "He just poured himself into making Steel Vineyards the best boutique winery ever and then training Uncle Ryan to take over. That was his life. He certainly doesn't seem any worse for the wear."

"No. He does seem happy." Maddie looks around the room. "This is a beautiful home, after all. And I'm sure your family gave him an excellent retirement package."

"Oh, we did," Donny says. "According to Uncle Ryan."

About twenty minutes later, Brock returns with Ennis. Ennis looks okay. His eyes are a little glassy, but he's all right.

195

"I suppose you all know where we've been," he says.

"We do, Ennis," Donny says. "We just thought it would be best for you to hear it from Brock, someone you've met before."

"You forget. I've met all of you before." He turns to Maddie. "Except you, my dear."

"True," Donny says, "but we were just kids."

Ennis clears his throat. "Thank you for telling me everything. It's what I suspected, but it's good to finally have closure after all these years."

"May I ask you a question?" I say.

"Of course, my dear."

I draw a breath. "Why didn't you ever marry, Ennis? I've seen pictures of you. You were a handsome young man. You still are."

It's not even a lie. Even in his eighties, Ennis Ainsley is still brightly blue-eyed with a sculpted jawline.

"Bree . . ." Donny begins.

Ennis holds up a hand. "No, it's all right. It's a valid question, and I've had to answer it many times over the years. I don't mind answering it again."

Ennis takes a seat next to me, and he pats my hand. "I think I could've found love again if I'd tried. I was young—dashing, as we say over here. And I happened to walk into the cushy job of assistant winemaker at your brand-new winery. Your family is very generous, as you know, so I made very good money, and I lived on the ranch. But . . ." His gaze darkens, and he tips his chin down. "Life got difficult during those years. Your grandfather got into some dealings he probably shouldn't have, and your dear grandmother . . . Well, I watched her spiral downward. None of us knew, at the time, what was wrong. How ill she truly was. She was my last link to Patty, so I watched over her."

"Kind of like a guardian angel," I say.

"Except I wasn't dead." He clears his throat again.

"Right. That's not what I meant."

"I know that, my dear." Ennis stares at me, almost transfixed. "My, you do look just like Daphne."

"Thank you," I say. "I've seen pictures. She was very beautiful."

"Oh, she was. Her hair was the same color as yours, and it was even longer. It was a different time then, and she wore it straight. It nearly reached her bottom. She had such deep and expressive brown eyes, just like yours."

"Did you ever . . ."

He chuckles. "When I first met her, yes. But once she met your father, there was no one else for her. When Patty and I got together and I fell for her, I understood." He rises, walks to the mantel, leaning on his cane, and gazes longingly at an old photo. Is it Patty? It's in black and white, so I can't tell. He returns. "So while I probably could have found love as a young man, I didn't. I fell so hard for Patty, felt her loss so deeply, that I never wanted to."

"So you feel it's possible to meet the love of your life at such a young age?"

"Yes, of course. I wasn't yet twenty when I met Patty."

A feeling of warmth exudes through me.

"That's so very sad," Maddie says.

"It is," I say. "To find love like that is a miracle, but you only had it for such a short time."

Ennis nods. "That's how I've chosen to look at it, my dear. A miracle. Looking at it any other way would just be too sad. Patty was such a bright light. I never believed that she left me. I never believed the story her parents told."

"They were paid off," Donny says.

Ennis nods, sighing softly. "Yes, I see that now. And frankly, I'm glad they at least had some kind of financial benefit. It certainly doesn't take the place of the loss, but at least they didn't have to worry about money anymore."

Brock clears his throat then. "We should probably be going."

"No." Ennis turns to me with a twinkle in his eyes. "I'm fine. Really. I'm happy to answer your questions. And I get the feeling, young lady, that you have a reason for asking."

He doesn't know how right he is.

I shrug, but my cheeks warm. "I'm just interested. Curious. It's a beautiful love story with a tragic ending."

"Yes, I've often compared us to Heathcliff and Catherine of *Wuthering Heights*. Tragedy on the moors."

"Except on the western slope of Colorado," I say.

"Yes."

My heart goes out to Ennis. And to Patty as well, taken from her vibrant life at such a young age.

"Did you try to find out what happened to Patty?" Maddie asks. "Sean Murphy's nephew tried nearly his whole life to figure out what happened to his uncle. We only just found out the truth."

Ennis chuckles. "Sean Murphy. He was a character too. Hair almost as red as Patty's. They even dated a bit before I knocked her off her feet." He smiles. "And to answer your question, I tried for a while. I didn't want to believe that she had left, which was the party line at that point. Brad helped. But there was no trace. Nothing. So I poured myself into my work."

I smile. "Yeah. My brother Dale says you're the reason the winery is so great."

"I can't take all the credit. Your uncle Ryan is truly gifted, and he took the business to places I couldn't."

"Yes, but you taught him."

Ennis nods and closes his eyes. Then he rises, steadying himself on his cane. "I hope you don't think me rude, but I'm quite fatigued."

Brock stands. "Not at all. Like I said, we've got to get going ourselves. But we will see you tomorrow for tea then?"

"Yes, absolutely, and I'll make sure I nap beforehand so I will be in much better spirits."

As we leave Ennis's beautiful home, all I can think about is his tragic love story.

He loved once and then lost.

And I fear my story will echo it.

Because there's no one else on earth for me except Jesse Pike.

CHAPTER THIRTY

Jesse

I wake the next morning in my private room next to Brock and Rory's suite.

Seven o'clock.

I'm awakened by the alarm on my phone, which I wasn't expecting.

Damn it, Rory.

But oh my God ...

Finally.

Finally I slept.

I followed Rory's instructions to the letter. First, at the spa, I sat in the Jacuzzi for the hour before my massage. Then I lay on the massage table as skilled hands kneaded my sore muscles for an hour and a half.

I returned to my room, ordered room service for comfort food—a steak and fries—and then I ran myself a bath.

I hate baths. I still do.

But I did it, and once I was out and dried off, I slipped between the sheets of the king-sized bed, laid my head on the fluffy pillow, and the last thing I remember is the image of Brianna Steel's deep brown, long-lashed eyes.

I stretch, wanting to close my eyes and sleep some more. It felt amazing.

But Rory is right. I'm not on my game, and I have to be. So I'm going to meet her and Brock for breakfast as she instructed.

I force myself to get up, and I stretch my arms above my head again, groaning. Then I pad into the bathroom, brush my teeth, and take a shower.

Once I'm dressed in jeans and a black-and-white-striped button-down, I run my fingers through my still damp hair. I kind of miss my long hair, but it will grow back. Admittedly, it's a lot easier to deal with this way. It dries a lot more quickly.

I half expect to run into Brock and Rory as I leave my room, but then I check my watch and realize I'm a few minutes late.

Yup. The phone dings. A text from Rory.

Where are you? You're not oversleeping,
are you?

I text her back quickly.

On my way.

I'm tempted to give her shit about breaking into my phone and setting the alarm, but I decide to be the bigger person— which is way easier in a well-rested state.

Once I reach the dining room in the hotel, I spot Brock and Rory at a table near the back. I head toward them.

"Wow," Rory says. "You actually look refreshed. Please tell me my plan worked."

"It did. I slept like a rock." I stretch my arms above my head. "In fact, I'd like to go back and sleep some more."

"You can't," Rory says. "Not until tonight. This should get you over that jet lag and onto London time."

"How was your massage?" Brock asks.

"It was good. I've never had a massage before."

"Neither have I," he says.

"What?"

"I'm pretty sure I didn't jumble up the words."

"I just figured . . . "

"You just figured that with all the Steel money, we would do nothing but pamper ourselves on our time off."

"Well . . . yeah."

Brock chuckles. "It's funny how you think I have all this time on my hands."

"I know you guys work hard."

"We do. But I'm thinking I may try a massage while we're here."

"You totally should," I say. "This won't be my last one."

Brock grabs his phone. "Since you guys will be working today, maybe I'll try to get one in."

"Are you taking the girls sightseeing?" I ask.

"We saw a lot yesterday, and I think I deserve a little bit of a break. Actually, I'm sure I could convince Bree and Maddie to join me at the spa."

"Maddie would probably like that," Rory says.

"Oh, I almost forgot." He looks to Rory. "Ennis Ainsley invited us again for tea at four p.m. today. Will you guys be done rehearsing by then?"

"Probably, if everything goes well." She eyes me.

"Now that Jesse's finally had a good night's sleep, it'll probably go well." Brock glances at me. "Anyway, I'd love for you to come along. It'll just be you and me, Donny and Callie, and Brianna and Maddie."

She turns to me. "Yeah, I'd like to. Do you think we'll be done by then, Jess?"

I mimic holding a cup with my pinky extended. "Sure. I won't stand in the way of you getting the full high tea experience."

Rory laughs. "Why don't you come along? You think that would be okay, Brock?"

Brock shrugs. "Yeah, probably. I mean, he's your brother. Maddie and Callie'll be there."

Brianna will also be there . . .

"I'm not sure high tea is my thing," I say.

"Suit yourself," Rory says, "but I'm sure he'd love to meet you. The fourth Pike sibling and all."

I shake my head, rolling my eyes. "Why the hell would he want to meet me?"

"Because he's a nice guy," Rory says. "And you'll get to experience high tea with a real English butler in an actual English mansion rather than in some restaurant. This is local color, Jess."

I sigh. "Fine."

I do enjoy a cup of tea, though the whole high tea experience isn't something I thought I needed to have.

But I can't avoid Brianna forever. This way, at least I'll be with everyone else too—including her brother, who would probably grind me to a pulp if he knew what I'd done. I should have pummeled him for touching Callie—but at least she wasn't twenty-two and a virgin.

As if our high school rivalry weren't enough.

"When do we order?" I ask.

"We already ordered," Rory says. "Classic English breakfast."

"Which is . . . ?"

"Eggs, ham, bangers—"

I cock my head. "Excuse me?"

"Sausages," Brock laughs. "Plus roasted tomatoes and potatoes."

"Sounds fine to me."

"And coffee," Brock adds. "Rory and I tried tea with our breakfast yesterday, and though it's delicious, we both need our coffee."

"Thank God."

Our coffees come in a moment, and within another minute, our breakfasts are served. "You've got eggs sunny-side up," the server says, pointing, "streaky bacon, sausage, blood pudding, baked beans, and roasted tomatoes."

I take a bite of the bacon and then the sausage. Delicious. The roasted tomato is surprisingly good. It accents the other food nicely.

"You're hungry today," Rory says.

I try the blood sausage this time. Not bad. "Yeah, I am. I had a decent meal last night. I ordered steak and fries from room service."

"Your classic comfort food," Rory says. "Good man."

"I can't tell you how much better I feel," I say.

Rory takes a sip of coffee and smiles. "You look a lot better too. I think today's rehearsal will go much more smoothly, and we'll be in good shape for our debut tomorrow night."

I breathe in. "We have to be, Ror. I'm not going to blow this for us."

"Damn right you're not. That's what your little sister's here for. We take care of each other, Jess. We're going to make this work. We're going to make Dragonlock a household name."

I nod as I take another bite of eggs with roasted tomato.

We've come this far. We will *not* blow our one shot.

★ ★ ★

High tea with Ennis Ainsley turns out to be quite enjoyable. So far, I've managed not to make eye contact with Brianna, but it's been difficult since she and Maddie are sitting together in the large living room.

Mr. Ainsley brought in extra chairs to accommodate everyone.

His butler, Havisham, looks like he came straight out of *Downton Abbey*.

The tea is surprisingly good. Robust and flavorful. I drink mine plain. Brianna adds a tiny bit of lemon to hers. Maddie drinks herbal tea.

Blueberry scones, cucumber sandwiches, mini quiches with ham and spinach, and red velvet cupcakes.

"So the first lesson of high tea," Ennis says, "is that no one calls it high tea. We simply call it afternoon tea. It's more like an early dinner."

"We should've known that," Callie says.

"No reason for you to know." Ennis takes a sip from his cup. "The Yanks have taken over and now call it high tea. But to us, it's simply afternoon tea." He directs his gaze to Brianna. "Second rule is your saucer stays on the table."

Brianna reddens. She's holding her saucer and taking a drink. "Oh," she says.

"Not a problem, my dear. There's no reason for you to know."

Brianna sets her saucer down.

"The next rule—don't wrap your hands around the cup, which I can see none of you are doing. Use the cup handle. The handle of the teacup stays at three o'clock, unless you're left-handed. Then it stays at nine o'clock."

"Looks like none of us are lefties," Maddie says.

"Good. Keep those handles at three o'clock, and don't

over stir. You may have noticed that Havisham did not serve cream. We only add milk to our tea over here. We also don't use tea bags. Always loose tea. Havisham went ahead and put the loose tea leaves in the teapots for us, but sometimes, people serve tea directly into the cup."

"How?" Callie asks.

"You place a small strainer over the cup, add the tea leaves to the strainer, and pour hot water over them."

I take a sip as Mr. Ainsley continues.

"Now, for the order of the food. Sandwiches first, and then scones. This is all finger food. To eat a scone, you simply break it in half with your fingers."

He demonstrates, though I'm pretty sure we could have figured it out.

"Add your clotted cream first, if desired," Mr. Ainsley continues, "followed by jam or lemon curd if you so choose." He demonstrates, again, and then he laughs. "I almost forgot the most important rule of all. Never put your pinky out when you lift your teacup. For the life of me, I don't know where that horrid habit came from."

Way too many rules for me, but the women are having a great time, laughing and jovially following the directions. Especially Brianna and Maddie.

I regard all three of my sisters. This is the most amazing experience for them, and Maddie especially. I'm so glad she came along.

And I have Brianna to thank for that.

I wish I could've given Maddie this trip, but I don't have the resources. Brianna does.

Damn. Brianna. Already my groin is tightening just at the thought. The thing is, I'm angry as much as aroused . . . which makes the arousal all the more profound. I take the last sip of my tea and replace the cup on my saucer, and then I rise.

"Would you excuse me? I need to get some air."

"Jesse's still dealing with jet lag," Rory says, giving me an excuse.

"It's the worst," Ennis agrees. "I remember the first time I flew into Denver to go to university. I could barely function with the jet lag and the high altitude on top of it. I wholly understand. Just come right back in when you're ready. No need to knock."

"Thank you. The tea was excellent." I nod and walk out of the living room, through the foyer, and out the front door.

I breathe in the fresh air, drawing it deep into my lungs. The house is gorgeous, made of gray stone with ivy growing up the sides. The green lawn is nicely trimmed. In the front is a circular fountain with bushes all around it, though it's not running. The driveway is cobblestone, and our limo driver sits in the driver's seat, waiting for us to be done.

I don't want to think about how much Brock is paying him.

I walk to the black limousine, knock on the window.

It opens, and our chauffeur, complete with black flat cap, raises his eyebrows. "May I help you, sir?"

"I'm just wondering, how much do you make an hour?"

"Fifty pounds."

"So Brock Steel is paying you fifty pounds an hour to drive us around?"

"Oh no, Mr. Steel is payin' the company I work for." He looks past me out the window. "I shouldn't be sayin' this. But he's probably payin' more like two hundred pounds."

I drop my jaw.

"Don't worry, sir. Everything is paid for in advance."

"What about your gratuity?"

"A tip, you mean? We don't do that in England much."

"Okay. I'm sorry to bother you."

"Not a problem." He smiles and closes the window.

I need to get over myself.

I walk along the lawn for a while, breathing in more of the fresh air. Then I turn to walk back toward the door when—

Shit.

Brianna is out here. Looking beautiful, of course, in jeans and a tight T-shirt. No cowboy boots, though. Nikes. Walking shoes. They were sightseeing earlier. Brianna and Maddie, to my astonishment, didn't take Rory up on her spa offer.

"Jesse?"

"What?"

She blinks. "I wanted to make sure you're okay."

"Don't I look okay?"

"You look amazing as always. But you were so distraught the other night, and I—"

I shake my head forcefully. "The other night never happened, Brianna."

She chews on her bottom lip.

I don't want to hurt her. I have nothing against Brianna. She's a beautiful young woman, and she didn't deserve to have her virginity taken from her the way it was. I regret my hand— or other body part—in it.

She sets one hand on her hip. "Jesse, it *did* happen. If you want to never talk about it again, I can't stop you. But it did happen, and I don't regret it."

"I do." I walk past her, head toward the door.

But she grabs my arm and yanks me back. "I don't accept that. If you don't want it to ever happen again, there's nothing I can do about that. But I can't believe that you regret such a beautiful moment. I gave you something that I—"

"That I never asked for, Bree." I sigh. "How am I supposed

to live with that? Live with the guilt?"

"There's no reason for you to feel guilty, Jesse." She reaches for my hand and squeezes it. "I wanted it to happen. I don't feel any regret at all."

My cock aches at just her slight touch. I pull my hand away. "That makes one of us, then. I need to get back inside. My sisters will be worried." I turn toward the house.

"At least tell me one thing."

I stop, but I don't turn to face her. "What?"

"Did you at least... enjoy it?"

Regrets. Wishes. Lies.

I wasn't lying when I told her I regretted it, but can I lie now? Can I tell her that I didn't enjoy it at all?

Because that would be a big fat lie—as big as I've ever told.

"Are you going to answer me?"

I pause. Mull it over. What is the best way to respond? Finally, "Brianna, whether I enjoyed it really isn't the issue."

"It's an issue for me. I enjoyed it. I loved every minute of it. I'm glad it was you. I wanted it to be you."

I turn this time to face her. "You manipulated me."

"I didn't, though. I simply told you what I wanted."

"Yes, you did. But you didn't tell me you were a virgin."

"Why does that matter?"

"We've been through this. You know exactly why it mattered, Brianna. You knew that if you told me, I wouldn't take you to bed."

"But I wasn't—"

"That's a lie. You manipulated me. We both know it, so stop saying you didn't."

She bites on her lip again, and all I can think about is biting on it for her. Chewing on that luscious lower lip of hers, shoving my tongue into her mouth and kissing her, taking her again, this time aggressively, right on this manicured green lawn that belongs to an old friend of her family's.

"All right," she finally relents. "If that's your definition of manipulation—"

"That's *everyone's* definition of manipulation, Brianna."

She lets out a breath. "I suppose I *did* manipulate you. But you know what? You weren't entitled to know my sexual history."

"What sexual history?" I demand.

"Stop that. You know very well what I mean. If you'd asked me straight out—"

"Who the hell asks that question when they're about to take a woman to bed?" I shake my head.

"You could have. You know my age. You absolutely could have asked."

She's right. I could have. Should have, even. But I didn't, and I know exactly why.

I fucking wanted her.

This is on me. It's always been on me. I can try to blame her for not telling me, for manipulating me, but I bear the fault here.

"Don't you understand?" she says. "It didn't matter to me, Jesse."

I stare at her. Her beauty, her fire, her wild Colorado cowgirl nature. Of course I didn't ask. I never thought...

"You've been in relationships before, Brianna. I know you have. Maddie has mentioned it."

Her eyebrows jerk upward. "Maddie mentions my relationships to you?"

"She's my sister. We talk."

"Yes, but she's ten years younger than you are, like I am. When she talks about her friends, I can't imagine you would remember anything she says."

A chill hits my heart.

My God, she's right.

"If that's the case, how many relationships have Angie, Sage, and Gina been in?"

I can't answer.

I can't answer because I don't know.

I've never kept those three in my memory.

Only Brianna.

Jesus fucking Christ.

Is it possible I've let her inside me in some way?

"My point is that you've had relationships before. With men who were invested, who probably were in love with you, or if not, at least cared a lot about you. You could have given your virginity to any one of them if you wanted to be rid of it."

"I wasn't ready." She frowns. "That's a lie. I've been ready for a long time, Jesse. I just wanted it to be you."

My cock reacts to her words, to her presence, to everything about her.

All this time... have I been pining after Brianna Steel? The thought sounds ridiculous, but my body is certainly responding to it.

"You got your wish." I turn back toward the house. "We should get back inside."

"Jesse..."

"For the love of God, what?"

CHAPTER THIRTY-ONE

Brianna

So many things I want to say to him.

How much my dreams of him have meant to me over the last couple of years. How much his music means to me. How much I love watching him perform, how he moves with the music. How he's the melody in my mind.

How much that one night meant to me. And how I don't want to have sex with anyone else ever again.

How I didn't mean to manipulate him—because I truly didn't.

I just wanted him so badly. I wanted to be free of my virginity, and I wanted him to take it.

Because I . . .

I've always thought I was in love with him.

But do I really know him? Only as Maddie's brother. As a rock star. Although I can't really say he's a *star*. At least not yet.

As a rocker, then.

As a rocker who makes my heart sing every time his voice weaves its magic.

His voice is deep, with a subtle rasp to it. The perfect rock voice.

He stands before me, his perfectly sculpted jawline tense, black stubble gracing it. I miss his long hair, but he looks even more handsome with it shorter.

"Why did you cut your hair?"

He tilts his head. "*That's* what you want to ask me?"

"Yes. I loved your long hair. I like long hair on a guy, but so few guys can pull it off. My brother can. And *you* can."

"It's a pain in the ass to take care of." He looks at my hair, raises his hand, his fingers twitching. Does he want to touch my hair?

"Wouldn't you agree with that?" he continues. "Yours is longer than mine ever was."

"Yeah. But I like it."

"I liked it too." He breaks his gaze away from me, dropping his hand back to his side. "But I need this tour to be perfect, Brianna. I need to be focused. I want to get rid of anything that takes time away from my music."

"Your hair took time away from your music?"

"I don't expect you to understand."

I take another step toward him. "Help me understand."

"Help you understand why I cut my hair? No. My hair is no one's business but my own."

He's right. I'm just stalling. Talking about his hair is stupid. Even I can see that. "You're right."

"Exactly. In fact, everything about me is no one's business but my own." He shoves his hands into the pockets of his jeans. "Certainly not yours."

This time he turns, and as much as I want to, I do not ask him to wait.

I sniffle back some tears, and then I take a walk around the grounds. Ennis's place is beautiful and very quaint. Not as beautiful as our ranch, of course, but I can see why he wanted to come back here and live out his senior years in his home country.

The lawn is more like a lush emerald-green carpet, and it's expansive, stretching out across the estate, offering a sense of spaciousness. The edges of the lawn are sharply defined, forming a clear boundary between the grass and the surrounding flower beds, pathways, and hedges. The flower displays are splashes of color, with roses, hydrangeas, and lavender.

Deciduous trees provide shade in the summer, no doubt. Now their limbs are bare, though no snow is on the ground. It's an oddly mild winter in London, and though I'm chilly in only my T-shirt, I have no desire to go back into the house yet.

After exploring the grounds, I find myself at a gray stone bench that sits adjacent to the driveway. I take a seat.

I breathe in the fresh air and settle my stomach, which is full of cupcakes and quiches and tea.

Oh my.

I sit for a moment but then rise.

Time to go back in.

Time to face the music.

By the time I return, though, Havisham is in the living room cleaning up the tea, and Brock and Donny are shaking hands with Ennis. When Callie holds out her hand, Ennis's gaze drops to her left hand. He cocks his head a moment, but then shakes the right hand she offers.

Time to go, apparently.

Maddie walks toward me. "Everything okay, Bree?"

I force a smile. "Absolutely fine. Did you enjoy the tea?"

"It was everything I expected and more. And we still have tomorrow to go sightseeing and then the concert tomorrow night." She grabs my hands, squeezing both of them. "This is all so exciting, Brianna. Thank you for making it happen for me."

"I'm just sorry we couldn't get tickets to any shows we wanted in the West End."

"That's okay. This is all perfect. Thank you."

"No need to keep thanking me, Mads. I'm glad you're here with me. Truly."

The words are not a lie.

The only problem is that every time I look at Maddie, I see her brother. Of all the Pike siblings, Maddie and Jesse resemble each other the most.

Maddie is Jesse in female form, but she's also my friend—my friend I've unintentionally neglected over the years.

I'm going to be a good friend to her. She deserves that much. She deserves so much more than what she's gotten from me and the rest of the awesome foursome. I made this commitment to her—to accompany her on this tour—and I will not renege on that.

One thing's for sure.

I'm going to have to forget about Jesse.

Because he's already forgotten about me.

★ ★ ★

The next day…

Maddie, Callie, Donny, Brock, and I take our first guided tour the next afternoon to see the most touristy places, beginning with Buckingham Palace. Again I wish Diana were here as our guide explains the palace's neoclassical architecture that's adorned with intricate details and a balcony where significant royal events, such as the changing of the guard and royal announcements, take place. The interior isn't open to the public—not that I expected it would be. It's someone's home, after all.

Next we head to St. James's Park, where we walk and enjoy stunning views of the palace's gardens, a gorgeous lake, and charming bridges that span across the water. I wouldn't mind staying for a while, relaxing and soaking up the chilly sunshine, but the rest of my party are eager to continue on the tour.

Next is The Mall, a tree-lined boulevard that connects the palace to Trafalgar Square. We take in the Admiralty Arch and the Institute of Contemporary Arts, as our guide explains that The Mall serves as a ceremonial route for royal processions and parades.

When we reach Trafalgar Square, we see Nelson's Column, a towering monument dedicated to Admiral Lord Nelson, who played a pivotal role in the British Navy's victory at the Battle of Trafalgar. Beyond Trafalgar Square is Whitehall, home to the Horse Guards Parade, where the changing of the horse guards occurs, and the Cenotaph, a memorial dedicated to the fallen soldiers of World War I and subsequent conflicts. I'm no history buff, but I'm moved by the surroundings.

A short walk later and we arrive at the Houses of Parliament and the famous Big Ben clock tower. Maddie and Callie gush over everything and take lots of photos.

I smile, and it isn't forced. I've enjoyed the tour. Here our guide leaves us, along with instructions to get anywhere else on the Tube, London's subway system.

We return to the hotel and grab a quick dinner in the hotel restaurant before we head to the event center where the concert will be.

We haven't seen the band all day.

"How is Rory holding up?" Donny asks Brock.

Brock smiles. "She's determined. I'll give her that."

"Not nervous at all?" Callie asks.

"Rory doesn't get nervous. Or so she says, anyway." Brock rubs his jawline.

"I know. I mean, she always says she doesn't. But this can make or break the band's career. She's not showing even slight nerves?"

"Maybe a few. She was a little short with me this morning. Of course, maybe I was being a dick."

"Probably," Donny says dryly.

"I know." Brock grins. "It's pretty dickish of me to not put the cap back on the toothpaste tube, isn't it?"

Callie laughs. "Sounds like she's a bit nervous. I'm nervous for her. My pulse has been racing all day."

"Me too, Cal," Maddie says. "I want this so badly for Rory and Jesse. They both work so hard at their music."

"I know," Callie says. "If only Mom and Dad could be here."

"We would've gladly brought them over," Donny says.

I wait for Callie to say something about her parents not taking our money, but instead, she says, "I know. But it wasn't a good time for them to leave the ranch, after the fire and all. There's too much to do. Dad especially would've enjoyed it. Jesse and Rory got their musical talent from him."

After Brock and Donny take care of the check, we all head to our rooms to freshen up before the limo arrives to take us to the concert.

My nerves are jumping inside me.

Watching Jesse . . . Imagining that he's singing solely to me.

That won't happen. He can't see who's in the audience from the stage. The lighting is too bright.

But I *am* nervous. Nervous for him.

I want this to be everything he imagined and more.

Perhaps someone famous will be in the audience. Maybe Sir Elton John, whose music my parents adore. Or maybe Adele or Ed Sheeran.

Emerald Phoenix has a global following and a huge fan base in the UK, so this concert must go well. The UK has to fall in love with Dragonlock.

I close my eyes, sending wishes to the heavens.

"Bree?"

I pop my eyes open. Maddie stands, dressed in dark blue jeans and a Dragonlock T-shirt. I'm holding one just like it.

"Yeah?"

"You had your eyes closed, and you looked so ... "

"What?"

"I don't know, like you were concentrating hard on something. Is everything okay?"

"Yeah. I'm fine." I take my walking shoes off and replace them with a pair of sienna-colored ostrich cowboy boots.

"You're always the cowgirl, Bree," Maddie says, smiling. "You're going to be the only person at this concert wearing boots like that."

"You can take the cowgirl off the ranch, but you can't take the ranch out of the cowgirl."

I throw my Dragonlock T-shirt on. It's identical to Maddie's, but my boobs are a bit bigger. I can't help but smile about that. The Ts are cut for women, so our shapes are definitely visible.

Good.

We all have backstage passes, so when the concert is over, I want to look good for Jesse.

May as well let him see what he's missing.

I'm tempted to wear my hair down, as that's the way I think it looks best, but I know I'll get hot and sweaty at the concert, and my hair will end up being a bother. So I brush it until it shines and then pull it into a high ponytail. Maddie has hers in one long braid down her back.

She takes a peek at her watch on her left wrist. "We better get down there."

I shove everything I need into a tiny leather purse that I strap over my shoulder. "Let's go."

CHAPTER THIRTY-TWO

Jesse

When I was a little kid, before we moved to Snow Creek, we went to church every weekend.

Mom and Dad weren't overly religious or anything, but they had both been raised as churchgoers, so they began raising us that way as well. I learned to pray. I respect other people's religions, which is why we have a moment of silence and not a moment of prayer before every performance.

But even though I no longer go to church, I have a relationship with God, and I ask for His blessing before each performance.

I also express gratitude for all the good things I've received in my life.

Sometimes it's hard to see them, like right after the fire.

But tonight? Dragonlock is opening for Emerald Phoenix in London.

I have a lot to be grateful for.

So that's what I do during my moment of silence. I express my gratitude first and foremost, and then I ask for God's blessing that we may all be in top form. That we don't let this wonderful chance go to waste.

When I'm done, I open my eyes. Everyone else's eyes are open except for Rory's.

A few seconds later, she opens hers.

"We ready?" I ask.

"We are damned ready," Cage says.

I place my hand forward, and the others place their hands on top of mine.

"On three," I say. "One, two, three—"

"Dragonlock!" we all yell in unison.

Silly, I know, but it's been a tradition since we formed the band.

The sound check went well, and now the stadium is filling with spectators. Spectators here to see Emerald Phoenix, and who don't want to sit through the opening act.

We can't just be good. We have to be *spectacular*. We have to make them want more of us.

Talk about pressure.

We can do it. I've had Rory and all the guys practicing visualization since we got this gig. Something we've never done before, but it was our mother's idea. She told us how she used to visualize before her pageants when she was younger.

The pageants are a sore spot for her. She always wanted Rory to get into them, but she wasn't interested. Mom didn't even bother trying with Callie, who was such a brainiac and felt pageants were degrading, and by the time Maddie came along, she had let it go.

But she did talk to us about visualization, so I've got the band doing it. We see ourselves out on stage, performing each number perfectly, and then we see the audience going crazy.

And damn it . . .

That *is* what will happen tonight.

"Ten minutes, Dragonlock," the stage manager says.

Rory and I adjust our headsets.

"All good?" I ask her.

She nods. "All good, Jess."

I give her a hug and whisper in her ear, "This is our time, Rory. We're going to rock this hall."

She nods against my shoulder.

The worst part is the waiting.

The waiting until we take the stage.

Once we're on stage, the thinking is over. The nerves disappear. And we sing. Become one with the melody. With the harmony. With the rhythm.

We're singing original numbers—numbers Rory and I chose together to complement Emerald Phoenix's set.

"All right, Dragonlock. Take the stage," the stage manager says.

I draw in a deep breath, let go of Rory, and watch as first Dragon, and then Cage, and then Jake take their places.

Rory and I follow hand-in-hand.

The concert is sold out, and even with the bright lights, I can still see lots of heads bobbing. Heads who paid for Emerald Phoenix and have to sit through us.

Brock, Callie, Donny, Maddie, and Brianna are all in the front row.

VIPs.

I don't dare look. I probably wouldn't be able to see them anyway.

"Ladies and gentlemen ... presenting ... Dragonlock!"

The applause is deafening, which surprises me.

They're excited, their adrenaline is flowing, so we need to rock this hall and get them even more pumped.

Rory and I look at each other, and then I nod to Jake, who strums a few notes on his guitar, and then Cage comes in on the keyboard and Dragon on the drums.

The intro is a few measures long and then—

I sing. I sing the first lines, and then Rory.

And the audience disappears.

It's only Rory and me, singing.

And we rock.

We fucking rock like we've never rocked before.

Rory and I are in complete sync as we end our show with "Faint of Heart," a harmonious duet I composed that combines elements of pop and rock and a bit of alternative. I'd had the tune in mind for years, but not until the fire did I compose the lyrics about perseverance and overcoming adversity.

The audience fucking loves it, and as we end the song—and our set—the applause is thundering.

I don't expect a standing ovation. The opening act never gets one, but I can't help but look down.

And right in the front row is Brianna Steel, flanked by the rest of our party, all standing.

But my gaze drops on Brianna only.

Brianna...and suddenly she's the only person in that audience.

She's clapping for me.

Then she puts two fingers in her mouth and whistles shrilly.

I can't hear the whistle of course, but that's what she's doing.

I do hear it.

I hear it in my heart.

We're the opening act, so we don't do an encore.

The lights go dim on the stage, and we exit.

"Man, that was awesome!" Cage gives me a high five.

"We fucking rocked it," Jake agrees.

Usually, I'm the one who gives the notes after a performance. I could tell Dragon that he was about a second off on the first number. I could tell Cage that he was slightly late on the third.

Other than those two minor mistakes, we really did rock it. I'm going to give them this one show free of critique.

"It was perfect," I say. "Every one of you nailed it."

Rory launches herself into my arms, kisses my cheek. "I can't believe it, Jess. They loved us. They freaking *loved* us."

I turn around at a tap on my shoulder.

Jett Draconis himself stands there, meeting my gaze. "You guys rocked this place. I'm not sure how we're going to top that."

His comment makes me burst out into laughter. "You're kidding, right?"

He shrugs with a smile. "Hey, they're waiting for us. We could go out there and blow it, and they'd still applaud. But you guys? You just set the fucking bar."

"Thank you."

Jett pats me on the shoulder. "I knew I was right about you guys. The two of you—singing together—you can hit it big. Trust me on that one."

I didn't realize I've been holding my breath until I gasp in some air.

Jett has gone onstage, getting ready, along with Zane and the others.

Rory meets my gaze. "You okay?"

"Yeah. I'm just… I'm not sure I've ever felt this good, Rory."

No truer words. Fireworks are exploding in my brain, and

my emotions are all over the place. I'm happy beyond happy, and I've even been reduced to a tear or two.

"It was amazing, wasn't it?" Rory beams.

"It totally was. And we get to do it all over again tomorrow."

"Right. Another concert and then we're off to Edinburgh."

Cage gives me a big bear hug and then hugs Rory. Jake does the same.

"What did Jett say?" Dragon asks.

"He said we rocked it. He said we'd be a tough act to follow."

Cage's jaw drops. "Jett Draconis said *that*?"

"Yeah, and here's the weird thing. I think he actually meant it."

Rory smiles, her grin splitting ear to ear. "I need to go talk to Brock."

"Not until later," I remind her. "We're going to watch Emerald Phoenix, remember?"

Rory paces around, nearly dancing. "Right, right, right. How am I going to hold in this glee, Jess?"

"I don't know. It's fucking awesome."

And it dawns on me. I told my sister that this is the best I've ever felt.

But I realize that was a lie.

Because as wonderful as this feels—the endorphins running through me, my adrenaline on high...

It doesn't feel quite as good as when I came inside Brianna Steel.

CHAPTER THIRTY-THREE

Brianna

"Let's go talk to Jett." Maddie grabs my hand to go backstage after the concert is over.

"Didn't you meet him when he came to Snow Creek?"

"Only briefly. It was a quick intro. They had to get out quickly, or they were going to be mobbed by everyone in Snow Creek."

"Right, they were a surprise."

I love Emerald Phoenix. And Jett has an amazing voice. He's a former opera singer, like Rory. And he rocks the house.

But he doesn't hold a candle to Jesse Pike.

Jesse's voice isn't quite as deep as Jett's, but it has that sexy rasp. I get goose bumps every time I hear him sing.

Hell, I get goose bumps every time I hear him talk.

I look around. There are some other VIPs surrounding Emerald Phoenix.

Then I spy Jesse.

Jesse Pike, with two blond groupies pestering him and Cage.

And I don't like it. I don't like it one bit.

People are talking to Rory as well, with Brock at her side.

At Jett's side is his wife, Heather, a gorgeous blonde who's always smiling.

If only I were at Jesse's side . . . as his partner.

Sadness sweeps through me. That's never going to be. He's made it quite clear.

"Ugh," Maddie says. "We'll never get through to see Jett or Zane."

"We could talk to Rory and Jesse."

"Who cares about Rory and Jesse? They're my brother and sister. We can see them anytime."

I'm not sure how to respond to that. "Don't you think they did great?"

"Of course," Maddie gushes. "I'm not sure I've ever heard them perform better. Maybe it was just the acoustics here. It's probably a better venue than they've ever played. But they were awesome. They rocked so hard."

"They *were* awesome. I can't believe how talented they are."

"I know. They're amazing, and then there's Callie the super brain." Maddie sighs. "One day I'll find my special power."

"You will. In fact, I can already tell you what it is, Mads."

"What's that?"

I lightly touch Maddie's upper arm. "Your kindness. Your empathy. You feel things."

She feels things very deeply, something I failed to observe as her supposed friend. I won't let that happen again.

She rolls her eyes. "That's hardly a superpower."

"I think it is." I give her a quick hug. "It's amazing, isn't it? All these VIPs came to see Emerald Phoenix, but they're paying attention to Dragonlock as well."

"It *is* pretty cool. I never imagined that . . ." She smiles, closing her eyes for a moment. "The only thing better than this would be if I met my true love on this trip."

"You're certainly in a sea of European hotties."

She grabs my wrist. "What if we both fell in love on this trip, Brianna? I mean, it doesn't even have to be the everlasting kind of love. Think of it. Maybe a romance in Paris."

I wish I could get excited with her, but I'm already in love, and he doesn't feel even close to the same way. "Maddie, we're only going to be in Paris for a couple of days."

"I know. Haven't you ever heard of love at first sight?"

"You're romanticizing it."

"But Paris is the city of romance. And we're going there in a mere"—she counts on her fingers—"four days."

"No, it's longer than that. We have to get to Edinburgh, do a concert there, then Glasgow for another concert, and then back to London for an encore concert. *Then* we go to Paris."

"Yes, I know. I can count, you know. I'm just too excited. I guess more like five days, right?"

"Yeah. Or a week. It's a long time. I can't believe we're going to be gone for so long. Don't you think you're going to start missing your ranch?"

"Not really," Maddie says. "I don't even miss Mom and Dad that much. If things had gone as planned, I'd still be at school. Of course, they'd be a lot closer and I could see them whenever I wanted. What about you? Do you miss your mom and dad? Dale? Diana?"

"Since Diana lives in Denver, I don't see much of her. And I've always been closer to Donny than I am to Dale. But yeah, I miss them all. I miss my dad especially. I still feel pretty guilty about leaving him. He was so excited to get me started in the orchard when I graduated early."

I do miss Mom and Dad. And Dale. And Dee. And the

orchard. Dad says he's going to expand the Granny Smith orchard, which is my favorite apple. I love the light-green hue, and I love the crisp flavor that's a perfect combination of sweet and tart.

Kind of like how I'm feeling about Jesse at this moment. I'm thrilled for his success with this performance, so happy for him that he's realizing his dream. But I'm sad, so sad, that he doesn't return my feelings. That he doesn't want me.

Waxing poetic over a green apple... This is what Jesse has reduced me to.

I have no doubt that I'll go back to the ranch. Ranching is my life. Performing is Jesse's life, and if Dragonlock makes it big after this concert, and I have no doubt that they will, he'll be traveling all the time. Would I be willing to leave everything behind? Leave the ranch, to travel with him?

Doesn't really matter.

Jesse's made it clear where he stands as far as I'm concerned.

I have to accept it.

But tonight... as I watched him... I felt he was singing directly to me. Especially those lyrics from "Flyaway," the song Dragonlock sang before "Faint of Heart."

I never knew it was you. All this time you were right there around me, and I never knew.

That song could've been written for Jesse and me.

Maddie and I grab a glass of champagne from the servers who are mingling in an area near the dressing rooms. A few tables are set up, but they're all occupied. We stand against the wall, and as soon as Jesse is free from his admirers—

"Let's go congratulate your brother."

Maddie torpedoes toward him. "Jesse!"

"Hey, Mads." He embraces her in a big brother hug. "Brianna," he says once he lets Maddie go.

No big hug for me, I guess.

"You guys were so fabulous," Maddie gushes. "I've honestly never heard you play better."

"We were on fire for sure. But the acoustics here are also incredible."

"Acoustics shmacoustics," Maddie says. "It was all you guys. You and Rory were never more in sync."

"I'm glad you enjoyed it, little sis."

"Oh, we did, didn't we, Brianna?"

I nod. "It's the best I've ever heard you guys play. Seriously. You and Rory were absolutely astounding together."

"Thank you, Brianna." Then he looks away from me.

"So I see you already have a bunch of female admirers," Maddie says.

A jolt of jealousy hits me right in my gut.

"Only a few," Jesse says.

"What did they say?"

"Nothing that's fit for my little sister's ears," he says.

The jolt of jealousy again, and this time it slices right into my heart.

Groupies.

They were probably offering him sex.

No. Jesse can*not* go to bed with groupies tonight.

He wouldn't, would he? He and Rory are completely serious about making this tour a springboard for something more.

It would be stupid of him to use it as a chance to bed a bunch of European women.

"You're not serious," Maddie says.

"Hey, I think it's a rite of passage. Any rock star worth his salt gets a proposition." He deliberately looks away from me.

"You're not going to—"

"Maddie, of course I'm not going to do anything. But even if I were, do you really think I'd be telling you?"

I hold back a sigh of relief. It's true, he wouldn't be telling Maddie anyway, but I don't get the feeling that he's lying.

"You were amazing," I say again, and then I take a drink of my champagne.

"Thank you. That means a lot to me." He turns. "Excuse me for a moment."

Maddie watches him go. "What's eating him?"

"He probably didn't want to talk with his little sister about groupies."

Maddie rolls her brown eyes. "I know, right? I'm perpetually two years old as far as Jesse's concerned. We're only ten years apart."

"Only ten years apart," I say, more to myself than to Maddie.

"I'll always be the baby of the family," Maddie says. "No matter how hard I try."

"I know the feeling."

Boy, do I ever.

I will always be a child in Jesse Pike's eyes. After all, his baby sister is slightly older than I am.

If only I could be his groupie for the night.

Just one more time. One more time, when I'm not a virgin waiting for my cherry to be popped.

I'm healed up now, and I would like to experience sex with someone I care about—even if he doesn't care about me.

I want to experience sex as *not* a virgin.

The crowd is beginning to die down, and Jett leaves with his wife. The other two members of Emerald Phoenix go, and the only one left is Zane Michaels, and he's heading straight toward us.

"My God, Maddie . . . " I glance toward him.

Maddie gasps. "Is he really coming toward us?"

"Looks that way," I say. "Be cool." My heart is thumping a mile a minute.

"Hello, ladies," Zane says.

Zane is no Jesse Pike, but he is gorgeous and so talented on the keyboard. He has long blond hair, a sculpted jawline, and searing blue eyes.

"Hello," Maddie says. "You guys were amazing."

"Thank you." He holds out his hand. "It's wonderful to meet you both."

"I'm Maddie," she says. "We met briefly in Snow Creek. This is my friend, Brianna. Do you remember us?"

He takes Maddie's hand and kisses it. "Of course I remember you both. Do you ladies have plans for later this evening?"

"What kind of plans?" I ask.

Maddie gives me an evil eye.

Oh God . . .

"I have a suite at the hotel," he says. "Would you like to join me for the night?"

"In your suite?" I ask.

"That sounds amazing," Maddie says. "How about it, Bree?"

"Tonight?" I say.

"Yes. I have a full bar in my suite. But if you're more comfortable, we can stop at the main bar for a drink first."

"That would be nice," I say.

"Or your suite," Maddie says. "Either. We're up for anything."

Anything?

Maddie... I never took *her* for a groupie. Where is this coming from?

She's more experienced than I am, though. Pretty much everyone is.

I only lost my virginity a couple of nights ago, but my mind returns to what I was just pondering.

I want to have sex without worrying about losing it. Sure, I'd like it to be with Jesse, but he's made it clear where he stands.

What Maddie and Zane are suggesting is a threesome. Meaning I would see Maddie naked. She would see me naked.

And knowing Zane... He's pretty much a player.

He'll expect us to do things with each other.

Yeah. That's not going to happen.

Maddie's beautiful and all, but women aren't my cup of tea. I found that out the first and only time I hooked up with one.

Although, with some alcohol in my system... maybe...

What the hell?

I'm in London. Far away from home. My virginity is a thing of the past, and Zane Michaels is... Well, he's Zane Michaels.

I paste on a smile. "I'd love a nightcap."

"That's awesome, ladies. I'll give you a lift in my limo."

"That'd be super," Maddie says.

"Come with me." He offers both his arms.

Maddie takes his right, and I take his left.

I do a quick scan of the room for Jesse.

He's talking to Dragon.

He doesn't even see me. I may as well be invisible.

Well? I'm not invisible to Zane Michaels.

I'm going to drive in a limo with a real rock star.

And yeah . . .

Threesome here I come.

CHAPTER THIRTY-FOUR

Jesse

Dragon pulls me aside. "I've got some babes lined up for us."

"You've got to be kidding."

"Do I look like I'm kidding?" He penetrates me with his dark gaze. "Four of them, Jesse. All ready and willing to come back to the room with us."

"I'm not interested."

"You kidding me? This is the dream, bro. A rocker's dream. Groupies, man. They're ready to spread their legs."

"You can have them all."

"I could deal with two. But it's our room, Jesse, and I'm offering to let you in on the fun."

Something about Dragon appeals to women. Always has. It's that darkness he has about him. That brooding intensity. I have no doubt all four of these babes he has lined up would be happy to go back to the room with just him.

"Go for it. Rory got me my own room, remember?"

"They want us both."

"For Christ's sake, Dragon."

"Come on, Jess. Your adrenaline has got to be riding high. The only way we'll ever get any sleep is if we get our rocks off."

He's not wrong.

I sigh. "Fine. Where are they?"

"I've already put them in one of the limos. All I need is you."

Things are beginning to die down backstage. Jett and his wife left, along with two other members of his band. Only Zane is still here, talking to fans. Maddie and Brianna are still here, speaking together.

I can't help but stare at Brianna in that Dragonlock T-shirt. She looks scrumptious.

I'm already aching for her.

So what the hell? I can take the ache, go back to Dragon's room, fuck the groupies, and then leave.

Except I've never had sex with a woman—or women—with another guy in the room.

There are things I'll have to *not* look at.

I take one last glimpse at Brianna, and I find her staring straight at me.

I want to offer her a smile, but I don't. I follow Dragon off the stage and out of the venue to the waiting limo.

The "babes" Dragon has lined up don't look any older than Brianna. Am I going to have to ask for ID?

"Girls, this is Jesse," Dragon says, as the chauffeur shuts the limo door.

"You were fabulous," one of them—a blonde with pink tips—gushes.

All four of them are pretty, but they're not beautiful. Not Brianna Steel beautiful.

"Thank you," I say.

"You guys are both so hot." This from a goth-looking chick—dark hair, dark eyes, lots of eyeliner.

"Thank you," I say again, as if I'm stuck on repeat.

We get to the hotel, and I feel like everyone is staring at

me. As if everyone knows what Dragon and I are taking these women up to the room to do.

Which of course, everyone *does* know. Our only salvation is that the people in the hotel weren't at the concert, so they don't know who we are. They're paying us no mind.

Still, my skin feels itchy, as if their gazes are giving me hives.

We reach the room, and Dragon pulls out his key card and lets us in.

The blond girl frowns. "We thought you'd have a suite with an open bar and everything."

"Afraid not," Dragon says. "This will have to do."

"I'm afraid it won't do at all." Pink tips girl leaves, and goth girl follows her.

The other two—both brunettes, one brown-eyed and one blue—don't leave. In fact, they're smiling.

"Well, that works out well for us," Blue Eyes says.

And it works for me as well. Now I have an excuse to get out of this. What was I thinking, anyway? That I could be the guy who fucks women indiscriminately? That was my plan initially, and then Brianna happened. It was my plan for tonight...but...

"I'll take my leave," I say. "You can handle two women, Dragon."

"Sure I can."

"I don't think anyone will miss me."

Brown Eyes grabs my arm. "I'll miss you. Please stay."

"Sorry, ladies. I'm out. You all enjoy your night."

I pull my arm away from her and leave the room without looking back.

I've got to get rid of this adrenaline somehow, and jacking

off in my room doesn't sound like the right thing. On a whim, I head downstairs to the bar. A drink may help, and then I'll go back upstairs and turn to Rosie Palm and her five friends.

I get there and—

I stop in my tracks.

My sister and Brianna have just entered, each on the arm of Zane Michaels.

Oh. Hell. No.

I head right toward them.

"Maddie, Brianna," I say.

"Oh...hi, Jesse," Brianna says, her voice shaking. "You know Zane, right? From Emerald Phoenix?"

"I do." I shoot darts at him with my gaze. "What exactly are you doing here?"

"I thought I'd purchase these lovely ladies a drink."

I absently close my hand into a fist. "It might interest you to know that *these lovely ladies* are only twenty-two years old, and that one"—I point—"is my sister."

Zane's eyebrows shoot upward. "Sorry, dude. I didn't know."

"You want to buy them a drink? Knock yourself out. I'll be coming along."

Zane pauses a moment. He didn't have a drink in mind, and we both know it. I weigh the pros and cons of my actions in my head. Zane is Jett's second-in-command. If I piss him off, we could be kicked off the tour.

But this is my sister...

And Brianna...

Yeah, I know where my loyalty has to lie.

"Sure," Zane says, trying to save face. "Come on. Let's head to the bar."

I pull Maddie back. "You two go ahead." When they're out of earshot, I place my hands on her shoulders and lower my voice. "What the hell are you thinking?"

"I..."

"Madeline Jolie Pike, I forbid this."

She swats my hands away. "You're not my father, Jesse. And even if you were, I'm a grown woman."

"Grown women don't take strange men up to their rooms."

"We weren't going to—"

"Save it. You think I don't know what rock stars are like? Zane Michaels is a player. Everybody knows it. I can't believe you and Brianna were going to go through with it."

She glances down at the floor. "Don't blame Brianna. I talked her into it."

"I blame you both. What the hell were you thinking?"

"It's not like I've ever done anything like this before, Jesse."

"Good. You're not going to start now."

"But it's Zane Michaels," she says.

"You think I give a fuck? You're my little sister, Maddie. This is *not* happening."

"You can't stop it."

"The hell I can't." I step toward the bar, Maddie following me meekly. Zane and Brianna are already sitting down at the table, talking to a server.

"Bring the best bourbon you've got for the lady," Zane says. "And I'll have the same." He looks to us. "Oh good, the rest of our party is here. What will you have?"

"I'll have what you're having," I say dryly.

"Awesome, and you, beautiful?" He eyes Maddie.

"Sidecar," she says, her lips trembling.

"Excellent," the server says. "I'll get those up for you in just a moment. Did you want to order anything from the bar menu?"

"No, thank you," Zane says.

The women both shake their heads.

But I raise my hand. "Yeah. We'll have a large pizza, pepperoni and mushrooms."

"Perfect. That will take about fifteen to twenty minutes."

"Perfect," I echo.

"I didn't know you were hungry, man," Zane says.

I force a smile. "There are a lot of things you don't know."

I'm not hungry, but the pizza will take time, and maybe by then Maddie and Bree will have come to their senses. Or, more likely, Zane will get bored and get off elsewhere.

I'm determined to keep this from happening however I can.

"Jesse," Maddie says, "can I speak to you privately?"

I gape at her. "Nope."

She huffs.

Does this woman not know what's good for her?

Then I look to Brianna.

She hasn't said anything, and she's looking down at the table.

She doesn't want this.

My sweet little sister really *did* talk her into it.

I can't wrap my head around any of this.

"So, ladies," Zane says, "tell me about yourselves."

I'm no lady, but I reply anyway. "Maddie is my little sister. She's twenty-two, and she's missing her last semester of *college* to be here on the tour with me."

Maddie scowls at me.

"And Brianna is our neighbor. She's been a friend of Maddie's since we moved to the western slope of Colorado, which was a while ago. She's a cowgirl. A rancher. Works with her father."

"I got that vibe from the boots." Zane smiles.

"I think he asked *us*, Jess," Maddie says.

Again, Brianna says nothing.

"I'd rather hear about you," Maddie says to Zane.

"Sure. Most of what you read in the gossip rags about me has no merit at all. I trained as a concert pianist. Jett and I went to grad school together. That's where we met. He's a classical singer. When neither of us got anywhere in the classics, we decided to try rock and roll, and we were discovered by a woman who became our benefactor."

"That's exactly how it was for Rory," Maddie says. "She wanted an opera career too, but it didn't work out for her."

"And you?" he asks me.

"I've always been a rocker. A true rocker." I can't help puffing out my chest a bit.

I don't know why we're having this discussion. Zane knows all of this. We talked about it when they first discovered us at that little bar in Utah where we played.

The devil and angel on my shoulder taunt me again. Emerald Phoenix can make or break us . . . and I'm not being very nice to Zane.

Then again . . . he's trying to fuck my sister and Brianna.

At the same time.

In his room.

My jaw is clenched so tight I may crack a tooth.

The server brings our drinks, and Zane hands her a credit card. "Run a tab, and anything these three want, put it on there."

"You got it." She runs the credit card through her handheld machine and hands it back to Zane.

Once she's gone, Zane stands. "I'm afraid I can't stay, but please, have whatever you want on me."

"I'm sorry," Maddie says.

"No problem, little lady. I have a big day tomorrow, as does your brother." He nods to Brianna and to me, and then he whisks away.

The yoke lifts from my shoulders.

"Thanks a lot, Jess." Maddie sulks.

But it doesn't escape my notice that Brianna looks visibly relieved. She takes a sip of her bourbon.

"Do I really have to have this talk with the two of you?" I ask.

"Not with me you don't," Brianna says.

I ignore Brianna. "You, Mads? You're better than this."

"Oh, come on. This is a once-in-a-lifetime opportunity, and you blew it for me. Zane will never come near me again, and neither will the others."

"Works for me. What would Callie and Rory say?"

Maddie crosses her arms. "They'd be a lot cooler than you're being."

I turn to Brianna. "Did you really want to do this?"

She meets my gaze. "As a matter of fact, yes I did."

"Really."

This woman just lost her virginity two nights ago. I feel badly enough about that, but she's clearly not easy. Not that I ever thought she was, but I didn't figure she was a virgin.

"Yeah, really," she asserts. "Like Maddie said, it was the opportunity of a lifetime."

"Are either of you even attracted to Zane Michaels?"

"Of course," Maddie says. "He's gorgeous."

He's kind of a pretty boy, but whatever. Long blond hair, which is obviously colored.

"And you, Brianna?"

"Sure. It's not like I have a *type*."

Her emphasis on the word *type* is not lost on me.

What the hell? This is completely insane. The thought of my little sister . . . I'd like to pummel that pretty boy's face.

And Brianna?

I'd like to throw him into next week.

I'm not sure which of them upsets me more.

My little sister . . . or Brianna.

Brianna shouldn't bother me at all.

Maddie downs her sidecar quickly and rises. "I've had about all I can take of this brotherly talk. I'm going back up to the room, Bree. Stay and finish your drink if you want. See you in a few."

She huffs and walks away before Brianna can stop her.

Then Brianna sighs. "I'll finish my drink quickly."

"Hell no. Have one or two more. It's all on Zane. Besides, we've got a pizza coming. You hungry?"

"Not especially." She takes another sip of her bourbon. "I don't know what this is. Zane ordered the best bourbon they've got here. It could be expensive, and it's delicious. I'd like to take my time with it."

"Go right ahead. I'm not going anywhere until I finish my pizza."

She nods, not smiling, and then takes another sip.

Oddly, I don't feel weird being with her.

I should talk about tea at Ennis Ainsley's house. I was damned rude to her, and I should apologize.

I should do a lot of things.

But all I can think about right now is getting her back in bed.

And my God… I have a private room. I even have everything I need since my luggage was finally delivered yesterday.

She takes another sip. And then I take the first sip of mine.

She's right. It *is* delicious. Perfect caramel and smoke with no harshness on the finish at all. I swirl it in my glass, watching the amber liquid flow. Thinking about how I might give my entire burgeoning career up for just one more time with Brianna Steel.

What the fuck is wrong with me?

She takes another sip of her bourbon. "Jesse, I have a question for you."

Here it comes. Why can't we be together? Why don't you want to be with me? What's wrong with me?

I brace myself for all the possibilities.

"Go ahead," I finally say after taking another sip of bourbon.

"Why didn't you want Maddie and me to go with Zane?"

CHAPTER THIRTY-FIVE

Brianna

He doesn't hesitate. "Because the two of you are better than that, Brianna."

"Is that the real reason?"

"Maddie's my little sister. I don't like to think of her having sex with anyone. Least of all a player like Zane Michaels."

"And what about me? *I'm* not your little sister."

"Maybe not. But that's how I always thought of you."

I set my glass on the table. "*Thought* of me? You used the past tense, Jesse."

"Of course I have to use the past tense. There's no way I can think of you as a little sister anymore, Brianna. Not after what happened."

My heart thumps. "We've been through that. It wasn't a mistake."

"In your opinion."

"It wasn't a mistake for either of us. You didn't do anything wrong, Jesse. I know you think you did. I know you think you stole something from me, but you didn't. I gave it to you. I knew what I was doing. I'm a big girl."

He doesn't say anything. Just takes another sip of his bourbon.

"For what it's worth, I wasn't really into the whole thing with Zane."

"Oh? Then why did you go along with it? And why did you say you were?"

"It seemed as good a way as any to forget the person I really want."

He looks away from me, takes another sip. Then he draws in a breath and meets my gaze. "You're better than that."

"Better than using sex with someone I don't care about to forget someone I *do* care about? Yeah, I'd agree with you."

"Then why were you going to do it?"

I shake my head. "Because I'm not freaking perfect, Jesse. I'm a human being. I watched you tonight, women surrounding you, and it broke my heart a little."

He says nothing. Simply takes another sip, finally draining his drink.

"I get it. You're not interested. I can accept that. But that doesn't make it easy. Tonight there *was* a man interested in me."

"There will always be men interested in you, Brianna. Since when have you been lacking in male attention?"

I can't answer right away because he's right. I've always had plenty of men trying to get in my pants. I want something more. I know I'm attractive, and I know I carry the Steel name. Two things that make men want me. But none of them really *know* me. I've had a few relationships, and they've gone okay. I cared about them, and they cared about me. But I never gave them the gift I gave Jesse, and the relationships eventually fizzled out.

Most men don't want to wait around to have sex.

I can't blame them really. I wanted to have sex as much as they did. Just not with them.

Finally Jesse speaks again. "What I witnessed tonight

wasn't you. And it wasn't Maddie either."

"Maybe not. But it's easy to get caught up in the glamour of it all. You saw that yourself. I saw the women flocking to you."

"You think I could have taken any of them to bed?"

"I know you could've. But apparently you didn't."

"I almost did, Brianna. Dragon and I had four girls ready to service both of us. Two of them are up with Dragon right now."

I try to ignore the lump in my throat that forms as he tells me this. "So why didn't you do it?"

"Because it's not me any more than it is you."

"You took *me* to bed," I say boldly.

"I did."

"So why not the other women, then?"

He rubs his hand up and down his face and holds up his glass up to the server as she walks by.

"Are you going to answer me?"

"I don't have a fucking answer for you, Brianna. I wish I did. I wish I could tell you there was some reason that I allowed it to happen. I shouldn't have. It's not my style. And I don't think it's yours either."

"Maybe the answer is staring you straight in the face. You just don't want to acknowledge it."

He rolls his eyes. "What answer might that be?"

"That you *did* want it. That you wanted it as much as I did. If this isn't you and it isn't me, then maybe we both just *wanted* something badly enough and we made it happen."

"Damn it, Brianna."

"What? Prove me wrong then, Jesse. Tell me there was another reason. You say you don't do things like that.

Indiscriminate sex isn't your thing. I told you it's not my thing either. Yet we both let it happen."

"You were about to let it happen again tonight."

"You don't know that. Don't presume to know what's inside my head. I might have called the whole thing off before we got up to the bedroom."

"God, I hope you're right. I wish I could say the same for my little sis."

"I don't know that she would've gone through with it either. Neither of us will ever know now."

"That doesn't make me feel much better."

"She's a grown woman, Jesse. Just like I am. I'm sure Dale and Donny feel the same way about me as you do about Maddie."

"Yeah . . . which is why I can't ever look either of them in the eye again."

"You're being stupid."

"Seriously? You want to play that game?"

"I'm not playing any games. That's my whole point. I'm a grown woman, and you're a grown man. Sure, my brothers wouldn't like it. They wouldn't like me having sex with anyone. Just like you don't like the idea of Maddie having sex with anyone. Just like you hated when Callie started sleeping with Donny."

He curls his hands into fists, his knuckles going white.

Yeah. I just proved my point.

"It's different."

"How the hell is it different? Because Maddie's so much younger?"

He runs his hands over his hair. "That's part of it, I guess. I was ten when Maddie was born. You're even younger than

Maddie, Brianna."

I let out a soft scoff. "Do I have to go through all of this? Brendan and Ava are together. He's thirty-five and she's twenty-four. My own parents are ten years apart in age. Uncle Bryce and Aunt Marjorie have an even wider age gap."

"Were any of them twenty-two when they got together?"

He's got me there. "My mom was twenty-five. Ava's twenty-four. It's close."

"Those two years mean a lot. Twenty-two is just a baby, Brianna."

"Do I look like a baby to you?"

He looks at me then, his gaze smoldering as he rakes his eyes over my entire body.

"No," he finally says. "You do *not* look like a baby to me, Brianna Steel. And right now, all I can think about is getting you out of those clothes and into my bed."

My entire body burns. I ache between my legs, and I know this time there will be no pain and no blood.

"I don't see anything stopping you."

"I'm stopping myself."

"Where are you sleeping tonight, Jesse?"

He remains silent.

"I can't take you to my room. Maddie is there. But you have a room."

Again, he says nothing.

"We can both have what we want. Through the whole tour if you want. And I promise you I won't consider it any kind of commitment. It will be sex, Jesse. Sex that we both want because we're extremely attracted to each other."

"I've told you. I don't have indiscriminate sex."

"And I've told you that I don't either. This isn't

indiscriminate sex. We've already been together, and we know each other. I'm willing. Are you?"

CHAPTER THIRTY-SIX

Jesse

My God, she's fucking killing me.

Does she really think this is indiscriminate between us? Because it's not.

I'm feeling something, and I don't like it. Not one bit.

I could take her now. I could pound her into the fucking morning, just to get Donny Steel back for taking my sister.

I'll even throw Brock Steel in for taking my other sister.

That's not my style.

Still... It will give me a reason to take her.

A reason that has nothing to do with the burgeoning feelings that I'm having, which make me extremely uncomfortable.

She may look grown up—even act grown up—but she's a twenty-two-year-old.

I'm not sure I can live with the guilt.

I'm not sure I can live with the stupid ache in my cock either.

I have a room. My own room, where only I will be tonight.

"What will you tell Maddie?"

"About what?" she asks.

"If you go with me. What do we tell her?"

"I don't have to tell her anything. I don't answer to her."

"Yeah, but the last time she was worried sick."

Brianna bites her bottom lip. "That's true. I don't want her to worry."

"So you see? This can't happen."

"Are you saying it *would* happen if there was a way to do it without worrying Maddie?"

I rake my fingers through my hair. "I don't know what the hell I'm saying. I'm trying to convince myself there's a good reason not to do this. You know, a good reason other than my profuse guilt and the fact that you're only twenty-two. But damn... I want you so much right now that I ache, Brianna. I yearn for you."

Her eyes widen, and a slow smile spreads across her face. "I want you too, Jesse."

"Text my sister. Tell her you won't be back in the room tonight. Don't offer any other explanation."

"So you mean—"

I raise both my hands. "I mean we're both damned to hell, Brianna. This is so fucked up. But I want to take what you're offering, because as God as my witness, I don't think I've ever wanted a woman this much before."

She grabs her phone and taps onto it.

It dings back.

"She says okay."

"She didn't ask where you'd be?"

She looks up from her screen and smirks. "No, but she probably wanted to."

"Good enough." The server returns with my second drink, and I shoot it quickly, letting it burn my throat in a good way. Then I rise. "Let's go."

Brianna stands as well, and we walk, not touching each

HELEN HARDT

other, out of the bar, through the foyer lobby to the elevators.

Still not touching her, I press the up button.

The elevator doors open, and I allow her to step in ahead of me.

We're the only two on the elevator, and when the doors close, I can't help myself.

I grab her, crush our mouths together.

She opens for me instantly and melts into me as we kiss.

The air seems to thicken with an unspoken tension, and time slows down, amplifying every heartbeat. Heat radiates from her body, and an invisible force seems to draw us closer.

Her hands creep into my hair, tugging on it, and I close what little gap is left between us.

I deepen the kiss as passion and desire surge through my veins. Our lips move like a perfect melody, a dance of tongues and breath.

We speak volumes in this kiss—volumes I've refused to acknowledge until now.

Volumes I won't be able to forget, no matter how hard I try.

The elevator reaches my floor, and the doors open.

We break apart, and neither of us speaks.

Again I let her walk out before me, and then, without taking her hand or touching her in any other way, I lead her to the room that Rory reserved for me.

I open the door quickly, let her in first, and then shut the door behind us. I then slam her against the wall and kiss her.

She tastes of her bourbon, and for a split-second I remember the pizza that I ordered on Zane's tab.

But then I don't care.

I don't think at all.

I simply kiss her, cupping both her cheeks, grinding the bulge of my cock against her.

She groans into my mouth, which makes my cock tighten further.

My God, I want her. I want her so badly.

We kiss and we kiss and we kiss, until she finally pushes at me and gasps in a breath.

"Jesse . . ."

"Please don't say you've changed your mind."

"No . . . Of course not. I just need to . . ." She sucks in another breath. "Need to breathe . . ."

She's not wrong. I need to breathe as well. My heart is racing, and even a few deep breaths don't slow it down.

Brianna takes a few steps away from me, and then she pulls her Dragonlock T-shirt over her head.

Her hair is in a high ponytail, but I desperately want to see it flowing over her milky shoulders.

She unclasps her bra, removes it, revealing her luscious breasts.

I stalk toward her, grab her ponytail, and yank so her chin tips forward, and I slide my lips over her neck as I pull the band out of her hair.

I throw the band on the floor, still kissing her neck as I cup her breasts.

My cock is aching inside my jeans.

She pushes away at me again.

"Please, Jesse. I want to look at you."

"You first," I growl.

I've seen her, of course—beautiful breasts, her shapely hips, her nice firm ass, her luscious pink pussy.

But I want to see it all again. Take it all in. As if I were looking at her for the first time.

She doesn't smile, simply smolders at me as she removes her boots, her socks, and then her jeans, sliding them over her hips, revealing a red lace thong.

I growl. "God, you're fucking perfect."

She blushes all over—a warm and rosy pink from the top of her breasts to the swell of her abdomen to her beautiful cheeks.

"All of it," I say.

She slides her thumbs underneath the waistband of her thong and lowers it first over her shapely thighs, then the beauty of her calves, until she steps out of it with her red polished toes.

I stare at her. I can't help myself. I rake my gaze over every inch of her flesh, my cock getting harder with each passing second.

She closes her eyes and sighs. "Please. Now you."

"Then I suggest you open your eyes, Brianna."

I remove my clothes quickly, not even attempting to prolong her torment. When I free my aching cock, it juts out.

And she gasps in a breath. "Beautiful," she sighs.

I stop myself from letting out an animalistic growl. "You're the beauty standing here."

A pinker blush spreads over her body. "I've always thought you were the most beautiful man I ever laid eyes on, Jesse. I've thought it for a long time."

"Your beauty knows no bounds," I tell her. "I could write a song about the color of your cheeks. About the curtain of your hair. About those deep brown eyes that see into my soul."

She melts into me then. "My God . . . "

I hear the words coming from my mouth, and I mean them. Every one. I can already hear the lyrics forming in my mind.

In the crowded room, she stood alone, a vision of splendor, like no other known. Her cascading hair, like a midnight sky, her eyes so deep, they....

My God...

What am I doing?

CHAPTER THIRTY-SEVEN

Brianna

He stares at me, and then he shakes his head. He picks up his jeans. "We can't do this. Not again."

"You've got to be kidding me."

"I'm not. I just... This can't happen, Brianna."

"Jesse"—I walk toward him, cup his cheek, run my fingertips over his dark stubble—"you just told me that my beauty knows no bounds. You've told me how much you want me. Plus, I can see the physical evidence of that with my own eyes." I drop my gaze to his massive erection.

"What I want doesn't have any meaning."

"What?"

"You're not mine to take, Brianna."

"I'm pretty sure that ship has sailed." She touches my cheek. "And you're not taking me. I'm giving myself to you."

"You are, with no expectation of anything in return."

"Absolutely. Nothing more than tonight. And maybe the next night. Whatever you're willing to give me, Jesse. I'll take whatever you're willing to give me."

"You're better than that, Bree. You and I both know it."

"Fine." I turn, sway my firm ass because I know he's looking. I pick up my thong. "Just try to resist me, Jesse Pike. I dare you."

He advances toward me then, throwing his jeans back down. "You don't know what you're asking for."

"I said I do."

"I'm not some college boy, Brianna. I *will* take you, and I will take you violently. I'll smack that firm little ass of yours."

"Go ahead," I dare. My skin is tingling all over. I've never been spanked before, and the thought...

Let's just say I don't hate it.

"You're playing with fire, Brianna. And I know a hell of a lot about fire."

He's no doubt thinking about the fire that torched his family's vineyards. His family is strapped now, and they need the money from this tour.

And here I am... toying with him, trying to manipulate him.

He's right. I deserve better, and so does he.

I drop my gaze and step into my thong, pulling it up around my hips. Then I touch his cheek once more.

"I apologize. This isn't who I am, Jesse." I move my hand away from his cheek. "It's just... I want you so much. But I won't manipulate you. I'm very sorry."

He pulls me to him, his nose in my neck, inhaling.

"If you only understood..."

I pull away then, force him to meet my gaze. "Help me understand, then. I want to understand you. I know I'm young. I know I come from incredible privilege. I know all of these things about myself. I wish I were more like my cousin Ava. She does things out on her own, without the help of our family's money."

"What's stopping you?"

"Nothing, I suppose. But Ava left the ranch. I never

wanted to. I love working with my father. I'm the only one of his four children who shares his love of the orchard."

"I can see that." He nods. "I mean really, why *should* you live without your family's money? It's there. It's yours. You're entitled to it."

"By virtue of being born a Steel, yes. But I didn't do anything special to earn it."

"I'm glad you see that."

"I'm sorry that I'm sometimes insensitive about what you and your family are going through. I saw how much the partial loss of our vineyard hurt Dale, and—"

He raises his hand to quiet me. "Please don't go there. I have nothing against Dale. Nothing against your family. But it's not the same thing."

I don't bother trying to explain to Jesse what I mean. He's seeing things in dollars and cents, but what those vineyards meant to Dale went way beyond their monetary value. They were part of *him*. A place he went to for solace, peace. After everything he's been through…

Does Jesse even know about all that?

It's not my story to tell. It's Dale's.

"I understand." I nod. "I mean, I'm trying to understand. I won't ever fully understand, because I've never been in your shoes, Jesse. But you've never been in Dale's either."

He sighs. "Brianna, please don't—"

I place two fingers over his firm lips to quiet him. "I won't. This isn't about Dale. This is about you and what your family has suffered. And it's about me wanting to understand."

He grabs me then, throws me on the bed, and hovers over me. "I want to tell you, Brianna. I want to try to help you understand. But I can't. Not with this raging hard-on. I have to have my release."

I slip out of my thong. "I'm not stopping you."

He plunges inside me then, and I gasp out. He's so large, and though I'm still aroused, talk of Dale and the vineyards and Jesse's family tightened me back up a bit.

"Okay?" he rasps against my neck.

"Yes. I'm okay."

"Thank God." He pulls out and pushes back in.

This is a hard and fast fuck, nothing like my first time.

He made that special for me after he found out I was a virgin.

This time isn't for me. This is for him.

He's suffering, and I want to give it to him.

I wrap my arms around his neck, massage his shoulders, as he thrusts, thrusts, thrusts . . .

When he pushes in hard, I feel him spurting his release inside me.

I smile against his neck.

He stays inside me for a moment, and then he rolls off me onto his back, flinging his arm over his forehead.

I stay quiet a moment. Let him bask in his afterglow.

Until—

"Let me know when you're ready to talk."

He grunts.

So I stay lying next to him, biding my time, trying to be patient. Until he finally turns, propping himself up on his shoulder.

"Try to imagine what it might be like to *not* have everything your heart desires. Not to be able to go into any store and buy whatever you want."

"I can imagine that."

"Can you? You're probably thinking of someone who's

gone hungry. That isn't me or my family. We've always had enough to eat."

"I'm glad of that."

"But the difference is that I have to think before I go to Taco Bell for a meal. I have to think before I go to Lorenzo's for some lasagna."

"But I just saw you in there, with Ava, Brock, and Rory, before the holidays."

"Yeah, I was with Brock and Rory, so Brock picked up the tab."

"I know you're not going hungry, Jesse."

"No, I'm not. I never have, and I'm very grateful for that. I'd sell my soul to the devil if I had to if it meant feeding my sisters."

"I believe you would."

"Of course I would. But that's not even the point. Our small ranch is everything to my mom and dad. Uncle Scott and Aunt Lena as well. Our vineyards were destroyed. All of them. Our winery operation isn't as good as yours, isn't as big as yours, and we don't produce fine wines like Ryan and Dale do. We produce table wines. Wines that people buy in bulk, and we sell a lot of them. It's the major source of our income, and now it's gone."

I gulp audibly. "But you keep beef as well."

"We do. But our operation isn't like yours. We have enough beef to feed ourselves, and to sell to local markets. But it's not our operation's major focus. We don't have orchards, like you guys do. It's just wine. That's our business." His lips twist into a frown. "And it's gone, Brianna."

"I think Callie said something about you guys buying grapes from other vineyards to keep your business going."

He shakes his head, laughing sarcastically. "And you don't see the issue with that? Those grapes cost money. Money we don't have. We've had to go into debt to keep our operation going. Plus, we have no control over the quality of the grapes we buy. When they come from our own vineyards, we do. We know their quality. Now we have to start from fucking scratch, Brianna."

My heart breaks.

Mom and Dad, and my aunts and uncles—they taught us how to value our money. We all grew up working on the ranch, learning good family values, learning that nothing comes free.

But it's not the same.

Even though we all worked our fingers to the bone when we were kids, learned how to run the ranch, we never wanted for anything.

We never worried about where any kind of income was coming from. On Christmas morning, there were always piles of gifts under every tree for each one of us.

And the parties... The infamous Steel parties, where barons of Steel roast were served along with Dom Pérignon and Uncle Ryan's best Bordeaux blends. Practically the whole town was invited to feast on the Steel riches.

It's a part of my life. It always has been and always will be.

It's not a part of Jesse's life. Or Maddie's. Or Callie's or Rory's, for that matter, although it will be once they marry into our family.

I open my mouth, ready to tell him that I understand, but then I realize that's not what he needs to hear.

"I won't insult you by saying I understand, Jesse. But thank you for telling me this. I *want* to understand."

"I didn't tell you all this to make you feel sorry for me," he says with a growl.

"I know that."

He sits up. "Do you? Because the last thing my family needs is your family's pity. But here's the thing, Brianna. My family's well-being depends on the success of this tour. And I can't be distracted. And frankly? You're a distraction."

My God . . .

Now I *do* understand, and I feel like a big dirtbag for trying to manipulate him.

I reach for his hand. "Jesse . . ."

He holds my hand for a moment, gazes deep into my eyes, and for a split second I think he's going to smile, but he doesn't. He snaps his hand away. "Do you understand what I mean? I can't get my head wrapped around you right now. I need my head wrapped around the band, our music, our performances."

"My God . . . I'm so sorry. I shouldn't have come."

"You're here now, and you brought Maddie with you. I'm not going to insist that you leave because Maddie is looking forward to this trip. Although, I really ought to send you both home after the thing with Zane Michaels."

"I'll talk to Maddie. I'll make her understand that neither of us can be a distraction, and that includes her. You can't be worrying about her trotting off with some celebrity."

He touches my cheek then, trails his lips around the shell of my ear. "Thank you. Maybe you truly do understand."

"Thank you for opening up to me. I . . ."

"Please. Don't say what I think you're going to say."

I love you.

I keep the words to myself. It's way too soon.

It was a mistake to come here, but he's right. I can't take this experience away from Maddie. So Maddie and I are here for the duration.

And I need to make sure Jesse is free from distractions.

CHAPTER THIRTY-EIGHT

Jesse

I'm tempted to ask her to continue sleeping with me just as a physical release, but as I said before, she deserves better.

Plus, I need her looking after Maddie. Donny and Callie will be going back to the States once we leave the UK, and Rory will be too busy with the band.

I'll have only Brock to watch over Brianna and Maddie. He can do it. He's changed a lot since he got serious with my sister. He was probably the worst womanizer of the bunch, but somehow, he and Donny both got tamed by two of my sisters.

Brianna smooths my hair. "I suppose I should get back to my room."

Stay.

My God, the word is hovering right on the end of my lips.

But I force it back.

"I'll take you up."

"There's no need, Jesse. I'm perfectly capable of going back to my room alone."

"You want something to eat first? We didn't stick around the bar long enough to get that pizza."

"No, I'm fine." She rolls off the bed, finds her thong, eases it up over her perfect hips.

Such a shame to cover up that beautiful pussy.

God... I haven't wanted a woman like this in a long time. The thought of...

When I saw her and Maddie with Zane Michaels, my protective instinct raged through me for my little sister.

But for Brianna?

It went way beyond a brother protecting his baby sister.

It was more like a wolf protecting his mate.

And that scares the hell out of me.

She's too young, first of all, and this tour... This tour is too damned important for me to get distracted by falling in love with anyone, especially Brianna Steel.

I slide off the bed as well, throwing on my jeans, sliding into my shoes, and pulling my shirt over my head. "I'll see you to your room," I say. "Just keep Maddie safe. I can't be worrying about her ending up in bed with one of Emerald Phoenix. Or even with Dragon."

"You and Cage are here."

"I know that. And I'd like to think Jake and Dragon would leave my little sister alone. They probably would. But at this point? I just want you to take care of her."

"You can count on me, Jesse. I promise."

She's dressed now. Her Dragonlock T-shirt accents the gorgeous curve of her breasts and her indented waist.

I push her hair back behind one ear. "Thank you again. For understanding."

"Thank you for helping me understand. I promise, Jesse. The tour will be a success."

Against my better judgment, I brush my lips over hers, my cock reacting.

Damn it.

This is going to be a lot more difficult than I thought it would be.

★ ★ ★

The next morning, I rise at eight a.m., take a quick shower, and head back to my original room. I use the key card and walk right in. If Dragon's not done by now, I don't give a flying fuck.

Indeed, he's sprawled out on one of the queen beds, entwined with the two girls, all three of them naked.

I clear my throat.

Not one of them stirs.

Jesus fuck.

We have a fucking show again tonight, and my drummer is passed out with two naked women whose names he probably doesn't even know.

I just got done lecturing Brianna on distractions last night. Seems I'm going to have to lecture Dragon as well.

I walk over to his bed. He's lying face down, thank God, so I don't have to ogle his junk.

I push at his shoulder. "Dragon. Wake up."

Nothing.

"Come on, man. We've got rehearsal. Get your ass up. It's breakfast time."

One of the women stirs, opening one eye, her tits on display. Her eyes are smoky with mascara smudges.

"Well, hi there, handsome." A slow smile spreads across her face.

"Good morning. I hope you had a great time. But it's time for you to leave now."

She yawns. "What time is it?"

"Time for you to leave. Time for your companion to wake up and leave as well. And time for Dragon—"

"Dragon?"

266

"That guy in bed with you?"

"Yeah..." She caresses Dragon's ass through the bedsheets. "He's hot."

I roll my eyes. "Come on. Get up. And take your friend with you."

I turn my back.

"Don't like what you see?"

"Ladies, just get the hell out of here. Dragon and I have to get to rehearsal."

"Yeah... The concert... Jenny and I have tickets tonight too. Can't wait to see you all again."

"I'm hoping we get to go to bed with one of the real band members tomorrow night," Jenny says.

I resist the urge to comment. Just as I suspected, Dragon and I were sloppy seconds. The groupies are gunning for Emerald Phoenix. Do they not know that Jett Draconis is happily married? Zane would take them, though. I'm just glad I kept him off Maddie and Brianna.

The first woman—I have no idea what her name is—gathers her clothes and heads into the bathroom, while Jenny finally sits up in bed, her tits dangling.

"Who are you?" she asks, her voice raspy from cigarette smoke.

"You don't remember me from last night? I'm Jesse. Time for you to leave."

"I have to wait for Andrea to be done in the bathroom."

"I think you can join Andrea in the bathroom," I say. "You two clearly don't mind sharing."

She giggles with a rasp. "Fine." She gets off the bed, and I look away again as she gathers her clothes, traipses into the bathroom. She knocks on the door. "Andy, let me in!"

The door's lock clicks, Jenny enters, and I hear giggling and then some smooching.

Yeah, I don't have to guess what went on here last night. I just hope they get the hell out of here quickly.

Now to deal with Dragon.

He's still lying face down, and I don't want to pull the covers and see his bare ass, but I don't have a choice.

I rip the covers off and nudge his shoulder. "Dragon! Get your ass up!"

He doesn't stir.

"Jesus Christ. Come on, Dragon!" I roll him over, avoiding looking at his junk. His face is pale. "Oh, shit!"

I reach for his neck. Thank God. I find his pulse, but he doesn't look good.

"Dragon." I slap his face several times. "Dragon! What did you do? Wake up!"

I run to the bathroom and pound on the door. "What did you guys take last night?" I demand.

No response.

I twist the doorknob. Thank God it's not locked. I open it and—

"Jesus Christ," I say again.

Jenny is sitting on the counter, and Andrea is kneeling, her face buried in Jenny's pussy.

I yank Andrea away. "You two need to listen to me right now. I can't wake up my friend in the other room. What the hell did you guys take?"

Andrea's eyes go wide. "We... We didn't take anything. We just drank."

"Did you see him take anything?"

"No. He drank a little. Not as much as we did, to be sure."

"All right. Call 9-1-1."

They both widen their eyes at me.

Right. We're not in the US. "What do you do when you need emergency help?"

"9-9-9," Andrea says, her voice trembling. "You call 9-9-9."

I reach into my pocket—

"Fuck!" My cell. I must have left it in the other room.

I leave the bathroom and dart my gaze around the room. A phone sits on the desk.

I pick it up and dial 9-9-9 quickly.

"Emergency," an English-accented voice says into my ear. "Which service do you require—police, fire, or ambulance?"

"Ambulance. Please."

"Please allow me to assess the situation. Where are you located?"

"The Regalia Hotel in London. My friend. He's not responsive. He has a light pulse. He may have ingested some kind of drug."

"I see. I'm dispatching an ambulance now. What is your room number, please?"

Robotically, I give her all the information she asks for.

"Emergency help is on the way, sir. Please do not leave the patient. Make sure . . . "

I listen with half an ear to her instructions. Finally she hangs up.

I have no idea how quickly they'll get here. At least someone answered.

Andrea and Jenny leave the room after that, thank God. I don't need them to be here when the ambulance shows up. The dispatcher asked me to scan the room to see if I could find any pill bottles or anything, so I do so. I look under the bed, in the nightstand drawer, and then I race into the bathroom, scouring it as well.

Nothing.

About ten minutes later, I hear the sirens in the distance. They sound different from American sirens.

Then a pounding on the door.

I open the door, and two paramedics greet me. They head toward the bed.

The first paramedic checks Dragon's vitals. "How old is he?"

"He's thirty-two."

"History of drug use?"

"Yes. But he's been clean, other than pot and booze, for a while."

"Got it." The man checks his neck. "Light pulse." He shakes Dragon. "Sir, can you hear me? Sir, can you wake up?"

The other two bring a stretcher, and they get Dragon situated on it.

"You a family member?"

"Friend. We're members of a band that's playing with Emerald Phoenix here in the UK. He's my roommate. We've been friends forever."

"Good, you can come in the ambulance with us. If he comes to, he'll want to see a familiar face."

I gulp, nodding.

"Emerald Phoenix, you say?" the female paramedic asks.

"Yeah, we're their opener."

"I have tickets to the concert tonight."

"You may not see us if we don't have a drummer."

My heart is racing. Dragon's not just my bandmate. He's

my friend. He's shared secrets with me that he hasn't told anyone else.

I can't believe he would screw up five years of sobriety from narcotics. So he has a drink once in a while, smokes a joint.

But I should know better. Those are gateway drugs. When you've got a narcotics addiction under your belt, you really need to stay away from everything.

Why didn't I try harder? Why didn't I intervene?

Because I know Dragon's history. I know what he's trying to escape. And frankly, I'd need a drink every now and then if I were him.

We leave the room with Dragon on the stretcher, and of course doors open in the hallway, guests wandering out to see what the commotion is.

I keep my eyes on one door—Maddie's and Brianna's room.

Please don't open. Please don't open.

Cage opens the door to his and Jake's room, which is right next to ours.

Brock and Rory and Donny and Callie are a few floors up in suites. Thank God they won't hear this.

"Cuz?" Cage says, his voice shaking.

"Dragon. I think he may have OD'd on something."

"Fuck!" Cage rushes alongside me.

"You a family member?" the male paramedic asks.

"Friend. Bandmate," Cage says.

"I can only let one of you ride along."

I nod to Cage. "I'll keep you posted."

We're almost to the elevator when what I was dreading happens.

Maddie and Brianna, both dressed in lounge pants and tank tops, come running toward me.

"What's going on?" Brianna demands. "Jesse, are you all right?"

CHAPTER THIRTY-NINE

Brianna

"It's Dragon," Jesse says, his voice low, slightly shaking.

"What happened?" Maddie asks.

"I don't know. He may have OD'd on something. I'll keep you all posted as well as I can."

I reach out to touch Jesse's arm, but he yanks it away.

I'm hurt, but we had this chat.

No distractions.

And this—whatever just happened to Dragon—is a *major* distraction. Jesse doesn't need me on top of that.

The elevator doors close, and Maddie clasps her hand to her mouth. "Is Dragon going to make it?"

"God, I hope so." My heart is racing.

"What are they going to do for a drummer?"

"I don't know. Brock used to play the drums. He and David and a couple other guys had a garage band."

"Were they any good?"

"Hell no. They sucked."

"Then how is that going to do us any good?"

I shake my head. "I don't know, Mads. But Brock may be all we have."

"Maybe Dragon's okay. Maybe he's just drunk or something."

"God, I hope so," I say again.

I stand against the wall, trying not to hyperventilate. I don't know Dragon well. No one does, really.

Except Jesse. I've spotted him and Dragon alone and talking many times—mainly because I'm always watching Jesse. The two of them seem to be close friends.

This must be killing Jesse.

"It's eight thirty," Maddie says. "We're supposed to meet Brock, Callie, and Donny for sightseeing in half an hour."

"Right. I guess I forgot to set my alarm."

"Me too. I was so angry after Jesse broke up that date—or whatever it was—with Zane that I came up here and pouted. Now none of that seems important now."

"No, it's not important. In fact, it never was. We should be thanking your brother, Maddie, and we've got to fix this for him."

"How are we supposed to fix this? We can't go back in time and make sure Dragon stays away from whatever he took."

"No. But we can find a drummer. What floor is Emerald Phoenix on?"

"What are you suggesting?"

"We have no choice. We have to see if their drummer can fill in for Dragon."

"Emerald Phoenix's drummer is not going to fill in for Dragon," Maddie says. "He has his own band."

I sigh. Maddie's right. "Then Brock is their only choice."

"If they have to cancel this tour... Jesse and Rory are going to be so disappointed. This tour could have meant their careers, and it meant so much to our family."

"I understand more than you know. I'm going to fix this, Maddie. If it's the last thing I do, I'm going to fix this for your brother."

ACKNOWLEDGMENTS

Welcome to a new Steel trilogy! I hope you're enjoying the antics of Jesse and Brianna. We'll see more of Ennis Ainsley in *Harmony*, where an old mystery will be solved, and a new Steel will join the tour as well.

Huge thanks to the always brilliant team at Waterhouse Press: Audrey Bobak, Haley Boudreaux, Jesse Kench, Jon Mac, Amber Maxwell, Michele Hamner Moore, Chrissie Saunders, Scott Saunders, Kurt Vachon, and Meredith Wild.

Thanks also to the women and men of Hardt and Soul. Your endless and unwavering support keeps me going.

To my family and friends, thank you for your encouragement. Special shout out to Dean—aka Mr. Hardt— and to our amazing sons, Eric and Grant. Special thanks to Eric for helping with *Destiny* before I handed it in to Scott at Waterhouse.

Thank you most of all to my readers. Without you, none of this would be possible. I am grateful every day that I'm able to do what I love—write stories for you!

Harmony will be out soon!

CONTINUE THE STEEL BROTHERS SAGA

WITH BOOK TWENTY–NINE

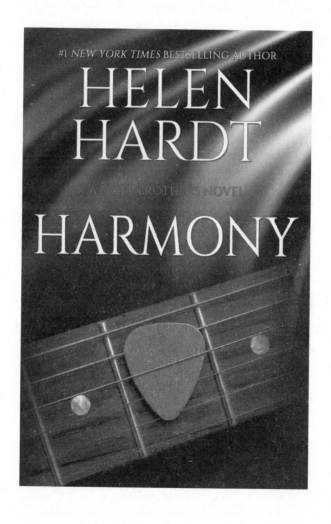

KEEP READING FOR A PREVIEW OF:

MISADVENTURES

WITH A

ROCK STAR

BY
HELEN HARDT

CHAPTER ONE

Jett

Janet and Lindy tongued each other in a sloppy, openmouthed kiss. Lindy, platinum-blond with fair skin, smoothed her hand over the strap of ebony-haired Janet's soft-pink camisole before pulling it down and freeing one of her plump, dark tits. Her nipple was a deep violet, and Lindy skimmed her fingers over its tip before giving it a pinch.

Janet let out a low moan, sucked Lindy's bottom lip into her mouth, and released her creamy tits from the scant blue tube top she wore. They kissed each other more frantically, groaning, pinching and twisting each other's nipples.

"That's hot, man," Zane said, stroking the bulge under his jeans.

Zane Michaels was the keyboardist for our band, Emerald Phoenix. I loved him like a brother, but he hadn't matured past his teen years. I couldn't deny the ladies looked great, but this wasn't anything I hadn't witnessed many times before.

Lindy was now nestled between Janet's firm thighs, her pink tongue sliding between the folds of Janet's purple pussy. Zane looked about to explode.

And I couldn't have cared less.

Oh, Janet and Lindy were hot as hell. I'd had them separately and together, and they both gave killer blowjobs and let me fuck not only their pussies but their tight asses as well. Janet loved to be handcuffed to the bed, and Lindy let me spank her as hard as I liked.

Tonight, though? I wasn't interested.

Same old, same old.

I still had my post-performance high, but I wasn't looking for the usual orgy, despite Janet and Lindy's show and the rest of the scantily clad groupies milling around looking for attention. A redhead was perched on the lap of Bernie Zopes, our drummer, and the backup guitarist, Tony Walker, was getting a BJ from two women who looked like they might be twins.

Nah, couldn't be.

I'd already pushed a few hotties away after one shoved her tongue into my mouth and grabbed my crotch.

"What's with you, man?" Zane had asked.

I hadn't given him a response.

Truthfully, I didn't have one. I just wasn't in the mood. Not for this, anyway.

Zane passed me the joint he was smoking, but I waved it away. I no longer smoked. Bad for my voice. I'd already turned down his flask as well as the many drinks and drugs offered by the chicks in attendance. No booze. Not tonight. And I didn't do anything harder than that.

Not in the fucking mood.

One more concert, and one more drug- and booze- and groupie-filled after-party.

If anyone had told me five years ago I'd be tired of this scene, I would have laughed in his face.

Now?

Janet and Lindy finished their show and stood. Janet

strode to Zane and unbuckled his belt, while Lindy walked toward me.

"Hey, Jett. You have way too many clothes on." She cupped my crotch, my lack of erection apparent. "Not happy to see me tonight?"

"Nothing personal, sweetheart. Just not in the mood."

"I always did love a challenge." She nipped at my neck.

"This isn't a challenge."

She pulled back and glared at me with her dark-blue eyes. "*Everything's* a challenge. I want you tonight, and I'm going to have you." She snaked her tongue over my bottom lip.

Well, what the hell? Fucking Lindy was no hardship, and I didn't have anything else pressing to do. My groin began to tighten.

But was it because of the blonde grinding on me? Or the auburn-haired, brown-eyed goddess I caught a glimpse of across the room?

CHAPTER TWO

Heather

Several hours earlier...

"I know you love this band," Susie said. "Come on. Please?"

Susie was my roommate and a good friend, but she was a notorious rock and roll groupie. The woman had a pube collection, for God's sake. She'd sworn me to secrecy on that one. She hadn't needed to bother. Who the heck would I tell? Pubic hair didn't regularly come up in conversation. Also, keeping locks of rock stars' gorilla salad in zippered bags made me kind of sick. I'd turned her down when she offered to show it to me.

"Sorry, Suze. Just not up for it tonight."

"I'm so sorry Rod Hanson turned down your rewrite. But sitting around wallowing in self-pity on a Friday night won't make it any better."

"And going to a concert will?"

"A concert *and* an after-party. And watching Jett Draconis and Zane Michaels on stage is an experience every woman should have at least once."

I did love Emerald Phoenix's music, and yes, Jett Draconis and Zane Michaels were as gorgeous as Greek gods. But...

"Not tonight."

She pulled me off the couch. "Not taking no for an answer. You're going."

★ ★ ★

Why was I here again?

I stifled a yawn. Watching a couple of women do each other while others undressed, clamoring for a minute of the band's attention, wasn't my idea of a good time. The two women were gorgeous, of course, with tight bodies and big boobs. The contrasts in their skin and hair color made their show even more exotic. They were interesting to watch, but they didn't do much for me sexually. Maybe if I weren't so exhausted. I'd pulled the morning and noon shifts, and my legs were aching.

Even so, I was glad Susie had dragged me to the concert, if only to see and hear Jett Draconis live. His deep bass-baritone was rich enough to fill an opera house but had just enough of a rasp to make him the ultimate rock vocalist. And when he slid into falsetto and then back down to bass notes? Panty-melting. No other words could describe the effect. Watching him had mesmerized me. He lived his music as he sang and played, not as if it were coming from his mouth but emanating from his entire body and soul. The man had been born to perform.

A true artist.

Which only made me feel like more of a loser.

Jett Draconis was my age, had hit the LA scene around the same time I had, and he'd made it big in no time. Me? I was still a struggling screenwriter working a dead-end job waiting tables at a local diner where B-list actors and directors hung out. Not only was I not an A-lister, I wasn't even serving them.

When I couldn't sell a movie to second-rate producer Rod Hanson? I hadn't yet said the words out loud, but the time had come to give up.

"What are you doing hanging out here all by yourself?"

Susie's words knocked me out of my barrage of self-pity. For a minute anyway.

"Just bored. Can we leave soon?"

"Are you kidding me? The party's just getting started." She pointed to the two women on the floor. "That's Janet and Lindy. Works every time. They always go home with someone in the band."

"Only proves that men are pigs."

Susie didn't appear to be listening. Her gaze was glued on Zane, the keyboardist, whose gaze was in turn glued on the two women cavorting in the middle of the floor. She turned to me. "Let's make out."

I squinted at her, as if that might help my ears struggling in the loud din. I couldn't possibly have heard her correctly. "What?"

"You and me. Kiss me." She planted a peck right on my mouth.

I stepped away from her. "Are you kidding me?"

"It works. Look around. All the girls do it."

"I'm not a girl. I'm a thirty-year-old woman."

"Don't you think I'm hot?" she asked.

"Seriously? Of course you are." Indeed, Susie looked great with her dark hair flowing down to her ass and her form-fitting leopard-print tank and leggings. "So is Angelina Jolie, but I sure as heck don't want to make out with her. I don't swing that way." Well, for Angelina Jolie I might. Or Lupita Nyong'o. But that was it.

"Neither do I—at least not long-term. But it'll get us closer to the band."

"Is this what you do at all the after-parties you go to?"

She giggled. "Sometimes. But only if there's someone as hot as you to make out with. I have my standards."

Maybe I should have been flattered. But no way was I swapping spit with my friend to get some guy's attention. They were still just men, after all. Even the gorgeous and velvet-voiced Jett Draconis, who seemed to be watching the floor show.

Susie inched toward me again. I turned my head just in time so her lips and tongue swept across my cheek.

"Sorry, girl. If you want to make out, I'm sure there's someone here who will take you up on your offer. Not me, though. It would be too ... weird."

She nodded. "Yeah, it would be a little odd. I mean, we live together and all. But I hate that you're just standing here against the wall not having any fun. And I'm not ready to go home yet."

I sighed. This was Susie's scene, and she enjoyed it. She had come to LA for the rockers and was happy to work as a receptionist at a talent agency as long as she made enough money to keep her wardrobe in shape and made enough contacts to get into all the after-parties she wanted. That was the extent of her aspirations. She was living her dream, and she'd no doubt continue to live it until her looks gave out ... which wouldn't happen for a while with all the Botox and plastic surgery available in LA. She was a good soul, but right now her ambition was lacking.

"Tell you what," I said. "Have fun. Do your thing. I'll catch an Uber home."

She frowned. "I wanted to show you a good time. I'm sorry I suggested making out. I get a little crazy at these things."

I chuckled. "It's okay. Don't worry about it."

"Please stay. I'll introduce you to some people."

"Any producers or directors here?" I asked.

"I don't know. Mostly the band and their agents, and of course the sound and tech guys who like to try to get it on with the groupies. I doubt any film people are here."

"Then there isn't anyone I need to meet, but thanks for offering." I pulled my phone out of my clutch to check the time. It was nearing midnight, and this party was only getting started.

"Sure I can't convince you to stay?" Susie asked.

"Afraid not." I pulled up the Uber app and ordered a ride. "But have a great time, okay? And stay safe, please."

"I always do." She gave me a quick hug and then lunged toward a group of girls, most of them still dressed, thank God.

I scanned the large room. Susie and her new gaggle of friends were laughing and drinking cocktails. A couple girls were slobbering over the drummer's dick. The two beautiful women putting on the sex show had abandoned the floor, and the one with dark skin was draped between the legs of Zane Michaels, who was, believe it or not, even prettier than she was. The other sat on Jett Draconis's lap.

Zane Michaels was gorgeous, but Jett Draconis? He made his keyboardist look average in comparison. I couldn't help staring. His hair was the color of strong coffee, and he wore it long, the walnut waves hitting below his shoulders. His eyes shone a soft hazel green. His face boasted high cheekbones and a perfectly formed nose, and those lips . . . The most amazing lips I'd ever seen on a man—full and flawless. I'd gawked at photos of him in magazines, not believing it was possible for a man to be quite so perfect-looking—beautiful and rugged handsome at the same time.

Not that I could see any of this at the moment, with the blonde on top of him blocking most of my view.

I looked down at my phone once more. My driver was still fifteen minutes away. Crap.

Then I looked up.

Straight into the piercing eyes of Jett Draconis.

Continue *Misadventures with a Rockstar*
Available Now!

MESSAGE FROM HELEN HARDT

Dear Reader,

Thank you for reading *Melody*. If you want to find out about my current backlist and future releases, please like my Facebook page and join my mailing list. I often do giveaways. If you're a fan and would like to join my street team to help spread the word about my books, please see the web addresses below. I regularly do awesome giveaways for my street team members.

If you enjoyed the story, please take the time to leave a review on a site like Amazon or Goodreads. I welcome all feedback. I wish you all the best!

Helen

Facebook
Facebook.com/HelenHardt

Newsletter
HelenHardt.com/SignUp

Street Team
Facebook.com/Groups/HardtAndSoul

ALSO BY HELEN HARDT

The Steel Brothers Saga:
Craving
Obsession
Possession
Melt
Burn
Surrender
Shattered
Twisted
Unraveled
Breathless
Ravenous
Insatiable
Fate
Legacy
Descent
Awakened
Cherished
Freed
Spark
Flame
Blaze
Smolder
Flare
Scorch
Chance
Fortune
Destiny
Melody
Harmony
Encore

Blood Bond Saga:
Unchained
Unhinged
Undaunted
Unmasked
Undefeated

Misadventures Series:
Misadventures with a Rock Star
Misadventures of a Good Wife (with Meredith Wild)

The Temptation Saga:
Tempting Dusty
Teasing Annie
Taking Catie
Taming Angelina
Treasuring Amber
Trusting Sydney
Tantalizing Maria

The Sex and the Season Series:
Lily and the Duke
Rose in Bloom
Lady Alexandra's Lover
Sophie's Voice

Daughters of the Prairie:
The Outlaw's Angel
Lessons of the Heart
Song of the Raven

Cougar Chronicles:
The Cowboy and the Cougar
Calendar Boy

Anthologies Collection:
Destination Desire
Her Two Lovers